J.J. HERNANDEZ

ONE NIGHT IN FEAR CITY

This is a work of fiction. Names, characters, places, and incidents either are the product of the author's imagination or are used fictitiously. Any resemblance to actual persons, living or dead, events, or locales is entirely coincidental.

Copyright © 2022 by Julio A. Hernandez

All rights reserved. No part of this book may be reproduced or used in any manner without written permission of the copyright owner except for the use of quotations in a book review.

One Night in Fear City

Published October 2022 by Moon Reign Publications

www.jjhernandezauthor.com

Edited by Jodie Renner

Book Cover Design by ebooklaunch.com

ISBN 978-1-7371013-3-8

ISBN 978-1-7371013-4-5 (paperback)

ISBN 978-1-7371013-5-2 (ebook)

To my father Julio. Thanks for being a rock through hard times and for introducing me to the many cool things that have influenced my imagination and writing.

acknowledgments

I would like to thank my Titi Sonia and Uncle Ray for always being there through difficult times, no matter how far away you may have been. And for sharing some of your memories that helped in the writing of this book. Thanks to my brother David for always showing support and love. And as always, I am forever thankful to my ladies Hazel, Nikki, and Kat. None of this would have been possible or worth doing without all of you.

one

Sunday, July 10, 1977

CAROLINA LYNCH COULDN'T HELP but stare at the woman's lipstick-stained teeth. The drunk woman had spent the last few minutes narrating her stream of consciousness through slurred words and alcohol-induced hiccups. Carolina was already regretting she'd agreed to attend the event, and the woman's inane ramblings about Leif Garret's good looks were not helping her feel better about her decision.

Her father, oil tycoon, Wall Street player, and puppet master extraordinaire Josiah Lynch, had urged her to attend the fundraiser in his place for New York City mayoral candidate Joe Renfrow. Her father had convinced her it'd be an opportunity to mingle among the political and social elite and let everyone know she was one of them. But Carolina had been at the party for nearly two hours and had yet to interact with any of the real players.

It hadn't been from lack of trying. Carolina had made the rounds when she'd first arrived, but as usual, had found herself staring at a lot of cool shoulders. Ever since her father had started pushing her to become the face of his company, which required her attendance at social events such as this one, Carolina had felt more like an observer than a player. Unless her father was around, the old white men who sat atop the food chain ignored her. And since she was a young and single woman, their wives usually did the same.

Usually being the key word because Carolina now found herself cornered by someone's twenty-two-year-old trophy wife. The inebriated woman had apparently not received the memo about Carolina being on the "someone to ignore" list and had spent the last fifteen minutes droning on about a teenage pop music star. Carolina was ready to leave.

She looked around and spotted her bodyguard, Joseph Millers, standing by the wall. Carolina was always self-conscious about how she was perceived, so she'd reminded him not to hover too close during the party. She didn't like the attention that came with having a six-foot-five former member of Australia's Special Air Service Regiment attached to her hip. She'd thought of herself as a strong person and hated that anyone would think she needed rescuing. But when the tipsy trophy wife segued from Leif Garrett to her favorite Charlie's Angel, Carolina gave Joseph a wide-eyed stare, signaling him to rescue her now.

Joseph made his way over to her, and with his back to the tipsy trophy wife, leaned in close so only Carolina could hear him speak. "Am I safe in assuming this conversation has run its course?"

Carolina made a face as if he'd reminded her of something. "Oh my. I completely forgot about that," she said loudly. She glanced at the drunk Barbie. "Will you please excuse me? I forgot I have to be somewhere early in the morning, and I really must speak with Mr. Renfrow before I leave." Carolina walked away before Leif Garrett's number one fan could respond. "Thank you for that, Joseph."

"Of course, Miss Lynch."

"Now where is our esteemed mayoral candidate? Dad would have a coronary if I left without speaking with him."

"I'm pretty sure I saw him go into the study."

"All right then, let's get this over with, shall we?"

With Joseph close behind, Carolina made her way to the study at the other end of the apartment. They were on the twenty-fifth floor of a thirty-story high-rise on Park Avenue, just north of East Forty-Ninth Street. It was one of only two apartments on the floor and took up the entire east wing, making it bigger than most single-family homes. Its opulent décor consisted of marble floors, Persian rugs, and, in what she thought was the worst decorating decision since the late sixties' lava lamp craze, crystal chandeliers in every room.

The large oak doors leading to the study were closed but there was a murmur of voices coming from the other side, so Carolina knocked once.

"Come in," a male voice said from behind the closed door.

Carolina entered confidently and without hesitation. She heard Joseph's heavy footsteps behind her as she scanned the room. It was a large space, lined with floor-to-ceiling bookshelves and filled with beautiful dark wood furniture. In the center of the room, four expensive looking high-backed leather chairs were arranged conversation style around a large oak coffee table. Four middle-aged men, including Joe Renfrow, sat in the chairs smoking cigars, drinks on the table.

They all glared at Carolina, not bothering to mask their annoyance that she'd interrupted their billionaire boys club meeting. Despite the thick cloud of cigar smoke that irritated her eyes and filled her nostrils, Carolina approached the group of men, enjoying the obvious discomfort her presence caused.

"Gentlemen," she said. None of the men stood to greet her and Joe Renfrow was the only one who bothered to fake a smile. He was a tall, heavyset man with icy blue eyes, thin blond hair, and a pale complexion. Carolina guessed he must have spent hours looking in the mirror perfecting his smile. And it was probably a good thing he did too, because it was his only attractive feature. "Forgive my intrusion. I was on my way out and wanted to say good night and thank you for the lovely evening."

"No, no, Miss Lynch. Thank you for coming and to your father as well—for sending you of course," Mr. Renfrow said.

Carolina smiled politely at the remark despite the obvious condescension in his tone. Her father had plans for Mr. Renfrow, and she knew better than to upset those plans. A center-straddling, fiscally conservative Democrat running on a law-and-order platform, Joe Renfrow was the clear favorite to win the New York City mayor's seat in November.

She was aware that having politicians in his pocket was a hallmark of her father's business, so despite wanting very much to tell this room full of egomaniacs what she really thought of them, Carolina was going to do her part and kiss the ring.

"Of course, think nothing of it. Dad wished he could have come himself, but there were some last-minute issues with one of the sites in Houston."

"Yes, those last-second site issues can certainly be a headache," Renfrow said. He took a long drag off his cigar and looked her over as if he were appraising an item up for bid at an auction. "Good thing the view in here is so very pleasant."

Carolina heard Joseph shift his weight behind her and figured Renfrow had one more misogynistic remark before Joseph pounced on him. "Yes, well, I must be leaving now. It was good seeing you, Mr. Renfrow."

"You as well, Miss Lynch. Have a good evening."

"Gentlemen." Carolina smiled and nodded at the others, but except for Renfrow's forced grin, none of the other men acknowledged her. Embarrassed, and annoyed at herself for letting their dismissive attitude bother her, Carolina walked out of the room and headed straight for the front door. All she wanted now was to get home and into a hot bath.

Alfredo "Pito" Baez watched the front entrance of the building from the driver's seat of his sky-blue 1967 Dodge A108 van. Pito loved his van. He'd even named it Carla, after the first girl he screwed in the back. He'd won it betting on fights down at the Navy Yard eight years ago, and even with over a hundred and sixty thousand miles on the odometer, she still ran like a champ.

The only issue was that the air conditioner didn't work. Which, with the city in the middle of a massive heat wave, was a problem for some people. Despite it being close to midnight, he was drenched in sweat.

Pito didn't mind the heat, or the sweat for that matter. He dug how it made him feel like one of them big-game hunters stalking prey out in a jungle somewhere. He'd been hunting the uptown bitch for a few weeks now, ever since Abaddon had put him on her.

He'd stand on the corner, blending in with the rest of the winos and riffraff, and watch her. He took pride in being able to do his thing without getting spotted. Even got his nickname Pito, Spanish for whistle, from being so good at staying out of sight and warning his people of coming trouble. When he was a kid, he'd stand watch while his boys were putting in work. He'd whistle whenever he peeped out the cops walking their beat, letting his crew know the heat was coming.

Rich people like her lived and played high up in the clouds and didn't pay attention to people like him—the ones holding on to the last rung. The cloud people walked around them like they did the garbage bags stacked up on every corner. Even her expensive-looking security team didn't pay him any mind. After a while, Pito had gotten a real good feel for her schedule, and it didn't hurt that Abaddon seemed to have someone feeding him information from the inside.

Pito was parked on the southeast corner of Park Avenue and East Fiftieth Street, right in front of St. Bartholomew's Church. From where he sat, he could watch the front doors. The doorman stood there in his funny hat with his nose in the air, looking down on the world like the rest of the rich people even though he probably didn't have a pot to piss in. Pito smiled to himself when he thought about how their uppity attitudes were going to help him and his boys.

He couldn't see them from where he was parked, but he knew Talon, Tony G, and Bamboo were waiting inside Talon's 1970 Mercury Cougar on the northeast corner of Forty-Eighth and Park. Pito had eyes on Machai, Runner, and Little Cory standing not ten feet from the building's front door. So long as they didn't block the entrance, the doorman didn't pay them no attention. All his boys were in place, and soon she would come down out of the clouds and they would grab her.

Carolina appreciated the silence as they rode the elevator down to the building's lobby. Except for using a small two-way radio to instruct the rest of the security team they were on their way down, Joseph hadn't said anything. He wasn't much of a talker anyway. They had never engaged in idle conversation, and whenever she'd asked him questions, his answers were usually succinct and direct.

They stepped out of the elevator and into the building's expansive and, with its Roman columns and gold furnishings, pretentiously decorated lobby. With Joseph a step behind, Carolina walked toward the front entrance. She could see her limousine and the black Cadillac Seville the rest of her security team used parked in front of the building. She spotted Joseph's right-hand man Oscar standing outside to the left of the front door. Another member of the team, whose name she couldn't remember, stood by the open back door of her limousine.

The doorman pulled the front door open just as Carolina reached the entrance, holding it as she and Joseph walked out of the building.

"Good evening, Miss Lynch," Oscar said.

Still lost in her own thoughts, Carolina was somewhat surprised by Oscar's greeting. "Oh. Good evening, Oscar." He grinned widely and the hotel's lights reflected brightly off his bald head.

She stopped walking when she noticed three young men watching her from the street behind Oscar. They stood close to the curb behind the Cadillac. They all wore denim vests and jeans. Two of them wore red-and-white bandanas around their heads, tight against their long dark hair. The third, who wore his hair in an afro, had no shirt underneath his vest. With wide, broad shoulders and a barrel chest, he was a lot bigger than the other two. His dark, puffy hair made him seem even taller and strangely regal.

Carolina felt someone grab her gently by her elbow. She looked to her right and saw Joseph standing beside her.

"Let's keep walking, Miss Lynch." He kept his eyes focused on the three men as he spoke.

Carolina didn't respond. She glanced back at the three men as she continued walking toward her limo. They had moved closer and were now standing on the sidewalk. The two with the bandanas were expressionless, staring at her with dead eyes. But the one with the afro had a strange smirk on his face, as if he knew something no one else did.

She noticed Oscar walking beside her, between her and the three men. They maintained their hard stares, but none of them spoke. Carolina, suddenly feeling very frightened, quickened her pace. She was just about to get inside the limo when she heard the gunshots.

When he saw her exit the building, Pito was so excited he had to squeeze the steering wheel to keep his hands from shaking. He turned the ignition key and the van's 318 V8 engine roared to life. He pulled away from the curb, keeping the headlights turned off.

He cut across the intersection at East Fiftieth Street and headed south on Park Avenue. The whole thing had to be timed perfectly, so Pito was careful not to get there too fast. He tapped the gas pedal lightly with his foot, and the van moved slowly toward the uptown bitch.

Machai, Runner, and Little Cory were standing on the side-walk, and as Pito would have expected, Machai was standing tall in front. He was the vice president of the Savage Kings, second in command behind Abaddon, and normally wouldn't even be on a job like this. But Machai was big, vicious, and well-trained—exactly what they needed to deal with the uptown bitch's expen-sive looking security.

Pito was about twenty-five feet from Machai and the others when Talon's Mercury Cougar turned onto Park Avenue and headed north. Pito made a looping right turn and steered the van toward the side of the limo. He leaned forward in his seat, trying to gauge the distance between the two vehicles. He figured he was close enough, so he slammed on the brake pedal and brought the van to a screeching stop a few inches from the limo driver's door. Pito let out a small, tension-relieving breath as he checked the view outside the van.

The Cougar cut across the grassy median and sped toward the front of the limo. Pito turned back to his right just as Machai was raising the .32 snub nose revolver he'd been holding in his left hand. Machai pointed the gun at the bald security guy's forehead and squeezed the trigger.

Pito jumped in the back and pushed the van's side doors open. He stepped out onto the street as Runner and Little Cory were flaring out to Machai's right, trying to get behind the uptown bitch and the big security guy. The thin security guy who was standing by the limo door reached inside his jacket.

Pito pulled the .38 Special Revolver out of his jacket pocket, but before he could raise it up, Little Cory put a round from his Colt Python revolver in the thin security guy's face. Pito jumped when he heard the concussive blast from the powerful handgun. The back of the security guy's head disappeared in a red mist as blood and flesh exploded outward and landed on the roof of the limo.

A high-pitched ringing filled Carolina's left ear and droplets of warm blood landed on her face and neck. She looked to her left and was paralyzed as she watched Oscar's lifeless body fall to the ground. She felt Joseph's strong grip on her right arm and his other hand on top of her head as he shoved her into the limo. Carolina landed face down on the back seat with Joseph on top of her, using his body as a human shield. Another gunshot, louder and more powerful than the first one, rang out.

"What the fuck—" the limo driver screamed.

"Go! Go!" Joseph yelled.

The limo's tires screeched loudly as it reversed a few feet and then exploded forward. There was a loud crashing sound, and Carolina was jarred to her right when the limo collided with something. She felt the limo veer to the left and then accelerate.

Pito watched as the lady and her big security guy disappeared into the back of the limo. Talon stopped his Mercury Cougar in front of the limo, trying to block its path. Pito heard the limo jump into gear and then the skidding of tires.

The limo rolled backward a bit and then lurched forward, colliding with the Cougar. The limousine turned slightly to its left and headed south on Park Avenue. Talon maneuvered his car through a three-point turn and went after the limo.

"Get in the van!" Pito yelled as he made his way back to the driver's seat.

Machai, Runner, and Little Cory jumped in the van through the open side doors as Pito gassed it and sped after the limo. After about ten seconds, the Cougar's taillights appeared ahead of them, changing lanes aggressively on Park Avenue.

The limo and Cougar disappeared into the tunnel at the base of the New York General Building on East Forty-Sixth Street. Pito followed them into the tunnel and onto the Park Avenue Viaduct. He caught up to the two other vehicles just as they were passing The Met Life Building.

The limo was traveling in the right lane of the narrow two-lane street. The driver had a hard time getting around a few cars and was forced to slow down. Talon moved the Cougar into the left lane and pulled even with the limo. He yanked his steering wheel to the right and the two cars collided. The limo veered slightly to its right before swerving back and banging the Cougar.

The Cougar skidded and squealed, then curved violently into the left lane, narrowly avoiding a collision with another vehicle. Talon got the Cougar straightened out and continued forward, but the limo driver had used the near collision to create some distance. All three vehicles sped around the corner in front of Grand Central Terminal and continued south on Park Avenue.

The Cougar pulled up on the right side of the limo just as they were passing East Thirty-Fifth Street. Talon cranked the steering wheel to the left and rubbed the limo. The friction from the two vehicles caused bright orange sparks to dance in the air. The limo made a hard left turn onto East Thirty-Fourth Street, almost colliding with the concrete median.

"Holy shit," Pito whispered. He white knuckled his van's steering wheel as he watched the near collision.

The Cougar fishtailed into a left turn and followed behind the limo. The vehicles continued east on East Thirty-Fourth Street, the limo snaking between the lanes, trying to block the Cougar from moving up. The cars sped past Second Avenue and made a left turn on Tunnel Approach Street, toward the Queens Midtown Tunnel. With Pito's van at the rear, the three vehicles sped down the narrow, one-lane street. There weren't any vehicles ahead of their caravan at the turnoff for the tunnel at East Thirty-Sixth Street.

The limo went through the intersection and made a wide right turn toward the tunnel entrance. It fishtailed and almost spun out, but the driver slowed down and regained control. The split-second loss of control gave Talon the time he needed to pull his car up beside the limo.

The two cars were nearly side by side as they sped downhill toward the tunnel entrance. Talon cranked his car's steering wheel to the left and slammed the rear of the limo. The force of the impact caused the limo to spin out of control. Round and round it spun until it crashed into a stone wall near the tunnel entrance.

***

Carolina was sitting up when the car hit them from behind. She felt the limo spin, and the force of its momentum caused her to slide into Joseph. A split second later, she was thrown back the other way when the limo crashed into the wall. She hit her head on the window and felt a sharp pain just above her hairline. Warm liquid trickled down her forehead and face, and she tasted the blood on her lips.

Everything went quiet, and Carolina was more concerned now than she'd been during the chase. Although her vision was blurry, she saw Joseph holding his handgun up and near his face as he peered through the vehicle windows. She was dizzy and thought she might pass out, but the fear-inducing silence kept her awake.

"Wait here, miss," Joseph said.

Carolina reached for him. "Don't go—"

Joseph ignored her touch and spoke to the driver. "Connor, you ready, mate?"

She listened for Connor's response but heard gunfire instead.

Tony G and Bamboo were out of the Mercury Cougar and headed toward the limo before it stopped spinning. Pito stopped the van about twenty yards from the limo, facing it head on. The limo's headlights were on so he couldn't see if anyone was still in the front seat. He made sure to keep his headlights on so they couldn't see him or his people either.

The van's side doors opened, and Machai, Runner, and Little Cory exited with their guns drawn.

"Stay in the van, Pito. Bring it up when we grab the bitch," Machai said.

They crept to the front of the van but stopped behind the headlights, uncertain what waited for them in the limo. After a few tension filled seconds, Talon exited the Cougar. He stood in the shadows, away from the lights, holding something in his hands. From the shape of the silhouette, Pito figured it was his HK MP5SD submachine gun.

The cherry on Talon's cigarette brightened. He raised the machine gun up to his shoulder, paused for a second as he took aim, and squeezed the trigger. Bullets exploded from the muzzle at 935 feet per second and tore into the front of the limo, destroying its headlights and windshield.

Pito could see into the front seat now. The driver lay motionless, his head on the steering wheel. There weren't any signs of life inside the limo. He found himself praying the Lynch woman was just hiding and hadn't caught a stray round. Because if she was dead, Abaddon would kill all of them.

It was eerily quiet as Tony G and Bamboo started inching forward. The right rear door flew open, and two gunshots broke the silence. The big security guy was out of the limo before Tony G and Bamboo's bodies hit the ground. He took cover behind the open car door and managed to get off two more rounds before Talon opened fire.

A series of three round bursts tore through the limo door like a warm knife through butter. The big security guy stumbled backward a few steps before falling to the ground. Machai, Runner, and Little Cory made their way to the open door. Machai disappeared into the limo and reemerged a few seconds later, clutching the girl.

Pito breathed a deep sigh of relief. Although she was covered in blood and she looked unsteady, the woman was alive. They threw her into the back of the van, and Pito drove into the tunnel—away from the wreckage and toward the safe harbor of Hemlock Gardens.

two
Monday, July 11

VIC ESPADA WATCHED the front entrance of Dario's Tavern from his black 1969 Pontiac GTO. The faded gold lettering on the storefront window advertised it as a bar and billiard hall, but he suspected they were pushing more than cheap whiskey and failed dreams. Vic, along with his trainee Teri Nelson, had spent the better part of the afternoon watching the bar from where they'd parked on Saint Ann's Avenue, just south of East 141st Street.

As a Fugitive Recovery Agent, he'd gotten word from an informant that Bobby Santini spent most of his days in the bar drinking cheap booze and betting long shots. Vic had been tracking Santini for the past three days, ever since he'd failed to show up for an appearance in the courtroom of tough-as-nails Judge Ivan Miranda. Apparently, being a no-show didn't sit well with the judge. Word was, the former New York Police Department beat cop had tossed his gavel at Santini's lawyer as he was issuing the bench warrant.

"I was just up here last week," Teri said.

"Uh huh." Vic answered without looking at her, his focus split between the bar and whatever Teri was talking about.

"Yeah. We were over at Pulaski Park, listening to music."

"You came all the way to the Bronx to listen to music?"

"It was more like a concert."

"They have punk rock concerts in the Bronx?"

He knew Teri was heavy into the punk rock scene and spent a lot of her free time going to live shows in different bars down in the Bowery section of Manhattan. Vic was aware he wasn't hip to the current music scene, but he would still be surprised if punk rock had made its way to this part of the city.

"Not yet. But they're coming, I can feel it. Anyway, that time was for a different thing. It was a DJ battle."

He glanced at her. "'DJ battle?' Are the disc jockeys throwing records at each other or something?" He chuckled as he turned his attention back to the bar.

"Damn Vic, sometimes you sound like an old man."

Vic flinched at the old man remark. He still felt energetic and youthful, but he had a decade on Teri. So, when she got to talking about what the kids were listening to these days, he felt a lot older than twenty-nine. "I've seen them in the park by the office. That's when they mix other people's music together and talk over the lyrics right?"

She chuckled. "Yeah, something like that. It was Busy Bee versus DJ Disco Wiz."

"Interesting names." A few silent seconds passed where he could have taken the off ramp and leave the topic behind, but to his surprise, Vic was curious about the outcome. "So, who won?"

"The battle? Man, they were both great. To tell you the truth, it doesn't matter. It was a great time, so we all won. You should come to a show with me sometime."

"Nah, that kind of music isn't my thing. I'm more of an Otis Redding, Willie Colón guy."

"Too bad. It's the future."

"If you say so."

They fell into an easy silence but after a few minutes she started fidgeting in her seat.

"How much longer do you want to wait, Vic?" Teri asked.

Vic kept his attention on the bar and didn't answer. He ignored her for two reasons: One, he didn't want to risk Santini getting past him because he'd gotten distracted. And two, after having Teri tied to his hip for the past seventy-two hours, Vic was all talked out.

He was showing her the ropes as a favor to his boss Chris, who also happened to be Teri's uncle. Chris had promised her he'd give her a shot as a Fugitive Recovery Agent, but only after she learned how to do the job. That's where Vic came in.

"Did you hear me, Vic?"

"Yeah."

"And?"

"And what?"

"How much longer are we going to be out here? It's hot as shit."

"As long as it takes."

He didn't want to admit it, but she was right. It was close to one in the afternoon and, despite having the air conditioning inside his car turned to its highest setting, it was oppressively hot. The news updates on the radio had announced it was already eighty-eight degrees outside and would get hotter before the day was over.

"How do we even know he's coming here?" Teri asked.

"That's the word I got."

"From who? A snitch? How can we be sure what he says is even reliable?"

He glanced at her, irritated. "We can't be. But it's all we have right now, so we're going to wait."

Teri stared out the windshield, seemingly annoyed with his answers. Beads of sweat dotted her forehead, and the white Ramones shirt she was wearing clung to the perspiration on her chest and arms.

"Can we at least go get an ice cream or something? I'm sure

that guy over there has something we could use." Teri pointed to the *piragua* man a half a block away.

Vic followed her finger to the man pushing his cart full of fruit-flavored syrup and ice, and felt the saliva build in his mouth. The truth was, as hot as it was outside, a cup of shaved ice covered in pineapple flavored juice sounded like a little piece of heaven to him.

"Tempting, but no dice. We need to be watching for Santini, not shoving our faces in a *piragua* cart. Besides, if he makes us and gets away, I'm gonna be pissed."

"Makes us how? There are people up and down this block all day. If you ask me, we look more suspicious sitting in this car."

"Maybe, maybe not. But from here we have a view of every angle of approach. And if in the off chance he's in a car and decides to take off, we're ready." She rolled her eyes and turned away. "I can see you don't like that answer, so how about this—we're not moving from this spot. Not till Santini shows up or the bar closes."

"Damn, Vic." Teri threw her head back on her seat, and her dark hair, which she wore afro style, shook on impact.

Vic turned his attention back to Dario's without responding. Teri was beautiful, intelligent, and tough as nails. But having just turned nineteen, she was like most people her age—impatient and self-involved. She was a good kid, and he liked her, but Vic was tired of the complaining.

"Listen, this is the job. Maybe you thought it'd be a nonstop chase, full of adrenaline and action, but it's not. It's mostly this—sitting around and waiting. And when we do find who we're looking for, they usually come quietly. If you don't like it, you can always catch a cab back to the office."

"I'm not saying I want to leave. But what was the bond on this guy anyway? Two grand? That means we clear maybe two hundred dollars on the recovery. We've put in three days on this guy already. I'm just asking if the juice is worth the squeeze?"

Vic appreciated how Teri's mind worked, but statements like

that made it clear she had some growing up to do. Santini had been a petty thief who'd recently graduated to committing nighttime burglaries. He'd been arrested for a series of warehouse burglaries in Mott Haven, in the South Bronx. But with the jails overcrowded, the judge had set his bond low. It wasn't the highest ticket Vic had ever chased but he needed the green, and there were more important things to consider.

"First, *I'm* going to clear two hundred. The only thing you're getting out of this is an education. Second, this is what we do. It's how we make a living. So yes, I'm going to squeeze every bit of juice out of every piece of fruit I can find." He turned and made sure she saw his face. "And last, and most important, your uncle built something here. He has his own business. You know how difficult it is for people like us to own their own shit these days?"

"Yeah, I guess," Teri said petulantly.

"Nah, you don't have a clue. But that's okay, you're still young and learning. It's about more than dollars and cents, it's about your uncle's reputation. He puts his name on every bond he writes. So, when a piece of shit like Santini decides they're going to skip, they're putting your uncle's name and business in jeopardy. After what Chris did for me—giving me a job when no one else would—I won't allow that to happen."

Something over Vic's shoulder caught Teri's attention, so he turned. Santini was crossing 141st Street, headed for Dario's.

"That looks like our boy right there. He's walking into the bar," Teri said.

"All right, you wait here. I'm going to go get him."

"What do you mean, 'wait here?' I want to go inside."

As much promise as she showed, Teri was still young and inexperienced. Judging from its exterior, Dario's was a low-end dive bar that was probably filled with bottom feeders like Santini. Vic had spotted three Harley Davidson Super Glide motorcycles parked on the sidewalk a few feet from the bar. He couldn't be sure how some bikers would react to people of his and Teri's complexion, and he didn't want to have to worry about her getting hurt.

"I need you to wait here. If I'm not out in ten minutes, drive to a pay phone away from here and call the cops. Then call your uncle and let him know what happened."

He exited the car before she could complain and headed for the bar.

Dario's was a long and narrow space, and Vic could see clear to the other side. He spotted Santini at the far end of the tavern, sitting on one of the short back stools that lined the front of the cherry-wood bar. Santini's attention was fixed on something in front of him. Either his reflection in the giant mirror that'd been mounted on the wall behind the bar, or the dozens of liquor bottles stacked on the shelf below the mirror.

Vic took a second to scan the room. The bar's glossy, maroon-colored walls were covered with framed pictures and shelves full of cheap looking trophies. An old jukebox, and two round cherry-wood tables filled out the rest of the interior.

The place smelled like stale beer and cigarettes. Two ceiling fans mounted about ten feet apart were barely moving and completely useless against the heat outside. Besides Santini and Vic, there were four people in Dario's, including the bartender who had disappeared into a back room when Vic walked in.

Judging by their garb, the other three patrons owned the bikes Vic had spotted outside. They were sitting at the bar, close to the entrance. They had eyed him when he walked in, but two of the three had returned to what they were doing after appraising him. The third stood up and did the mad dog thing as Vic walked by him—staring as if Vic had stolen his firstborn.

All three were stocky, but the mad dog was tall as well. Vic stood close to six feet tall and still had to look up to see his face. All three were wearing black leather vests with upper and lower rockers stitched on the back. The writing on the rockers identified them as members of the New York chapter of the Visigoths.

"You sure you in the right place? They don't serve fried chicken in here," the mad dog said.

One of the sitting bikers looked up. "C'mon Bear, let's just finish our beers and get back on the road."

Vic continued past Bear, but for about half a second, he contemplated turning around. He was tired and frustrated and wouldn't have minded getting a little workout in on the idiot with the unoriginal name. But Vic knew he wouldn't just be taking on Bear. It would be the other two as well and he didn't have the time.

What he had been looking for was sitting five feet from him, and Vic wanted to get Santini wrapped up and delivered to Central Booking. Vic figured if he was lucky, he and Teri could make it across the Macombs Dam Bridge and back into Harlem before rush hour started.

Santini had noticed the interaction with Bear and was looking in their direction. His eyes widened when he realized Vic was walking toward him.

"Bobby Santini?"

Santini eyeballed Vic suspiciously. "Who's asking?"

Santini was wiry and solid, with close-cropped hair and a heavy five o'clock shadow. There was a glass cup filled with a dark liquid resting on the bar top in front of him. Vic kept his eyes fixed on Santini, but through his peripheral vision, he spotted some softball bats mounted on the wall to his left.

"My name's Vic Espada. I work for Chris, your bondsman."

"Congratulations." Santini looked back down at his drink.

"This is an interesting spot. Very rustic."

"What's rustic?"

"This bar."

"No. I mean what *is* rustic?"

"Oh. It's a euphemism for shitty."

Santini tilted his head slightly. "Eupha-what? Those are some big words. I guess they're handing out dictionaries with welfare checks these days." He laughed at his own joke. "What can I do for ya, dictionary boy?"

"You missed your court date, so the judge issued a bench warrant. I'm here to take you in."

"You a cop?"

"No. Like I said—I work for the guy who put up your bond."

"So, you're a bounty hunter."

"I prefer Fugitive Recovery Agent."

"Oh, well excuuuse the fuck out of me." Santini turned in his stool, so he was facing Vic. "Listen here, Mr. Recovery Agent. I'm thirsty and I just sat down, so I'm not going anywhere with you. What I am gonna do is finish this drink, and then I'm gonna have three or four more. After I'm good and hammered, I'm gonna go home, jerk off, and go to sleep in my own bed." He lifted his glass and gulped his entire drink. "Door's that way fucko." Santini motioned toward the entrance as he turned away from Vic.

Vic sighed. He wasn't being entirely truthful when he told Teri the job was boring and that the people they tracked usually came along quietly. Yes, tracking fugitives could be tedious—a lot of hours spent waiting and watching. But when Vic found them, they almost never came along quietly.

They were criminals after all. People hardened by lifetimes of crime and violence, and every one of them thought they were the toughest person in the room. No, they hardly ever came along without a fight and if Vic was being honest, he loved when they didn't.

"I don't drink, and I don't have time to wait for you to finish yours, so get up. We're leaving."

"I already told you, spook—I'm not going anywhere with you." Santini glared at Vic. "Fuck off!"

Vic had expected the response and was preparing to take the conversation to the next level when he heard heavy footsteps approaching. He turned to his right and saw Bear standing about a foot away, his large frame almost entirely blocking the narrow walkway. Just past Bear, the other two bikers were still seated but watching the show.

"It sounds like you're bothering my friend here. I suggest you do what he says and get the fuck out of here before I mess up your neat little afro," Bear said.

"I appreciate the advice, but this is a private conversation. Why don't you go back to your seat and have a drink on me."

"You're an uppity little spook, ain't ya? Listen here, ni—"

Vic raised his leg and drove the heal of his foot into the side of Bear's left knee. There was a loud crack, and his knee went forty-five degrees in a direction God had not intended. Bear went down instantly, letting out a loud grunt as he grabbed for the bar top to try and catch himself.

As soon as his foot touched the floor, Vic dropped his one hundred and eighty pounds of body weight into his heals, rotated at the waist, and threw a left punch. The blow landed flush on Bear's temple. He fell forward and was out cold before his face bounced off the cheap linoleum.

The hefty ones stumbled out of their chairs and headed toward Vic. He grabbed one of the softball bats off the wall, stepped over Bear's unconscious body, and went to meet them head on. They were too big to stand shoulder to shoulder in the narrow walkway, so one stood behind the other. Vic heard movement behind him but didn't want to take his eyes off the threats. Half a second later Santini, using the bar top as his own personal runway, sprinted past Vic and the big bikers and out the front door.

Vic drew back as if he was going to swing the bat at the first guy's head, but when he raised his arm to block the blow, Vic brought the bat crashing down across the man's knee. Vic thrust his knee into the guy's face as he tumbled forward. Big boy reached for his nose with both hands and let out a pained wail as he fell to the side, against the bottom of the bar.

Vic's momentum from the knee strike carried him to his left, so he switched to a left-handed grip on the bat and swung it across the other guy's elbow. There was a loud cracking sound, and he uttered a yelp as he fell into the wall. Vic ran past the downed bikers, dropping the bat as he exited Dario's.

Teri was trying to find a radio station she liked when she sensed movement to her right. She looked toward the vacant lot filled with debris and trash and spotted dozens of rats, all clustered together feeding on some sort of waste. New York City was infamous for the giant rats that brazenly prowled its streets and took up space in its buildings as if they paid rent. Large, puppy-sized vermin, up to a foot long and weighing over a pound, infested every part of the city.

Teri, as she imagined most people did, hated rats. But as if hate wasn't enough, she also had a deep fear of them that could be traced back to her childhood. She couldn't have been older than nine or ten when it'd happened.

She'd been playing in a trash-filled lot with some other kids when she'd heard a soul-piercing scream. They'd all ran over and had found one of their playmates being attacked by rats. The girl had somehow fallen and there were dozens of them crawling on her, scratching and biting in a feeding frenzy. The experience still haunted Teri. She shuddered and turned her attention back to the car radio.

Before the cast from the horror film *Willard* had made their appearance and distracted her, Teri had been making her way through the radio stations. She didn't mind the stuff Vic listened to on 101.9 WPIX. Songs by Jim Croce and The Temptations were cool for what they were, but she preferred the tunes being played on 102.7 WNEW. Music from The Sex Pistols, The Ramones, and Blondie. The station was even playing cool new stuff from Springsteen. It was the kind of music that got her fired up, and after three days of following Vic around like a lost puppy, Teri needed some firing up.

Vic was a good guy, and she was learning a lot from him. But outside of work stuff, they hadn't had much to talk about. Even though he was only ten years older than her, it felt like they came from different worlds.

Teri knew Vic and her Uncle Chris were close, but she felt like Vic took the "overprotective big brother" routine too far. Making her wait in the car while he went in the bar was complete and total bullshit. Teri had grown up on these streets too and was confident in her abilities. She knew Vic meant well, but she resented being treated like a damsel in distress.

Teri heard "White Riot" by The Clash come on the radio. She was about to reach down to turn up the volume when Santini dashed out of the bar and headed north on St. Ann's Avenue. It took Teri half a second to decide her next move. She grabbed the car keys out of the ignition and took off after Santini.

Vic pushed open the front door of Dario's and rushed to the corner of the block, looking for Santini. He spotted Teri hauling ass north on St. Ann's Avenue.

"Goddamit."

He dashed across the street and got in the driver's seat of his GTO. He went to start the car, but the keys were gone. *Damn.*

Vic had one foot on the pavement and was about to take off after Teri when he remembered the extra key he kept stashed under the driver's seat. He reached down and groped around for the key, pulling it out of its hiding spot. He inserted it in the ignition and started the car. The engine turned over and roared to life. He slammed on the gas pedal with so much force, the GTO fishtailed as it peeled away from the curb.

He headed north on St. Ann's Avenue, catching up to Teri as she ran into St. Mary's Park. Vic was awestruck by what he was witnessing. The long-legged Teri, athletic and fast as hell, was about thirty feet behind Santini and closing fast. He continued driving on St. Ann's but slowed down and paralleled them.

After a few seconds Teri was right behind Santini. She kicked his heel. Santini lost his balance, fell face-first, and rolled. She was on him before he stopped rolling.

Vic parked his car along the curb, vaulted out, and ran toward them, hurdling the park's four-foot-high, cast-iron fence. When he reached them, Teri was on Santini's back and testing the laws of physics by trying to connect Santini's left hand to his right shoulder.

Vic tapped Teri on her shoulder and gave her a "cool it" expression when she looked up at him. He took out his handcuffs and handed them to Teri, who placed them on Santini's wrists with a little more force than was necessary. Santini let out a squeal and a barrage of curse words as they helped him off the ground. Vic noticed Teri wasn't breathing hard, and looked energized, like someone who'd just finished up a light jog before starting the serious part of their workout.

Teri reached into her jeans pocket, pulled out his car keys, and handed them to Vic. "Here, you might need these for later."

Vic grabbed the keys. "Man, I am never going to hear the end of this one."

They both smiled as they escorted a limping Santini back to the GTO.

three

THEY'D GOTTEN in and out of Central Booking faster than usual, and traffic on the Macombs had still been light, so Vic and Teri made it back to the office just before four in the afternoon. Sugar Hill Bail Bonds and Investigations was on the first floor of a three-story building on 154th Street, between Amsterdam Avenue and St. Nicholas Avenue. Four walk-up apartments made up the second and third floors.

The building and business were both owned by Vic's boss, Christopher Nelson. A former heavyweight boxer who once went thirteen rounds with Jersey Joe Walcott, he'd retired with a career record of twenty-two wins against eighteen losses. It wasn't the best win-loss record, but it'd been what Chris needed to earn enough money to buy a home and start his own business.

Vic had just closed the front door and was locking it when Chris's deep voice boomed out from his private office. "How'd it go?"

From where he stood, Vic had a clear line of sight straight back to Chris's office. The boss sat leaned back in his chair with his feet on his desk. A folded copy of his favorite paper, *The New York Times*, lay on his sizable stomach. Chris's office was one of four rooms that made up the base of operations for Sugar Hill Bail Bonds and Investigations, the other three being the bathroom, kitchen, and the large room that Vic and Teri worked out of.

Vic glanced over at Teri who was busy settling into her desk. "It went all right."

"Did you pick up Santini?" Chris asked.

"Yeah." Vic walked into the kitchen and pulled an ice cube tray out of the freezer.

Chris stepped out of his office and poked his head into the kitchen. "Then I'd say it went better than all right."

"He's just mad that the skip got chased down by little old me, Uncle Chris," Teri said.

"First of all, I'm not mad. And second, you had a head start on me." Vic folded a few ice cubes into a dish towel and wrapped it around the knuckles on his left hand.

Teri chuckled. "What are you talking about, Vic? You had a car."

Vic walked past Chris and sat down at his desk. "Which is useless without keys. It's a good thing I had the spare."

"Well, I didn't want that pretty little car of yours to get stolen."

"Thank you for that." Vic nodded and winked. "In all seriousness, Chris, the young lady did a good job today. She might have a future in this business."

Teri flashed a broad grin. "You got that right, jack—"

"If she can learn to calm down and listen," Vic interrupted.

Teri's expression went from joyful to dejected in a flash.

Chris motioned at Vic's hand with his chin. "What happened there?"

"Ah nothing. Some biker asked me on a date. Tried to break my hand with his head when I turned him down."

"Well, since you made it back here and your face ain't messed up, I'm guessing it wasn't that long of a conversation."

"Not at all."

Chris took a seat behind the desk across from Vic. "Listen to me, youngblood. You got to be careful at some of these spots. I know you think you're safe in The Fear 'cause you grew up in them neighborhoods. And on account most of the people who live there look like us, but that don't mean shit. There are still plenty of racist motherfuckers moving around out there that would love nothing more than to skin your red-boned hide. You're lighter than me young fella, but you're darker than them. And don't think them green-ass eyes of yours is going to get you a pass with them people."

"You know me better than that Chris. I'm always careful. People are starving out in The Fear, so it's pretty much every man for himself, regardless of skin tone. This was just one of those things. What the academics would call a 'confluence of unfortunate events.'"

"Call it what you want, just be careful—especially when you have my niece with you."

"Come on, Uncle Chris, I don't need a babysitter. I proved that today. Vic, will you tell him I'm okay on my own?" The childish whine of Teri's tone undermined the grown woman image she tried hard to project.

"Hold on there, grasshopper, you still have a lot to learn." Vic leaned forward in his chair and looked at Chris. "Anything come in today?"

Over the past few months, they had established an unfortunate routine. Vic would spend a few days tracking down a skip that would maybe net him a couple of hundred dollars after expenses. He'd ask Chris about new business, of which there was almost none, and then he'd spend two or three days waiting for the next job.

A thousand bail bond companies were all chasing the same clients, and most of the bonds Chris did post weren't worth the paper they were printed on. As far as the investigations part of Chris's business, Vic figured anyone who could afford to hire a private investigator wasn't looking to hire a fifty-five-year-old black man, no matter how good of an investigator he was—and Chris was a great investigator.

Chris stood up. "For the business? Nope. You had a visitor though."

"Who was it?"

"He didn't say. Tall white guy. He was dressed sharp and looked serious. Left this for you." Chris handed Vic a folded piece of notebook paper and walked back into his office.

"Did you read it?"

"Damn right I did."

Vic let out a small laugh as he unfolded and read the note. He sucked in a breath when he read the name Oran Burke signed at the bottom.

Pito had been sitting in the small, dark room staring at the thirteen-inch television for almost four hours. The black-and-white images appearing on the small screen were grainy and it was hard to make out the Lynch woman's features. She had been pacing back and forth almost nonstop since they'd put her in the room.

They had a few apartments set aside around Hemlock Gardens for prisoners. Abaddon had insisted on having somewhere to keep what he called their "prisoners of war." They were all small, two-bedroom apartments complete with kitchens and bathrooms for anyone on guard duty. The prisoners were kept in one bedroom, while the other bedroom was for watching the video feed.

He thought it was shit work, but Pito couldn't deny he liked watching her. He'd thought she was beautiful when he'd first spotted her a few weeks back. Pito had even thought they could put her to work on The Stroll over on Eleventh Avenue after all this was done. The johns looking for a good time would pay a hell of a lot for just a sniff of what she had between her legs.

But that was in the beginning, before he'd spent time watching her. She was beautiful, sure, but it was more than that for him. He'd seen how she'd acted since they'd nabbed her. She hadn't cried or begged like most of the others had done. She'd kept her head up and mouth shut. Not challenging any of the fellas with direct eye contact, but not showing fear by staring at the floor either. A lot like he'd done during his stretch in Auburn Correctional.

Pito had started to like the lady. So much so he had even stopped calling her the uptown bitch. But as much as he was digging her, he didn't appreciate getting stuck on guard duty.

He had been with the Savage Kings since they'd started up in 1963. There'd been only twelve of them then, a bunch of kids from the neighborhood spending their days robbing civilians for chump change in Howard Beach. But then Abaddon disappeared, and everything fell apart. Everyone had their own version of what'd happened to him—murdered, locked up, found love and took off for California—but no one really knew for sure. The Kings, never really that organized to begin with, had nearly fallen apart without Abaddon's smarts to guide them.

But then, in the summer of 1972, the man had returned. No explanation for the missing years was given. He was just back— bigger, stronger, meaner, and smarter, and so were the Kings. Only this time they weren't twelve kids hustling for chump change. It'd taken a little while, but eventually they were over two hundred strong, had money coming in from dope and women, and Abaddon was the supreme president.

He'd brought them back to life, like a doctor with them electric paddle things. With Abaddon running the show, they weren't ghosts any more—faceless, nameless reminders of what once was. With Abaddon at the head of the table, the Kings had purpose and were important—they ate first. Yeah, Pito appreciated everything. But that didn't mean he had to be stuck on shit work like watching cameras for hours on end.

The sound of the apartment's door opening and closing pulled him out of his trance. Pito walked out of the small room and toward the front. He was surprised to see Machai standing by the front door. Machai hardly ever left Abaddon's side, and he never checked on prisoners. He was Abaddon's number two, which pissed Pito off something fierce. He couldn't think of any reason Machai should be above him.

"How's the bitch?" Machai asked.

"She looks all right to me. Keeps walking back and forth, but that's it."

"Has she eaten?"

"Nah, we put some food on the table but she ain't touched it."

"Well, keep her fed. And don't let nobody touch her. That comes straight from the supreme president himself. That bitch is worth a lot of green, but only if she ain't hurt. You feel me, blood?"

"Don't worry about nothing. I got this shit."

"My man. I'm gonna check on her."

Pito didn't move. There wasn't any need for Machai to go in the room unless he was planning to take her. "Why?"

Machai looked down at Pito with a surprised expression. "What?"

"Why you going in the room?"

"That ain't none of your concern, Pito."

"We been doing real good not letting her see any of our faces. If you go in there, she's going to see yours. Be able to ID you to the cops."

"Believe me, that ain't gonna be a problem. Now get the fuck out of the way."

Pito couldn't think of anything else to say, but he held his ground. Machai pushed past him and walked toward the room.

Carolina had no idea how long she'd been in the room. She didn't have a clock or watch, and the only window in the small space had been covered with wood. Probably less than twenty-four hours, but that was just a guess. Three glasses of champagne at the party, followed by the sensory overload of being chased and the ensuing gunfire, had left her disoriented when they'd pulled her out of the limo.

She remembered being blindfolded and held down in the van, so she'd had no sense of direction. At one point, Carolina had heard a car horn echo, so she figured they had driven through the Queens Midtown Tunnel. She was probably in one of the boroughs outside of Manhattan.

As she paced back and forth thinking about what had transpired, her fear had turned to anger. The maniacs had killed Joseph and the rest of her security detail, but except for her dress being torn a little, she was unharmed. She'd spotted the camera mounted near the ceiling, so she knew they were watching her. But no one had said anything to her, and the silence was unsettling.

She looked around, taking in her surroundings. The walls were taupe colored and had a strange bumpy texture, as if someone had sloppily applied ten coats of the ugly semigloss paint. A child-size bed was in one corner of the room, and a small, metal bucket she had used to urinate in sat on the floor near the bed.

She heard the door being unlocked and stopped pacing. She recognized the man instantly when he entered the room. He was the tallest of the three thugs that'd been standing outside the building. He looked around the room but didn't say anything. He was wearing the same thing he'd worn last night and there were two patches over the right breast pocket of his denim vest. The bigger one on top read "Machai" and the smaller tag read "Vice President."

"Machai, huh? Interesting. Vice President of what, exactly?"

He ignored her question and glanced down at the food that was left on the table. "You gonna eat this or what?"

"Maybe later. What do you want with me?"

"Money. What else would we want? As long as your daddy pays up, everything's gonna work out just fine. Don't worry, ain't nobody gonna try anything with you. Unless you want it, of course." He looked her over hungrily.

His dead-eye stare made her blood run cold, but she was determined not to let her fear show. "Listen, none of this is necessary. My father will pay whatever you've asked for, I'm sure of it."

He lips twisted into a menacing smirk. "You better hope so, princess. 'Cause if we don't get that money, it's gonna be open season on you."

He walked out of the room, shutting the door behind him. Carolina waited till she heard the lock turn before she silently cried.

four

THE LAST TIME Vic saw Oran Burke he was boarding a plane for Tokyo. They had just spent two weeks on the island Oahu relaxing and recovering after surviving the hellscape called Vietnam. They'd said their goodbyes at the entrance to Honolulu International and promised to keep in touch. That was over seven years ago.

He dialed the number on the note. Oran answered on the third ring, and after thirty seconds of pleasantries, they arranged to meet in person. Vic suggested drinks at the 118th Street Rose in Harlem, half expecting Oran to give him a "that sound's great, but how about this" brush-off and suggest an alternative south of 110th Street.

While the bar was a happening spot, consistently filled with beautiful women and great music, it was in Harlem. A series of riots in the sixties had led to an exodus, leaving behind garbage-filled vacant lots and abandoned tenements. It'd become a community of desperate people living in poverty. Because of the high crime rate and pervasive danger in Harlem, the general sentiment among non-residents was that the only time to cross north of

110th Street was if someone was offering a cure for cancer. And even then, it was a maybe.

Only Oran Burke hadn't shied away. Hell, Vic thought, he'd even sounded enthusiastic about making the trip to Upper Manhattan. Originally a community with a large Italian population, Puerto Rican migration into New York City had skyrocketed after World War II, and East Harlem became a Puerto Rican cultural enclave. Outsiders took to calling the area Spanish Harlem, but for residents it would always be known as *El Barrio.*

The 118th Street Rose, a popular spot among the locals, was located between Second and Third Avenue in East Harlem. The spacious bar's décor and music were a fusion of the different cultures that made up Harlem. It was filled with small, round tables, a long mahogany bar, two pool tables, and a stage for live music.

Vic arrived at the smoke-filled bar a little after eight, early enough to find a table but not so early there wasn't already some eye candy to admire. Amber light emitting from the hanging lights reflected off the room's red brick walls, and "At Midnight" by Rufus and Chaka Khan played low in the background. He sat at one of the tables near the front and enjoyed the view while he waited for Oran.

He noticed the waitress standing by his table. Young and pretty, with big hips and an ample bosom, she wasn't wearing a name tag. And like the other two waitresses, her clothes seemed to be her own rather than a uniform.

"What can I get you, honey?" she asked.

"Beer. Whatever's on tap will work fine." Vic looked past her and spotted Oran walking in the front door. "And three fingers of Dewar's for my friend there."

She glanced toward the entrance, then turned back to Vic. "That's your friend?"

"Yeah. You say that like it's strange."

"I just don't see young, fine-ass brothers like you hanging out with white boys too often."

He chuckled at the remark. "What's your name?"

"Brandy."

"Well, Brandy, I have a lot of friends. If you have time after your shift ends, maybe we can be friends too."

She grinned and was about to respond when Oran sidled up to her.

"I'll be right back with those drinks," Brandy said as she walked away.

Oran squinted, his eyebrows arching ever so slightly. "Why do I feel like I just interrupted something?"

"Because you did." Vic stood up. "But it isn't anything I can't resume later."

"I bet it's not, you pretty motherfucker."

They both beamed and embraced in a hug. Vic stepped back and looked his old friend over. Oran's cream-colored linen pants, silk white V-neck shirt, and expensive-looking dark brown leather shoes seemed flashy and out of character from the man Vic remembered.

Aside from the early stages of crow's feet and flecks of gray in his full, dark brown mane, Oran hadn't changed much. He had the same wide, toothy grin and still looked fit and powerful. He stood a little over six-foot-two and possessed the size and—when Vic had known him before—violent disposition of an NFL linebacker.

"Man, look at you. You look good. What's it been? Six years?" Oran said.

They both sat down.

"Closer to seven, but yeah, it's been a while. You look good too. Some gray up top, but you look good, brother. That outfit is razor sharp."

"Yeah. Well, the gray hair and nice clothes both come from the same place—running a business."

Brandy placed their drinks down on the table and winked at Vic. Oran craned his neck in her direction as she sauntered away.

He turned back to Vic. "You're going to bang her later, aren't you?"

"Probably. I haven't decided yet."

They both laughed. Oran picked up his drink and eyed Vic's beer curiously. "Is that all you're drinking?"

"For now. I'm trying to pace myself, things might get interesting later." Vic glanced at Brandy as he picked up his glass of beer.

"That makes sense. Well, here's to old times and new pussy."

"*Salud*," Vic said.

They touched glasses and took sips of their drinks.

"This is a nice spot." Oran looked around the bar and back at Vic. "The neighborhood sucks, but this place is pretty cool."

"Yeah, Harlem's seen better days. But it's filled with resilient people. It'll find its way back."

"I'm sure it will. So, are you still in touch with any of the guys from Ariadne?"

Vic shook his head. He hadn't heard the name in a long time. Ariadne had been the code name of their eight-man team in Vietnam, one of the twelve teams that'd made-up 3rd Force Reconnaissance Company. Vic had been in the Corps for nearly two years when he'd joined 3rd Force Recon in 1968. He'd been assigned to third platoon where Oran had been one of the sergeants and Vic's team leader. They'd served together till 3rd Force Recon was deactivated in 1970.

"No, not really. I kept in touch with Bobby for a little while. He'd give me updates on some of the fellas. But after he died, I hadn't heard from anyone till I got your note today."

"Yeah. Bobby Seely." Oran's eyes glazed over. "Remember when we had to pull him off that Navy lieutenant in An Thoi?"

"How can I forget?" Vic said through a small smile. "The team had to pony up a lot of green to keep him out of squid jail."

Oran laughed at the memory. "Son of a bitch had the worst temper."

"Yeah. But to be fair, that lieutenant did shove him."

"I seem to recall the shove coming *after* Bobby called the lieutenant and his men dickless housewives, and very loudly suggested they have our meals ready before we went to work."

"Bobby wasn't very good at diplomatic relations."

"Yeah well, he didn't have to be. Fucking High Note," Oran said. He sipped his drink and stared foggy eyed at the glass. "When was that anyway? That he died?"

Private First Class Bobby "High Note" Seely had been one of Ariadne's riflemen. He'd been nineteen years old when he joined 3rd Force, the youngest guy on the team. Bobby had grown up in East Philadelphia, so his age and background had produced a combustible combination of loud, arrogant, and funny as hell. Despite his brash attitude, everyone loved the kid. But he and Vic were of similar age and backgrounds, so they'd been especially close.

"In 'seventy-five. Cancer."

"Yeah, seems like that got a lot of guys."

"Yeah. Probably all that Agent Orange shit they were spraying everywhere." Vic sipped his water. "So, what about you? You said something about running a business. What's that about?"

"Private security. Bodyguards for the rich and famous. That's kind of what I wanted to talk to you about?"

"I'm not really the bodyguard type, brother. And I already have a job."

"It's a contract job—for some serious money."

"Yeah?"

"Yeah. You up for a ride to my office? I need visual aids to explain everything." Oran finished the last of his Dewar's and placed the glass upside-down on the table.

"Sure, why not?"

Leviathan Security Consultants was on the fifth floor of a twelve-story commercial building on East Sixty-Seventh Street in Manhattan. It was a small, sparsely furnished, two-room office that Vic didn't think fit with the whole "security company for the wealthy" image Oran was trying to project.

"You want something to drink? Water? I think I have some beer in the fridge." Oran walked toward the back room.

Vic waved away the offer. "Nah, I'm good."

Oran emerged from the back room holding a video cassette in one hand and a white, paper-rolled marijuana joint in the other, close to his face. "How about a little Mary Jane?"

"Now we're talking."

They sat at a round conference table in the front reception area of the office. One of the new video cassette recorder machines sat on the table, next to a small television. Oran lit the joint, inhaled deeply twice, and passed it to Vic who proceeded to take in one long drag.

Oran grinned. "Pretty good shit, huh?"

Vic held the smoke in his lungs, finally exhaling after several seconds. "It ain't bad."

"Have you heard of Josiah Lynch?"

"No." He took another drag and passed the joint back to Oran.

Oran took three long pulls and passed it back. "Really? Oil, real estate, dirty politics. None of that rings a bell?"

He'd broken smoking protocol with the extra pull and left the tip of the joint moist. Vic dried the end with his fingertips. "Oran, I never heard of the guy."

"It doesn't matter. What does matter is that he's rich—really rich. I've been running his security for the past year."

"*Mazel tov.*"

"Don't congratulate me just yet."

"Why not?"

"His daughter was kidnapped yesterday."

"What do you mean, 'kidnapped?'"

"I mean a bunch of goons jumped her and the security detail last night. They grabbed her and wasted all of my guys."

He spent the next ten minutes filling Vic in on what he'd learned about the kidnapping. Oran's team had spent several hours interviewing the building's doorman and pulling video footage from hotel security cameras. When he'd finished with the back-story, Oran transitioned to the visual aids he'd mentioned in the bar.

Oran rolled his chair toward the VCR and TV that sat on the other end of the table. Vic eyed the brown-and-silver VCR. The things had become the newest craze, but Vic hadn't seen one in person till tonight. Oran pressed a button and a section on top sprang up, revealing a narrow, rectangular opening. He inserted the video cassette into the opening and pushed the whole section back down into the VCR. He turned the television on and pressed the "play" button on the machine.

"So, this is a few minutes before Carolina—"

"Carolina?"

"Carolina Lynch. My client's daughter. The victim."

Vic nodded.

"This is outside the place, a few minutes before she came downstairs," Oran continued.

The black-and-white footage was grainy and dark. The doorman was on one side of the screen, and every few seconds a male figure would appear on the other end of the screen.

"That's one of the fucks that did the kidnapping." Oran pointed toward the lower half of the TV screen. "See that? There's another one. The first guy looks like he has an afro. So, we're fairly certain there were at least two of them hanging out in front of the hotel during the party. Fucking doorman should've called the cops right then and there."

The doorman looked like he was ignoring the kidnappers, and

Vic figured the guy had been scared out of his mind. After a few minutes, two black cars, one of them a limo, pulled up to the front of the building.

"These are my guys pulling up here."

Two men exited the vehicles and took up standard security positions, one by the rear passenger door and the other closer to the hotel entrance, between the client and any potential threats. A few more seconds passed, then the Lynch woman entered the screen. There was a body man close to her, escorting her to the limo. The video didn't have any audio, but sound wasn't needed. The images were loud enough.

The kidnappers made their move. They worked fast but were sloppy and unorganized, shooting two of the bodyguards before allowing their target to escape. As soon as the limo sped away, the kidnappers jumped in a van and took off after them. They had spent enough time in the open for Vic to get a good look at them. The grainy image and distance made it impossible to identify their faces, but he was able to make out some markings on their clothing.

He sat back in his chair. "Oran, these guys look like fucking street gang members."

"That's what I was thinking. Can you tell what group?"

"Nah, the image is too grainy. And I can't tell what colors they're wearing. Did you find out what happened from here?"

"Fucking nightmare. We found the limo and two of my men full of bullet holes on the Manhattan side of the Queens Midtown Tunnel. Carolina was gone, but we found this on the back seat."

Oran handed him a folded piece of white notebook paper. Vic unfolded it and read the handwritten note.

ONE MILLION DOLLARS

72 HOURS

NO POLICE

YOU WILL BE CONTACTED

"That it?" Vic asked, placing the note on the table.

"As of right now, yeah. It's been over twenty-four hours and we haven't heard anything," Oran said.

"What about the cops? What are they saying?"

"The kidnappers said no police."

"So what? Fuck them."

"Not going to happen. Mr. Lynch wants to keep the police out of it."

"How did you clean up the mess outside the tunnel without cops getting involved?"

"Vic, Lynch is one of the richest people in this country. Believe me, keeping this private isn't a problem."

"So, are you going after her?"

"I plan to, but I don't know where she is. I need you to find out who they are, where they're keeping her, and lead my guys to her. We'll handle the rest."

"Why me? With the kind of business you're running, I'm sure you have some good intelligence people on the payroll." Vic hesitated a few seconds. "Look man, I appreciate what you're trying to do, but I don't need your charity."

"Come on Vic, you know I checked you out. How do you think I found my way to your office? And I know where you come from and what you were into before you joined the Corps. You trying to tell me you can't use the work? Everyone can use work. Especially now." Oran leaned in close to him. "It's not charity, brother, it's business. I want to hire you to provide a service for which you are uniquely qualified."

Vic nodded subtly. Oran had a point about the work thing. It wasn't exactly standing room only back at the office.

But something about Oran bringing up Vic's old life didn't sit right with him. He wasn't ashamed of it, not at all. But an outsider, even someone he loved like Oran, talking like they knew anything about his old neighborhood bothered him.

Vic had grown up across the river, in a three-story walk-up in Brooklyn. Young, stupid, and poor, he had been a founding member of the Ruthless Ones. A street gang full of kids who spent most of their time committing petty crimes, assaults, and pretty much anything to survive. That'd been Vic's life till he got involved in a gang fight and two people had ended up getting killed, one of them a civilian.

Spring of 1966, his boy Mousey had made the not-so-smart decision to throw up a piece in Slaughterhouse territory in Williamsburg. Twelve inches of graffiti art led to a violent gang fight that'd quickly turned deadly. Vic hadn't done the killing, but the cops were looking for everyone that'd been involved, so he'd needed a place to hide. With the Vietnam War going on and Uncle Sam desperate for troops, it hadn't been too hard to sign up, so he did.

Being a Marine had been rough in the beginning. Vic didn't have the required discipline or work ethic when he'd started. But he'd found a way to get there. He'd gotten stronger mentally and physically. Eventually he'd found something he was proud to be a part of, something bigger than him.

"That was a lifetime ago, Oran. Everyone I knew is gone. I hardly even go into The Fear anymore, except when I'm chasing a skip."

"The what?"

"The Fear. It's nothing, it's just a nickname for places in the city most people try hard to avoid. Which is mostly the outer boroughs." Vic could tell from his expression Oran had no clue what he was talking about. "The way this city is right now, if you're not one of the millionaires living in complete luxury, then you're living somewhere in The Fear. Depending on their circumstances, most New Yorkers are scared to death of something—not eating, not working, not being able to provide for their families. Being killed, having to kill to survive—"

"I noticed you didn't use the words 'living' or 'dying.'"

"Brother, when you're in The Fear, the concern isn't whether you live or die, it's *how* you live or *how* you die. Most well-off people don't have any real worries. They're mostly concerned with earning a good living and raising a healthy family before they grow old and die peacefully. But when people are scared shitless every day because they might be murdered over a cigarette, or they may have to kill someone 'cause their baby needs milk. Well, let's just say they're way past concern at that point."

"Well damn, you just took a big old shit on my buzz," Oran said. He leaned forward in his chair. "Listen. Putting all that other stuff aside, you know the neighborhoods and you know how to find people. Force Recon, baby. You go in, gather intel, and lead the guns to the enemy. That's it and that's that. Come on man, you're Vic 'The Sword.' This'll be child's play compared to the shit we did in Nam."

Vic shifted in his seat, a bit uneasy at hearing his old nickname said aloud. Back in Nam their team's radio operator, Lance Corporal Dominic Sanchez, had given it to Vic after one of their missions. They'd been out reconning a twelve-kilometer area of the demilitarized zone when Vic, the team point man, spotted a North Vietnamese Army patrol setting up an ambush. He'd locked eyes with one of the NVA soldiers and opened fire before the rest of the team knew what had happened. After a short gunfight, no member of Ariadne had so much as a scratch on them, but there were six dead NVA soldiers.

Vic had been fast and lethal, so Corporal Sanchez seemed to think the nickname made sense. Of course, it hadn't hurt that Vic's last name meant sword in English.

"Man, I haven't heard that name in a while. It doesn't really fit anymore."

"Brother, it'll always fit." Oran sat back in his chair. "And I'll give you fifty grand and cover all expenses. Whether we get her out or not."

Hearing that number caught Vic's attention. He enjoyed what he did, but he'd just barely been scraping by. Especially when he considered how much time he put into finding bail jumpers. A payday like this could change a lot for him—and for Chris. When he'd gotten back from Nam, Vic had been spinning. He had no job and zero prospects until Chris had given him a chance. Vic felt he owed Chris a lot and would do anything for him.

"Fifty grand plus expenses?"

Oran reached into his back pocket, pulled out a white envelope, and dropped it on the table in front of Vic. It landed with a thump and was unsealed, so the cash inside was visible.

"There's five thousand. For expenses of course."

Vic eyed the envelope and went through everything in his head one more time. "All right, man, you're on."

five

VELEZ WAS EXHAUSTED AND ANGRY. He was headed to his rack for some shut eye after pulling a long watch when Gunnery Sergeant Bukowski, looking uncharacteristically disheveled, ordered him to clear a tunnel half a klick past the tree line. He and the rest of the 1st Battalion, 7th Marine Regiment had found a few tunnels since they'd landed on the beach at Qui Nhon in south central Vietnam less than a month ago. The word had been the things were being located all over Vietnam—huge networks of caverns and caves that snaked through multiple levels and went on for miles in every direction.

The Gunny's order had surprised Velez. Clearing and destroying tunnels had been an engineer's job, after all. Hell, that's why they were called Tunnel Rats. He knew the One-Seven had suffered some casualties, so Gunny probably didn't have much to choose from, but Velez figured there had to be someone better suited for the job. From what he knew, most Tunnel Rats were short and skinny, like racehorse jockeys. Sure, he was on the skinny side—but, at a shade over six-two, he definitely wasn't short.

Velez took a deep breath and stared up at the morning sun,

already bright and warm in the sky, and tried to calm himself. Wasn't there a private somewhere nearby that Gunny could have dropped this on? He was a lance corporal, after all.

Arriving in country already an E-3 was the only good thing that'd come from his year in Maryland. After basic training, he'd left Paris Island ready to kick ass, any ass. But instead, Velez had spent his first year in the Corps stuck in Aberdeen, Maryland, answering pointless questions for people who hadn't seemed very interested in what he had to say.

He knew being angry was pointless. He'd been given an order, and regardless of how stupid he may have thought it was, the order had to be followed. Hell, maybe he'd get lucky and find a gook hiding in the tunnel. It'd been a while since he'd fed the hunger. It wasn't just about the killing—he'd done plenty of that since arriving in country. But firing 500 rounds into a tree line wasn't enough. He needed it to be like it was back home when he'd be close enough to hear their whimpers, and see the lights go out in their eyes.

Velez made his way to the tunnel, planning to meet up with Private First-Class Cornelius along the way. Apparently, Cornelius had drawn the short straw and been ordered into the tunnel too, stopping to pick up some C4 explosives on his way. Velez spotted his new partner in misery from a distance, and they glanced at each other. Cornelius stopped where he was, seemingly waiting for some help, but Velez smirked and kept walking.

Cornelius double-timed it till he was side by side with Velez, and the two men exchanged quiet nods. Cornelius's pockmarked faced looked red and irritated, and there was a cluster of moles on the left side of his neck, just beneath his ear. Velez winced at the thought of trying to shave over those moles.

Now Cornelius, on the other hand, looked like a Tunnel Rat. He wasn't short but he wasn't exactly tall either. And the guy was skinny as a broom, not to mention weird as hell.

It wasn't just that he was quiet—plenty of the fellas were quiet —but he was a cold fish. Always off by himself. And if Cornelius did happen to speak to anyone, he hardly ever made eye contact. He'd just stare foggy eyed past whoever he was speaking with, like he was looking at things no one else could see.

They made their way to the tunnel. At first glance, Velez couldn't make out what the two Marines standing sentry were guarding. But then he spotted it just in front of the Marine's feet, a small hole dug into the ground.

"What's up fellas," Velez said. Both guards pointed at the hole. "Is that it?"

"Yeah," one of the Marines mumbled. The pronounced circles under his eyes were a deep shade of purple, and small razor cuts peppered his chin and jaw.

"I wonder what took us so long to find this thing. Seems somebody would have seen it, with all the folks we've had march through here the past few weeks," Velez said.

"It was covered up with that thing." The sleep-deprived Marine pointed toward a shoddily made object lying on the ground near the hole. Sticks and leaves had been tied together with stripped pieces of bamboo to create a makeshift lid. "Somebody or something must have kicked it loose trudging through here. One of the scouts' legs dropped straight through—almost split himself in half."

Velez circled the hole. He had been imagining a tunnel like the ones back home. Giant underground, or underwater, passageways made of concrete and steel, big enough for eighteen wheelers hauling goods from state to state. What he was staring at now was made of packed dirt and looked like something out of a *Looney Tunes* cartoon. He half expected Bugs Bunny to pop his head out and yell, "What's up, Doc?"

He glanced at Cornelius who, as usual, had been staring off in the distance. "You ready?"

"Yes, Corporal, I am."

Velez lowered himself into a crouch and stared down into the black hole, trying to figure out the best angle of approach. "Give me some light," he said without looking up and to no one in particular.

One of the two Marines leaned over and used his L-shaped Fulton flashlight to light up the hole. There was a landing about six feet down, but Velez couldn't make out where it led. He took one last look around, pulled his .45 Colt M1911 semi-automatic pistol from his side holster, and lowered himself into the tunnel feet first, lifting his arms above his head to fit his upper body through the small hole.

He landed softly, squatting low inside a dust-filled sunbeam that provided enough light for him to make out his surroundings. The small space was made entirely of hard-packed dirt. He found it odd there wasn't any wood or stone helping to reinforce the structure.

Straight ahead, another opening had been dug into the dirt wall. Velez took out the flashlight he'd been carrying in his waistband and used it to light up the space past the hole. A passage had been dug into the earth—it was a tunnel. The flashlight's red lens turned the first few feet of the long and narrow space crimson before fading into an empty blackness. Velez felt as if he were staring into a gateway to hell.

"What do ya got?" Cornelius yelled from above.

"It's just a small trench, both of us won't fit in here. But I'm staring into another, bigger tunnel."

"What do ya want to do?"

Velez looked over his shoulder and rolled his eyes. "I *want* to go to my rack and get some shuteye, forget this place exists. But what I'm *going* to do is climb through this damn hole before the Gunny has my ass." He turned his attention back to the newly discovered tunnel. "I'm gonna climb in, give you some room down here."

Cornelius didn't respond. Velez heard him moving around up top, so he figured Cornelius was getting ready to climb down.

Velez dropped to his hands and knees. Holding his .45 in his right hand and the flashlight in his left, he crawled into the small space headfirst. He stopped moving after a few feet and waited for Cornelius to join him in the tunnel.

It hit him while he was waiting—an overwhelming feeling of panic that made it difficult to breathe. Velez had never thought of himself as claustrophobic, but he had never been in a situation like this before either. Crammed into a space so tight he could feel his back scraping against the ceiling—it was as if he'd been buried alive. Velez was about to back out of the tunnel when he felt Cornelius tap the bottom of his boot, letting him know that he'd entered the small space behind him.

Velez took a deep breath and started moving forward slowly, feeling for booby traps along the way. The warm air felt heavy in his chest, and it smelled like spoiled meat. He imagined a pile of dead gooks at the end of the tunnel, left to rot by their fellow Viet Cong.

They'd been crawling in total silence for about forty minutes when he spotted an opening ahead. He tapped Cornelius on the head with his foot and waited. A few seconds later Velez heard him pull the hammer back on his pistol.

Velez reached the opening and climbed down into the open space. He brought his .45 up and scanned the room for enemy combatants. The square room, dimly lit by a small oil lamp that hung from the ceiling, was surprisingly large and deserted. Two crude wooden chairs and a bed made from a pile of hay, covered with a tattered yellow blanket, were the only items. A gray canvas tarp was hanging opposite where he stood.

Cornelius lowered himself into the room. He bent over at the waist and breathed in deeply. The room was empty, but Velez had an uneasy feeling. There was an energy in the room, like people had just left.

They made their way to the tarp. Velez took a hold of it, and when Cornelius was in position with his pistol at the low ready, Velez snatched the tarp off the wall.

"What the fuck?" Cornelius whispered.

A square entranceway had been cut into the wall behind the tarp, and there was a descending staircase past the opening. Velez stepped closer to the staircase and felt a cool breeze on his face when he leaned over the edge. The rock and dirt staircase went down at a steep angle and disappeared into blackness, making it appear to have no end.

"Dude, what the fuck is that?" Cornelius took a step back from the entrance, sounding panicked.

"A staircase. What's it look like."

"Yeah, but this far underground? How much lower can these people dig?"

"Man, who knows."

"There ain't nothing down here. Let's just go back. Blow the whole thing shut from up top."

Velez was tempted to go with Cornelius's suggestion, but cowardice wasn't his thing. "We're not going back till we see what's down there. There could be something important."

"What the fuck is going to be important down there?"

"It could be anything." Velez peered down into the darkness. "Can't you feel that?"

"What?"

"There's something down there." He glanced at Cornelius, who was staring back blankly.

Velez sighed. Of course Cornelius couldn't feel it. The dipshit was one lost IQ point from living in a vegetable farm. But Velez sensed it. There was something alive down there in the darkness, and he wanted it. The thirst was building again. Driving him. "Look, it doesn't matter. We still have some time—let's just see where this goes."

Cornelius shrugged and nodded. Velez walked through the doorway first, and the two started down the narrow staircase. They took each step slowly, the crimson light from their flashlights lighting their way.

Velez had to crouch slightly so as not to hit his head on the low ceiling, and he took every small stair with his feet pointed sideways. "Fucking gooks. An entire country where nobody's taller than five-five. How the fuck does that happen?"

"I don't know. Bad genes?"

"Yeah, that makes sense. Every Gene I've ever known has been a prick." Velez chuckled awkwardly.

Every movement was agonizingly stressful, so the staircase seemed to go on forever. Finally, Velez spotted a landing and another hanging tarp. He inched closer. A soft orange light emitted from the other side of the makeshift door, creating an almost hypnotic glow around the tarp's edges. Velez took a hold of the tarp, and after receiving a nod from Cornelius, pulled it off the wall, revealing another room.

The putrid smell hit Velez hard and almost knocked him on his butt. A noxious mix of rotting flesh and human waste kicked his gag reflex into overdrive. He took a step back and used his left forearm to cover his nose and mouth. He collected himself and stepped into the room.

This dirt room seemed a bit smaller than the one they'd just left and was full of people. Their backs were to him, and they were all kneeling in front of a gold-colored statue. The statue, a sitting Buddha, stood on a large stone plinth, surrounded by a wall of lit candles. The people were making a strange, low-pitched buzzing that sounded like a swarm of bees.

Suddenly, they all turned toward him, and Velez lost a breath when he realized it was the goblins. It'd been a while since he'd seen them, so he thought they were gone. But somehow, they'd found him.

They were everywhere, taking up every inch of the small space. All of them were obscenely thin with large, dark eyes that bulged out grotesquely. Their grayish skin, covered in scars and scales, was visible through tattered clothing.

They advanced toward Velez slowly, reaching for him with bloody hands. Large, misshapen tongues protruded out from mouths filled with razor-sharp teeth. Velez, his knees weak and his heart racing, pointed his pistol at the encroaching herd as he staggered backward.

"Velez, what are you doing?"

Cornelius's voice came from behind him, but Velez didn't turn. His words sounded distant and hollow, so Velez figured Cornelius was retreating up the stairway. Velez continued walking backward, almost tripping over the tarp that lay on the ground. He heard a scream and realized it was his own voice.

The goblins had closed the distance and were almost on him. Velez aimed his .45 at the one closest to him and squeezed the trigger. There was a flash as the bullet exited his pistol, and loud gunfire filled the small space, causing a loud ringing inside Velez's ears.

The bullet pierced the goblin's right eye, and Velez felt warm blood droplets land on his hand and face. The goblin's body dropped to the ground, but the rest of the herd was undeterred and continued moving forward. Velez squeezed the trigger five more times, each round killing a goblin. He turned and sprinted up the staircase.

He reached the first room. There weren't any goblins following behind, so he took a second to catch his breath.

"Cornelius? You in here, man?"

He was startled when he heard the buzzing again. Panicked and breathing rapidly, Velez used his flashlight to check the dark space. He rotated his body in a circle, checking each section of the room.

He jumped backward when a goblin appeared in the red light, reaching for him with its mouth wide open.

"What are you doing?" the goblin hissed.

Velez fired his pistol twice. A bullet penetrated the goblin through one of the grotesque bumps that covered its neck. The goblin fell backward, letting out a high-pitched scream as it landed on the ground.

Velez hurried past it and climbed into the tunnel. On his hands and knees and in complete darkness, Velez crawled back through the small space. He didn't hear any movement behind him, but he didn't have room to turn and check if he was being pursued.

After what felt like an eternity, Velez spotted a narrow ray of light ahead. His hands felt bloody and raw, but he ignored the pain and crawled faster. He reached the end of the tunnel and crawled into the trench.

Light shone into the space from the entrance hole above him. He yelled up for help, and after a few seconds, hands reached down for him. Scarred, gray hands with long, curved nails—claws. Velez recoiled and stumbled backward. Arms, extending out from a dark hole, stretched unnaturally toward him—hands reached for him...

Abaddon realized he was dreaming when the hands disappeared and the hole receded into itself, like some sort of psychedelic episode of *The Twilight Zone*. The dream, more of a memory really, was so vivid Abaddon had felt the nails clawing at his face. He'd even heard his own screams. But he knew he was in the middle of another nightmare when everything went silent, and the images started to warp.

Abaddon forced himself awake. He was in a dark room, hyper-aware of every movement and sound, but, except for his eyes, which moved frantically in the darkness, he was paralyzed. Every muscle and limb felt heavy and weighted down, as if he was stuck neck-deep in cement. He yelled at his body through motionless lips for it to move, but it refused to comply. After several painfully long seconds, the struggle was over, and his body and mind seemed to become one again.

In one motion, he sprang up and out of bed. He moved his left hand across his bare, sweat-covered chest, using his thumb and forefinger to pinch the skin just above his right nipple. The sting confirmed he was awake now, and the feeling of paralysis he'd experienced had passed. He took a deep breath and ran his hands along his face and up through his long, damp hair.

By now Abaddon was used to the nightmares. He'd had them almost every time he slept since returning from Nam. Sure, some of the smaller details would change, like whether the Gunny looked sloppy or not, or the shape of the cluster of moles on Cornelius's neck. But otherwise, the dreams were all the same. The descent into the tunnel, the darkness, finding and killing the gray goblins. Hell, the only constants in his life were the nightmares.

After heading to the bathroom to urinate and then stopping to grab himself a beer from his fridge, Abaddon sat down in front of his video monitor and stared at the screen. Although the black-and-white images were grainy and the lights were off in the room, he could make out Carolina curled up on the bed, asleep. He'd taken to watching her whenever he could, and he was bothered that she wasn't more afraid.

He knew she was scared. Who wouldn't be after everything that'd happened? But she didn't show it, at least not enough for his liking. He knew Carolina cried sometimes when she was alone, but she'd stand tall whenever one of his boys went in the room. She'd look them in the eye—defiant and arrogant.

He wasn't sure what her deal was yet. Was it just that she knew her father was going to pay, so why waste time being scared? Or she really did just have ice in her veins, and everything she'd experienced the last couple of days was just another day at the office. Whatever the case, he had to admit she was beautiful—and classy. Not at all like the skanks he had around here.

Abaddon looked at one of them asleep in his bed now and felt nothing but contempt. She was weak like the rest of them. A shot of white magic, or better yet, a slap in the face—and they were on their knees, doing what skanks were supposed to do.

Abaddon ran his hand over his engorged and throbbing member. He walked over to the bed, turned the whore over, and thrust himself into her. He held her down by the back of her neck and cursed her till he was done.

six

Tuesday, July 12

"WHAT'D I tell you about bringing this mutt to the office?"

Vic peered up from his desk when he heard Chris's deep voice. He had been poring over still photographs of the kidnapping and hadn't noticed that Kubrick, his one-year-old Bullmastiff, had wandered off. He'd left his spot by Vic's desk and met Chris as he walked in the front door a little before eight in the morning.

Vic leaned back in his chair and stretched the cramps out of his back. "Mutt? I'd bet a month's salary that dog has purer blood lines than either of us."

"I don't care if his relatives can be traced back to Nefertiti herself, I don't want him in the office. It ain't professional."

Vic chuckled when Kubrick sat in front of Chris and tilted his head to the left in a "What's so bad about me?" sort of way. Kubrick had been in Vic's life for a little over six months, ever since he'd found him hiding under the bed of an armed robber named Teddy LeBlanc. Teddy had jumped bail after getting pinched for mugging senior citizens in Riverside Park. It'd taken Vic four days to track Teddy down to an apartment above the Carbajal Brothers bodega on 171st Street in Washington Heights.

Problem was, Teddy had a two-bag-a-day heroin habit that'd

finally gotten the best of him. When Vic found him, Teddy was sprawled out on the floor with the hypodermic needle still embedded in his arm. His skin had turned a strange shade of green and rigor mortis had started.

Vic was halfway out the door when he heard whimpers coming from the bedroom. Against his better judgement, he checked on the source of the noise and had found a large, brindle Bullmastiff puppy quivering in fear under the bed. Vic pulled him out from under the bed and double-timed it out of the apartment. He was holding the puppy when he made an anonymous call about the rotting corpse to the cops from a payphone outside the bodega.

It'd been late in the day when Vic found him, so the local dog pounds were already closed. He took the dog home, fully intent on dropping him at an animal shelter the first chance he got. But one night spent caring and playing with the pup was all it took for Vic to change his mind. Instead of dropping him at the nearest pound, Vic had named the dog after his favorite film-maker and spent the next day showing him off around the neighborhood.

"No, you're right. I had to come in early, so I brought him with me. I'll drop him back at the apartment before foot traffic picks up."

Chris eyed Kubrick for a few seconds before walking past him. "There ain't no rush. What business we do get usually doesn't start walking in till later anyway. I see your boy won again last night."

Despite the heat and humidity that had already enveloped the city, Chris held his customary cup of coffee in one hand and a folded early edition of the *New York Times* in the other. As usual, he looked happy to be at work.

"Yup. TKO in the fifth. That kid didn't have a chance against Gomez." Vic reached down and petted Kubrick's head and neck as he spoke, happy for the distraction. He'd been staring at the photos for nearly two hours and was ready for a break.

"Yeah, Wilfredo is good, but he wouldn't last two rounds with Duran."

"*Estas loco*? Are you crazy? Wilfredo Gomez puts Duran on his ass in five rounds—guaranteed."

"That's the problem with you Puerto Ricans, you all ride with other Puerto Ricans no matter what. No objectivity whatsoever. Duran is a knockout machine."

"Chris, Duran just went fifteen rounds with Javier Muniz, and that guy is a journeyman at best. Besides, Duran's a lightweight and Gomez is a bantamweight."

"So what? It's only twelve pounds difference. They can meet in the middle, fight at featherweight."

"It'll never happen. And why would Gomez go after Duran when he's still got to take on Carlos Zarate in his own weight class?"

"That's true, but in my day the best fought the best, we didn't duck no one. If there was someone out there that created even a kernel of doubt about your standing, you step in the ring and settle that shit."

"You know what? I cannot argue with that last statement."

Chris looked past him, at the photos on his desk. "What do you have there?" Before Vic could answer, Teri walked in the office and caught Chris's attention. "You're late."

Kubrick pulled free from Vic's grip and toddled over to Teri, his tail waving excitedly from side to side.

"Hey there, baby." Teri kneeled, wrapped her arms around Kubrick's neck, and hugged him warmly. After a few seconds she pulled back and set her eyes on Chris. "What are you talking about, Uncle Chris? It's eight, I'm on time."

"On time is late," Chris said.

Teri looked toward his office and then at the cup of coffee and newspaper he was still holding. "Seeing as how your office door is closed and you're still holding your comfort items, I'd say you just got here too."

"Yeah, but this here happens to be mine." Chris used the newspaper he held in his right hand to motion around the office. "I come and go as I please. You're an employee, or at least you want to be one. If you ain't early then you're late, and late don't work for me."

"Yes sir." Teri made her way to her desk.

He turned his attention back to Vic. "Now, let's get back to it. What's the deal with the pictures?"

"Pull up a chair, let's talk about it."

Chris sat across from him and, with Teri listening from her desk, Vic spent the next twenty minutes telling them about his meeting with Oran. He told them almost everything, including the amount of money he'd been offered. He left out his long history with Oran and the part about the shared joint.

Teri blew out a soft whistle. "Fifty thousand dollars? That's a lot of green."

Chris sat leaned back in the chair with his hands behind his head. "Yeah, it is. But something doesn't sit right with me—especially them wanting to keep the police out of it. I'm not the biggest fan of the boys in blue, but this sounds serious. You're saying this friend of yours—"

"Oran."

Chris continued as if Vic hadn't interrupted him. "—just wants you to find out where they're keeping the girl and then lead his people to her?"

"Yup. That's pretty much it."

"Sounds too easy, there's got to be a catch. What are you gonna do?"

"I'm going to take the job. We need the cash."

"Hold it right there, youngblood. That's your money. This friend of yours came to you. I don't want you thinking you have to do any of this for the shop. I've made it this far. I can make it the rest of the way."

"I know you can, but this is business and I work here—with

you. A piece of what I make goes in the shop. Same as before." Vic reached into his pocket, pulled out two thousand dollars, and placed it on the desk in front of Chris. "Here you go."

"What's that?"

"Call it a retainer. Oran gave me five grand for expenses, but I don't figure I'm going to need that much. The rest is for the shop."

"Youngblood, I—"

"Like I said Chris, a piece of what I make comes back to the shop, same as before. Well, almost the same."

"What do you mean by that?"

"Seeing as this is a lot of money—I'm thinking twenty percent for my end. Just this once."

"Well damn, just when I was getting all teary eyed." Chris tilted his head up and peered at Vic as if he was looking through reading glasses. "Deal."

"So, where do you want to start?" Teri asked.

"The best place to get information." Vic stood up. "Chinatown."

***

The drive south on Park Avenue wasn't too bad till they reached Union Square. Vic's grip on the GTO's steering wheel tightened when he spotted a traffic jam on East Seventeenth Street.

"I told you we should have taken the train. Driving in Manhattan sucks," Teri said.

"Yeah well, I thought it wouldn't be too bad this time of day."

"Driving in Manhattan is always terrible, it's just different levels of terrible."

"And what level is this?"

"I'd say we shot right past 'this fucking sucks' about two blocks back."

Vic leaned his head back against the headrest and took a deep breath. He knew she was right. It would have been faster to take the subway. But riding the subway was a pain in the ass, even at noon on a Tuesday.

Graffiti-covered train cars were filled with beggars and drug addicts, and the stations and platforms were overrun by criminals. Shitbags from all walks of life, emboldened by the lack of police presence, harassed and intimidated passengers into giving up their possessions. Predators lurked in every corner in search of prey.

"Listen, it was either this or take the train and risk getting into a fight. You know how the subway is, and I don't really feel like getting into it with anyone today," he said.

"If I have to sit in this traffic much longer, you may end up fighting anyway."

Vic looked over at her and they both laughed. Truth was, even though he was a little bothered by the traffic congestion, he liked the time it gave him to think about his next play. They were headed to Emerald Tigers territory in Chinatown, and it was a risky move.

Since its founding in 1625, New York City had always been a major destination for immigrants. People of different races and nationalities emigrated to the United States, most of them coming in through Ellis Island, establishing dozens of different ethnic enclaves around the city. Neighborhoods set apart from the main areas of the city by their food, language, and cultures.

Originally, these neighborhoods had been predominantly made up of hardworking people just looking to make better lives for their families. But racism and neglect from the city's rich and powerful buried these communities in poverty—and where there's poverty, there's usually crime. The underworld took over.

Gangs and mobsters used violence and intimidation to prey on their own people. Drug trafficking, extortion, illegal gambling, prostitution, assault, and murder became the norm. The Emerald Tigers were one of these gangs.

"I still don't get why we're doing this. The kidnapping happened in Midtown, and the doorman didn't say anything about the attackers being Chinese," Teri said.

"Because I don't know where else to start, and there's someone down there who's been really helpful in the past."

"Oh yeah? Who? When?"

"That's not important. What is important is finding out who took this lady. Once I know that, I can figure out where we need to go to get her back."

"So, how are we going to play this?"

"Honestly, I'm still working that out."

"Well, you better figure it out fast. We're almost there."

Vic parked the GTO on the northeast corner of Mott and Canal. He and Teri exited the car and headed south on Mott Street. The sun loomed large and bright in the sky, blanketing the city in an oppressive heat.

Automobiles flooded the narrow, one-way street, struggling to maneuver past legally and illegally parked vehicles. The usual sounds of the city—honking horns, screeching tires, and angry drivers—seemed amplified. Every inch of the sidewalk was covered with people, forcing Vic and Terry to walk single file. He glanced over his shoulder intermittently to make sure she hadn't gotten caught up somewhere as they navigated their way through the crowd.

Vic spotted the large, conspicuous sign from a block away. Bright yellow with red lettering that spelled out Yellow Springs Company. The rectangular sign was about twenty feet up and extended out from the building's side like a shark's fin protruding from the sea.

When they reached the storefront, Vic tried to pull the door open, but it was locked. The door was made of glass and it, along with the shop's giant windows, was covered in dark tint, making it impossible to see inside. YELLOW SPRINGS CO. had been spelled out in gold lettering along the top half of the windows.

Thunder rumbled in the distance. Dark gray clouds had filled the sky and covered the sun, threatening to send rain their way. A loud yell rang out. Vic turned toward the voice and saw a group of people walking their way. They looked Asian, probably Chinese, and most of them appeared to be young. None of them could have been older than twenty-five.

There were about twenty of them, mostly male, and all dressed in variations of the same garb—jeans, black or white shirts, and green leather vests. Some wore green and white bandanas, and they all seemed to be carrying weapons, either heavy metal chains or wooden baseball bats. Some of them likely had handguns and knives on them as well.

Teri's hands were balled into fists and Vic admired that, as far as the fight-or-flight instinct, the woman didn't seem to have any wings.

"So, I'm going to go out on a limb and guess these guys are the Emerald Tigers," Teri said.

"Good guess."

"You know, it's funny."

"What is?"

"I don't see any emeralds."

"Yeah well, you're probably not going to see any tigers either."

"What do you want to do?"

"Just hold on."

"Okay. To what?"

Vic stepped away from the front door and faced the approaching crowd. A man at the front of the group stopped close to Vic, encroaching on his personal space. They were about the same height and stood eye to eye. He had a crudely applied tattoo on the left side of his neck, just beneath his jaw. The cheap black ink had faded to an olive-green lettering that spelled the name Bullhead.

"What do you want here?" Bullhead asked.

"I need to speak with Gabriel."

"Who's Gabriel?"

"Don't play with me, you know who I'm talking about. I can pay."

"Oh, you're going to pay all right," a voice from the crowd yelled.

Vic looked past Bullhead to where the voice came from. The crowd parted down the middle, creating a pathway for a tall, powerfully built figure who was making his way through the group. He seemed to be wearing the same clothing as the rest of the gang, and it took a few seconds for Vic to recognize Kai Liu.

"Vic."

"How're you doing, Kai?"

Kai looked around at the crowd, making a show of noticing the stacked deck. "Right now? Better than you, that's for sure. What are you doing here, Vic?"

The first time Vic had met Kai Liu had been the winter of 1965. They were part of a large group of people who had been dragged into the Manhattan House of Detention, better known as The Tombs, after the cops had raided a coke and speed club in Alphabet City.

Their group hadn't been the only visitors to The Tombs that night. As luck would have it, ten members of the Shadow Dragons, a rival gang of the Emerald Tigers, had been locked up as well. Vic saved Kai from a late-night shanking and the two had been semi-cordial ever since.

"I want to talk to Gabriel. I need some information."

"From what I remember, you still owe Gabriel from the last time."

"That was a different thing, Kai. Shit got fucked up and I didn't have it. But I have the money to settle up. Plus interest."

Kai nodded subtly. "So what do you want to ask about?"

"Some shit that went down a few nights back. A kidnapping."

"What makes you think Gabriel knows anything about it?"

"When doesn't Gabriel have a handle on everything that goes down in the city? Come on, Kai, I only need five minutes."

"It's not going to happen. Gabriel isn't seeing outsiders anymore. Unless..."

"Unless what?"

"Unless you're prepared to show you're worthy of being in his presence."

Vic almost scoffed at Kai's choice of words but scanned the crowd and decided it wasn't a good idea. "I can't fight my way through twenty people."

Kai smiled a pirate's grin. "Who said anything about fighting? Let's take a ride."

seven

VIC AND TERI sat in the backseat of a black 1970 Mercury Marauder, uncomfortably sandwiched between two Emerald Tigers. Kai was in the front passenger seat, smoking a cigarette and watching the streets. The car didn't have air conditioning, so the two Tigers acting as the bread in the Vic-and-Teri sandwich were sweating profusely. The vehicle was as hot as a pizza oven and reeked of cigarette smoke and body odor.

The Marauder led a four-vehicle caravan south on Mott Street, then back up Mulberry Street, finally stopping in front of Columbus Park. Kai got out, pulling the seat forward as he exited so everyone in the back could squeeze out of the two-door car.

Vic scanned the area as he exited the Marauder. Kai was standing in the middle of the street, looking up at one of the buildings on the east side of the roadway.

"What are they planning to do with us?" Teri asked.

"I have no idea. This is a new one for me," Vic said.

"Look at that." Teri discreetly jutted her chin at two gang members removing gas canisters from the trunk of a yellow 1968 Chevy Malibu.

Vic glanced at them and then walked over to Kai. "What the fuck is going on, Kai?"

"Well, Vic, old buddy. It's like this. You're going to play a little game of Fire Mountain, and we're going to have some fun betting on whether you make it out."

"What's Fire Mountain? Make it out of what?"

"See that building there?"

Vic looked up at the seemingly abandoned building. It was an old, stand-alone, five-story walkup. Its graffiti-covered red-brick exterior was cracked and dirty, and the windows that hadn't been boarded up were filled with broken and cracked glass. The building's fire escape was on the front side, facing Mulberry Street, and extended from the second floor up to the fifth. Vic glanced over at the two guys carrying gas tanks and then back at Kai.

"You know what? I'm good. I can figure out how to get the information somewhere else."

Kai's mischievous grin was replaced with a sinister glare. "It's too late for that, Vic. You're here now and there's only one way you're leaving standing up."

"So, it's safe to assume I'm not going to get any rhythm on this? Because of how we met and all?"

"I paid that debt already. And yes, we know each other, but we ain't friends." Kai's lips curled into a friendly smile, as if he and Vic were meeting over drinks. "Look at it this way—all you have to do is run really fast. If you make it back down in one piece, I'll take you straight to Gabriel." He looked to his left. "And you get to play hero one more time."

Vic followed his eyes over to where Teri was standing. Three Emerald Tigers stood behind her, silent and motionless. Their menacing glares delivered the message loud and clear.

Shit. "Let's get this over with." They both started toward the building. Vic heard fast-moving footsteps behind him and guessed it was the two that'd been carrying the gas canisters, hurrying to catch up.

"Ain't nothing to it, Vic. Go up to the roof and wait for my signal. As soon as I give the word, make it back down here. Simple as that."

"Yeah, it sounds real simple," Vic said.

"One more thing—no fire escape."

"What?"

"You can't use the fire escape. Come on, Vic, you know the only way to the promised land is *through* the fire."

Vic knew he was out of options, so he walked into the old, run-down building. Small beams of daylight snuck in through the building's cracked façade and boarded-up windows, providing him with enough light to make his way around inside. He saw a narrow staircase a few feet ahead.

He started up it, heading for the roof. The smell of human waste, a vile mixture of feces, urine, and vomit, was overwhelming. Vic breathed through his mouth and tried to hurry, but the old wooden stairs squealed, threatening to collapse with every step he took.

He made it to the top floor of the five-story structure, pushing his way through the door leading to the roof. He took several deep breaths as he surveyed his surroundings. The roof was covered in black tar that'd spent the better part of a month under a merciless sun. Despite the dark gray clouds that had overtaken the sky, Vic could feel the heat radiating off the roof's dark surface through his sneakers.

He walked from one side of the roof to the other, checking his options. The gap between this roof and the next one over was too wide to jump. The building's brick façade was flat and offered no grip, so scaling down its walls was a no-go.

A sharp whistle pierced the air. Vic peered over the roof's edge, down at the crowd on Mulberry Street. Kai and Teri were staring back up at him, but the rest of the Tigers were laughing and holding money. Vic figured betting had opened on whether he would make it out.

"Stay right there till I say go," Kai yelled.

He looked toward the bottom floor of the building. Vic followed his gaze and watched as two of Kai's guys threw lit bottle bombs into the building. Vic took a five-dollar bill out of his pocket, balled it up, and threw it over the edge.

"Hey, Kai," he yelled.

"Yeah?"

"Put that on me. I'll be down in a few minutes to collect."

The crumpled five landed on the ground a few feet in front of Kai. He sauntered over, picked it up, and looked back up at him. "Hey, Vic."

"Yeah?"

"Go."

Vic ran into the building. Black smoke had already started filling the floors beneath him. He took the stairs two at a time and made it down to the fourth floor before he got his first look at the fire. Bright orange flames with sharp edges pointed toward the sky, like the sharpened claw of a demon reaching up from hell.

He pulled his shirt collar up, covering his nose and mouth. Vic sped down the stairs to the third-floor landing, his eyes burning from the smoke. He grabbed the newel on top of the banister, spun to his left, and started down the next flight without losing momentum.

Vic was side by side with the fire's tentacles, so close it singed the skin on his face. He could hear it inhaling the air—using the stairwell's oxygen to grow. The crackling and popping sounds reminded him the fire was a ravenous beast, intent on devouring the building around him. He kept his back tight against the wall and made it close to the second floor in three long strides.

A wall of fire stood between Vic and the second-floor landing. He hesitated for two seconds, then leapt through the flames. His left foot crashed through the wood floor when he landed, splintering the planks and trapping his ankle.

It was difficult to see and hard to breathe in the dark, heavy smoke. Vic felt panic bubbling in his stomach. He squatted and searched for breathable air as he tried to calm down, then reached out and felt a solid surface.

He ran his hand along the surface, felt patterns and indentions, and guessed it was an apartment door. Vic stood up. He yanked hard on his foot and freed himself from the splintered floor on the first try. He pivoted to his right, stepped back, and put all his weight behind a straight front kick, sending the apartment door crashing open.

The smoke inside the apartment was less dense, and gray daylight poured in from a glassless window. Vic shut the door, ran to the window, and thrust his head out into the open air. He took short breaths, trying to avoid breathing in smoke as he looked down. He was about twenty feet above a ground covered with large chunks of jagged concrete and broken glass.

He glanced back toward the door. Refusing to be denied entry, black smoke and orange flames invaded the apartment. Vic stepped over the windowsill, careful to avoid the sharp edges of broken glass still embedded in its frame. He lowered his head and shoulders, and while gripping the exterior sill, pulled the rest of his body outside the window. He held on tightly to the windowsill and lowered his body till it was fully extended.

Vic glanced over his shoulder at the ground below, searching for a safe place to land. He took a deep breath and let go.

Teri gasped in horror when the building's bottom floor ignited. Smoke plumed out from holes and uncovered windows, then bright orange flames spread quickly until they engulfed the entire bottom floor. She turned her heard upward, searching for Vic. He wasn't on the roof, so she took a step toward the building.

Kai grabbed her arm. "Don't."

She stopped and faced him. "Vic needs help."

"I'm sure he does, but he's not going to get it."

She snatched her arm from his grip. "What's the point of this?"

"The point? You mean besides you two coming here uninvited and asking for favors? There really isn't one. But you know what? It's all pretty pointless in the end."

Teri rolled her eyes. "Okay, Nietzsche. Listen, us being here isn't the same as some gang coming on your turf. We're civilians and don't roll with anyone. We're pretty much tourists."

He laughed. "I don't know how long you've known him, sweetheart, but Vic ain't no tourist. He may not be affiliated anymore, but he knows better than to come to Chinatown without permission."

Teri turned her attention back to the blazing structure. She couldn't see how he'd make it out through the building. And if using the fire escape wasn't allowed, Vic's only other option was to jump. Which, considering the debris from demolished buildings that covered the ground, wasn't much of an option.

She didn't know what they planned to do with her if Vic didn't make it out. So, in addition to worrying about him, Teri had to figure out her next move. She put her right hand inside her pants pocket, slipped her brass knuckles onto her fingers, and waited.

The knuckles had been a gift from her father. She called them a gift, although someone else might've referred to it as recovering abandoned property. It'd been the summer before her junior year of high school, and she and her mother had been evicted again. Teri had been going through some old things trying to figure out what was worth taking when she'd found a small box full of paperwork, pictures, a silver zippo lighter, and the brass knuckles. The paperwork had been miscellaneous junk, and most of the photos were of relatives she barely knew.

But there'd been one photo that'd caught Teri's attention. Black and white with frayed and yellowed edges, it showed a young couple posed in a tight embrace on a boardwalk somewhere—probably Coney Island. She'd recognized her mother right away. But the other person was a tall white man she'd never seen before.

Teri had asked her mother about the man in the picture, and after a few hours of prodding, her mother admitted he was Teri's father. She told Teri how the two had been young and in love, at least she'd thought they'd been in love. But times were different back then, and although he'd put up a brave front when it'd just been the two of them, things had changed when he'd learned of the pregnancy. Bringing a mixed-race baby into the world would've complicated things for him, so he took off.

Teri had heard all she needed to hear and burned everything, including the lighter. The only reason she'd kept the brass knuckles was because she and her mother often lived in not-so-great neighborhoods. The kinds of places where carrying a weapon for self-defense had been part of the social contract.

Teri watched the inferno through tear-filled eyes, her grip on the brass knuckles growing tighter with every passing second. She inhaled deeply when she spotted Vic climbing out a second-floor window. He lowered himself over its edge, holding on to the windowsill. With his arms stretched to their limit, he dangled helplessly for what felt like an eternity. After a few seconds, he let go and disappeared into a cloud of smoke and ash.

"Vic!" Teri started toward him, but Kai pulled her back by her shirt collar. She turned and swiped at his hand. "Let me go, you fuck!"

He motioned with his head at something behind her, so she turned. She exhaled a long, silent breath when she spotted Vic limping toward them. When he reached them, he bent over at the waist, put his hands on his knees, and coughed up black phlegm. He stood straight up, letting out small coughs and using his forearm to wipe his nose and bloodshot eyes.

"You're not going to need those," Vic said between coughs, motioning at Teri's brass knuckled covered hand.

She glanced down at her hand, slid off the knuckles, and placed them back in her pocket before turning her attention back to Vic. His soot covered clothes reeked of smoke, and he looked exhausted. She was proud of Vic, and it took everything in her not to hug him.

Vic stared at Kai. "So, what were the odds against my making it out? Cause I'm about to get paid."

Kai flashed a wry grin. "All right scarecrow, let's go see the wizard."

eight

ORAN WATCHED the elevator operator through his peripheral vision and wondered how he could spend all day riding up and down pushing buttons and making small talk. Oran imagined himself doing the job and knew he'd make it about an hour before he offed one of the building's rich and arrogant tenants. He'd been to Josiah Lynch's Park Avenue penthouse dozens of times since he'd taken over as head of Mr. Lynch's security, and it'd always been the same guy running the elevator. Two-inch gold lettering spelling the name Gordon had been embroidered in script over the left breast pocket of his sharply pressed navy-blue blazer.

Middle-aged and paunchy, Gordon always flashed the same uncomfortable smile—like the ones Oran had seen in high school yearbooks. As usual, Gordon's posture was ramrod straight, and the cheap-smelling aftershave he wore filled the small space. Judging from his pristine uniform and all-business stare, Oran guessed the man had served and was probably a former Marine.

Oran rode in the elevator at least twice a day every day. And for about ten of the ninety seconds it took to get to the top floor, he wondered the same things and made the same assumptions. He knew it would have been simpler to just ask the man about himself, make some friendly small talk. But Oran figured the back-story he'd come up with was probably a lot more interesting than the truth. The elevator's soft bell chimed, signaling they'd reached the top floor, and as usual, he stepped off without saying a word to Gordon.

Mr. Lynch's maid, Abigail, greeted him at the front door, then ushered him into the apartment's large foyer. She was an older woman of average height, with warm, brown eyes and a beautiful smile.

"Mr. Lynch's just sitting down for lunch on the balcony. He mentioned you'd be coming by, so I set two places."

"I'm not hungry, but thank you, Abigail. That was very kind of you."

He headed for the balcony, admiring the apartment as he walked. At over three thousand square feet, with seven rooms and twenty-foot-high ceilings, it was the smallest of the eight apart-ments Mr. Lynch owned in the city. Large paintings by Paul Gaugin and Caravaggio adorned the apartment's cream-colored walls. Its marble floor and stone columns reminded Oran of the churches he'd visited in Rome.

He stepped out onto the balcony where Mr. Lynch was reading the *Wall Street Journal*. Eggs Benedict sat untouched on the plate in front of him and there was an empty place setting across from him.

"Good afternoon, Mr. Lynch."

Mr. Lynch didn't take his eyes off the paper. "Have a seat, Oran."

Oran sat at the empty place setting and waited for Mr. Lynch to speak first. He knew better than to initiate the conversation, having been reprimanded during one of their first meetings for speaking before Mr. Lynch. After a minute of silence, he put the paper down on the table and glared at Oran.

"So, where are we with the issue concerning my daughter?"

Oran did not enjoy meeting with Mr. Lynch. It wasn't having

to provide status updates—keeping the people paying the bills informed was a necessary part of security work, and one he usually enjoyed. He just didn't like being around the man.

It wasn't that Oran had found him physically intimidating or anything. Mr. Lynch was in his sixties, slim, and a little under six feet tall. But he had some habits and physical traits that made Oran uneasy. Despite his slender frame, Mr. Lynch had an unnaturally deep voice and spoke in a strange song-like cadence. The singing thing wouldn't have been so bad on its own, little more than an annoying habit. But throw in the man's weird eye tick and being within ten feet of him made Oran's skin crawl.

Mr. Lynch's eyes moved rapidly side-to-side involuntarily, and Oran had noticed it the first time they'd met. Mr. Lynch must have picked up on some vibes because he'd taken a minute to explain the condition to Oran. He'd said it was an inherited condition called pendular nystagmus and there weren't any underlying physical or neurological issues. Just a lifetime of curious expressions like the one Oran had been giving him.

"We're still trying to figure out where the kidnappers are keeping her. I contracted out the locating responsibilities."

"To whom?"

"Vic Espada. He served under me in Nam."

"Is he capable?"

"More than capable, sir. We were part of a force reconnaissance company. The best of the best. Vic was one of the top guys in the battalion."

"Is he discreet?"

"He's a Marine, sir—we're all discreet when it comes to operations like this."

Mr. Lynch didn't respond, just looked past him. Oran was tempted to turn around but kept his gaze forward. After a few seconds the old man turned his attention back to Oran.

"Get this situation handled, Oran. Do what you've been paid to do. The clock is ticking."

"Yes sir, I understand."

Mr. Lynch picked up his newspaper and went back to reading. Oran had more to say and more questions to ask, but the old man's actions had made it clear their conversation was over. Oran got up and left without saying another word.

Josiah waited till he heard the front door close before he put the newspaper down. He stared out at the skyline and thought about the violence and poverty that had plagued the city, and how that situation had impacted his business. He had assets everywhere—hundreds of properties and thousands of acres of land throughout the five boroughs—that had become completely worthless.

He was willing to concede it'd been their own fault. The Council had invited the situation by being complacent. Too many years of keeping their noses turned up and getting fat had allowed for the current situation. All the mongrel races that made up too large a part of this city had been allowed to believe they had a voice and that they were somehow equal. It had gone too far, and now the rats had overtaken the ship.

But not for much longer. With his candidate, Joe Renfrow, on course to take over the mayor's office in a few months, Josiah would have just the right puppet in place to push whatever buttons he chose. All he needed now was something to fan the flames of public outrage.

The shocking kidnapping and horrible murder of a beautiful, young socialite would be just what he needed. Such an unspeakable crime would provide all the motivation New York's rich and powerful would need to lend their support to the cause. Calls for action to the highest office in the land would have to be answered and the cleansing would begin.

Policies of zero tolerance would be enacted, and the scourge of society would be locked away. Private prisons would have to be built to accommodate the rising inmate population, creating more opportunities for money to be made. With most of their number packed away in prisons, all that would be left to remove would be the beggars and the paupers. An easy enough fix in Josiah's opinion. With Renfro's help, Josiah would price them out, tax them out, and if needed, burn them out as he'd done in the old days.

It was all coming together. Josiah had the pieces on the board lined up exactly as he wanted, and he was five steps ahead. There was no move anyone could make that he hadn't planned for. He thought about Carolina, alone and afraid—the first pawn he'd sacrificed in his opening gambit—and felt no remorse whatsoever.

nine

VIC AND TERI followed Kai into the Yellow Springs Company. He told them to wait in the reception area and disappeared down a long hallway toward the back of the building. The walls inside the dimly lit room were painted a deep shade of purple and it felt strangely cold.

"All right Vic, I've had enough surprises for the day, so stop fucking around. Who are we waiting to see?" Teri said.

"An old acquaintance. Someone who's helped me in the past. Gabriel Yao."

"Helped you how, exactly?"

"Different ways. Information mostly."

"What's with the short answers? Why are you being so cryptic?"

"I'm just tired, Teri. This is—"

Kai emerged from the hallway, ending their conversation.

"All right Vic, you and the princess can follow me."

"Princess? Fuck you, punk," Teri said.

Kai smiled and led them down a long, narrow hallway filled with a soft, white flickering light. Synthetic sounding rain, mixed with dark, bass filled music, permeated the air. They followed Kai to the end of the hall.

He led them into the room the light and sounds were coming from. The actor Roy Scheider, behind the steering wheel of a large truck and wearing a fedora, was staring down at them. At first glance, Vic was a bit surprised by what he was seeing. But then the image changed to an exterior shot of the truck traversing a crumbling bridge in a jungle, and he realized it was a scene from the movie *Sorcerer* being projected onto a white bedsheet.

A film projector sat on a tall, wide table in the center of the room, behind a long, L-shaped couch. The sound of film moving from reel to reel was loud and had become part of the movie's audio. The silhouette of someone's head was visible just above the back of the couch, and Vic figured it was Gabriel.

The scene changed to a shot of the truck's front tires falling through the bridge. Just as it appeared as if the truck would fall through completely, Kai turned off the projector and the image disappeared. It was a great scene and Vic was tempted to ask him to turn the movie back on.

Kai stepped to the wall and flipped a light switch, illuminating the room in a soft amber glow. Gabriel stood up and faced them. He wore a sky-blue shirt and light gray dress pants, both of which had a silky sheen.

It'd been a while since Vic had last seen him, but Gabriel hadn't changed much. He was a little shorter than Vic and slightly built. His handsome face was delicate and smooth, and he wore his dark medium-length hair in a feather cut.

"Vicente Espada. This is certainly a surprise. How have you been?"

"Can't complain, Gabriel. You?"

"Complaining's never really been my thing. Who's the beauty?" Gabriel stared at Teri, but there was more intrigue behind his gaze than want.

"This is Teri. My partner."

"Partner? You? That's a new one."

"She's Chris's niece. I'm teaching her a few things about the job."

"Ah, that makes more sense. Do you mind if I call you Teresa? I'm assuming Teresa is your real name. It's such a beautiful name, and to be honest, I have no use for nicknames."

"I haven't heard it in a while, but it's fine if you use it."

"Very good." Gabriel nodded subtly and turned his attention back to Vic. "How is the old war horse anyway?"

"Chris? He's good. Big, strong, and mean as always."

"That's good to hear. He's a wonderful person, please send him my regards. All right then, you two, have a seat. Let's talk," Gabriel said, motioning them over to where he stood.

Vic and Teri stepped to the front of the couch.

"Hold on one second, Vicente." Gabriel glanced in Kai's direction. Vic turned around just as Kai was tossing a towel at him. He snatched the towel out of the air and looked back at Gabriel. "Do you mind, Vicente? I was told this couch was stain resistant, but I'd rather not find out."

"You're the reason I'm covered in this crap, you know."

"That's one way to look at it. Although, you wouldn't have been in that building if you did a better job of managing your debts. Cause and effect, Vicente."

"Fair enough." Vic spread the white towel on the couch and sat on it. Terri sat down next to him.

Gabriel waited a few seconds before sitting down on the other end of the L-shaped couch. He positioned his body so he was facing them, with his back resting comfortably against the armrest and his legs crossed in front of him.

"How'd you get a print of *Sorcerer*? It just came out a few weeks ago." Vic said.

"One of the perks of my position, Vicente. Getting movie prints isn't a problem. Have you seen it?"

"Yeah, it's great."

"It is, isn't it. The music score by Tangerine Dream is incredible. All right then, enough with the Pauline Kael routine. What can I do for you?"

"Didn't Kai tell you?"

"Of course he did. But I want to hear it from you."

Vic had known Gabriel Yao since they were teenagers and were both flying gang colors. But while Vic had joined the Corps and disappeared into the jungles of Vietnam, Gabriel had moved on to bigger things and had become a member of Hip Sing Tong, an organized crime syndicate on par with the Italian Mafia.

While to an outsider it may have seemed that criminal organizations were thriving businesses, the truth was often the opposite. Except for the upper echelon, syndicate members always had to hustle, engaging in one scheme or another for some sort of payday. When he had started working for Chris a few years back, Vic had learned Gabriel was a good source of information—for the right price.

"A rich socialite was kidnapped in front of a high-rise on Park Avenue two nights back. I'm pretty sure the attackers were a street gang, I'm just not sure which one. Or where they're keeping her."

"Is that all?"

"Yeah. For now. Do you know anything about it?"

"You know I do. Or else you wouldn't have come down here. Even though you still owe me from the last time. You always did have balls, Vicente. I'll give you that."

"I have what I owe you. Plus interest."

Gabriel stood up and walked to a small bar on wheels. He poured a dark-colored spirit into a glass for himself but didn't offer them a drink. "Vic, all these years I've been helping you, it was never about the money. Well, maybe it was a little. But really, it was about mutual respect." Gabriel sat back down and took a long drink from his glass. "The money was fine, sure. But it was more than that. It was about what the money represented. You and I had a good thing going, but the last time I helped you, you decided not to pay. And if that wasn't disrespectful enough, you didn't bother to show up and explain why."

Vic had always thought their arrangement was business, and like any business, money would get them back on the right track. But Gabriel seemed to have taken their last interaction very personally. The tone of his words made Vic uneasy and second-guessing his decision to come back to Chinatown. He glanced over at Teri, who looked concerned as well.

"Listen Gabriel, I get it—you're pissed. But I want to make this right, so tell me what I have to do."

"You did it, Vic. You made it through the trial of Fire Mountain and earned this opportunity right here. Another chance to do things the right way—to be resurrected, so to speak."

"Gabriel, what in the hell are you talking about?"

Gabriel flashed a toothy grin and finished his drink. "That's not important now. What is important is that if you settle up, I'm going to give you what you're asking. Pay what you owe me from last time, plus interest, and another five hundred for what you asked about today. That'll make you square. With everyone."

Vic wasn't sure what Gabriel meant by "everyone," but he didn't want to ask and risk not getting the information he needed. He counted out three thousand dollars and handed the money to Kai.

"The Savage Kings took her," Gabriel said.

Vic wasn't surprised when he heard the name. After all, the Savage Kings were probably the only gang in New York brazen enough to kidnap an heiress. Coming out of Howard Beach in Queens, they were the biggest gang in the five boroughs and as ruthless as their moniker would indicate. They were cold-blooded killers with a thirst for power.

"Do you know where they're keeping her?" Teri asked.

"The Hemlock Gardens Houses. Apartment 10B, on the tenth floor of the south tower."

Vic leaned forward at the news of where the Savage Kings were keeping the Lynch woman. "They took over the south tower?"

"Of course not. Why stop with one building when you can have six? They took over the whole thing. Hemlock Gardens is theirs."

"How does that happen? What about the cops?" Teri asked.

"What about them? Even if they wanted to do something, which they don't, they couldn't. They're outnumbered and outgunned and have unofficially taken a position of 'see no evil, hear no evil,'" Gabriel said.

Teri looked confused—and disgusted. It was no secret the city was on the verge of collapse. Rampant unemployment, crime, and violence had combined to create a monsoon of despair in which the city's citizens were drowning. They were living in strange times, and Vic had seen a lot of weird things in his life. But the idea an entire community could be overtaken without anyone batting an eye was shocking and almost unbelievable.

"All right, Gabriel." Vic stood up and looked at Teri, using his eyes to let her know it was time to go. "I think I got what I needed. We're going to get out of your hair."

"Before you go, there's something else you should hear. Call it free advice," Gabriel said.

"Oh yeah? That's good, because free is all I can afford."

"Take a second and really consider not going forward with this endeavor."

"What do you mean?"

"This is not going to end well for you, Vicente."

Vic wasn't sure how to respond. He'd known Gabriel a long time and had heard, and seen, enough to know better than to dismiss anything he said.

"What are you saying, Gabriel? Are you threatening me?"

"You know I don't make threats, Vicente. It's in the stars. Bad things will come your way if you continue on this journey."

"Thanks for the warning, I'll take it under advisement."

"I'm sure you will. See you on the other side, Vicente."

"What in the holy fuck was that, Vic?" Teri was confused, angry, a little scared, and worst of all—soaking wet. It was pouring rain when they left the Yellow Springs Company, so they were drenched by the time they walked the half block back to the GTO. Vic doing the strong, silent type routine as she sat uncomfortably in the passenger seat wasn't going to work for her. "I asked you a question. What was that back there? And don't be cute with your answers. I want to know what's going on."

He glanced at her, then back at the road. "That's just the way Gabriel speaks. It's part of the whole Vincent Price, Ziggy Stardust thing he's got going."

Teri scoffed. "That's bullshit. I saw your face when Gabriel gave you that warning. You believe what he told you."

"I don't know about all that. Like I said, it's just the way he speaks. Bottom line, Gabriel's information is always on point, so I believe what he told us about the girl. I get why you're upset, but we're running out of time. We're going to go with the information Gabriel gave us."

"So that's it? You're just going to ignore his warnings?"

"I don't know what you want to hear, Teri. It's Chinatown. The mystical mumbo jumbo is part of the ride and doesn't make much sense if you're not from there. To be honest, nothing makes a whole lot of sense right now, but we still got to do our thing. We'll make it through whatever the city throws at us."

Vic sounded confident and Teri appreciated his effort to make her feel better, but she wasn't buying what he was selling. Gabriel Yao, as beautiful and charming as he was, was dead serious about the things he'd said. After the trial-by-fire thing Kai put him through and his eagerness to ignore Gabriel's warning, it'd become clear that Vic was planning to go as far as he needed to finish the job. Teri wasn't sure she was willing to go with him.

She looked out her window and noticed the rain had stopped, and the sun had reemerged behind dissolving gray clouds.

ten

THE DOOR OPENED and the little man came in without knocking. He handed Carolina an old pair of jeans, a dark green t-shirt, and a pair of well-worn gray sneakers. He told her she had five minutes to change and then walked out. No doubt racing back to watch her on the monitor.

Carolina was determined not to become part of his mental spank bank, so she changed underneath the camera, out of view of its lens. He returned just as she was tying the shoelaces on the too-tight sneakers. Carolina thought she remembered him from the night they'd taken her, but she wasn't sure. He was a little shorter than her and had long, dark hair and a patchy beard.

"So, what do they call you? Danger Mouse?" Carolina asked snidely.

He approached her without responding and forcefully turned her around. He used a folded headscarf to blindfold her, tying it around her head tighter than necessary.

"Come on," the little man said, pulling her along by her right wrist.

Carolina heard heavy locks turning, followed by the squeal of rusty door hinges. She felt a hand on her back, nudging her forward. The sound of a heavy steel door crashing into its steel frame echoed from behind and startled her. After being pulled along for a few feet, Carolina felt the floor bounce slightly and guessed they had entered an elevator. There was a soft ding sound, and the elevator began its descent.

After about ninety tension-filled seconds, the elevator came to a stop, and someone shoved her from behind. Unsure of her surroundings, Carolina tried to walk slowly but someone yanked her along, causing her to stumble and almost fall. After a minute or so, she heard a door being pushed open and, judging by the smell of post-rain fresh air, they were now outside.

The heat from the sun hit her instantly, as if someone was pointing a blow dryer at her face. Besides the sounds of traffic in the distance, it was eerily quiet. Someone grabbed her left arm, their grip so tight it pinched the skin under her bicep. Now she was being led by both arms, the two guides moving so fast she had to jog to keep up or risk being dragged.

After several minutes, they stopped walking and she heard a door being pulled open. She was shoved forward a few steps, but Carolina dragged her feet, causing her sneakers to make a squeaking sound on the floor. Between that and not feeling heat from the sun on her face anymore, she guessed they were inside another building.

The blindfold was pulled away from her face and, after the blurriness cleared from her vision, she saw they were inside a giant, empty room. It looked to be the bottom floor of a large building—more wide than tall. There was a staircase in front of her leading up. The first step at the bottom was the longest, with each proceeding step narrower than the one below it—almost like a pyramid. At the top of the pyramid was a long landing with staircases on either side.

"Walk," one of her escorts said.

Carolina looked over and saw it was the little man who'd given her the clothes. He motioned with his head toward the stairs, so

Carolina started up them. The other man, heavy set and plain looking, raced ahead. He took the stairs two at a time, stopping when he reached the first landing.

When Carolina got close, he started up the staircase on the left side and she followed behind. The second-floor landing was at the center of a long hallway. The little man directed her to the right and they walked a few feet before entering a room on the left side of the hallway.

It was a huge room with four large, square windows on one of the walls. Aluminum bleachers had been erected in front of the windows. There were basketball hoops on each side of the long room, and the light brown parquet floor was dull and scratched. Carolina realized she was standing in an old gymnasium and guessed the building was a school or recreation center. It was warm in the room, and it smelled like mold and sour milk.

She heard doors being pushed open and looked toward the far end of the room. A tall, broad-shouldered figure was walking toward them. He was a large man, not muscular but not fat either. And he looked older than most of the people she'd seen, who appeared to be in their early twenties or younger.

He stopped a few inches away and glared down at her. He had a full, weathered face, with a few strands of gray in his black hair. His small eyes were dark brown and intense, and she felt like he was looking straight into her soul.

"She give you any problems, Pito?"

Carolina realized he was talking to the man who'd handed her the clothes. She turned her head slightly to the left and they exchanged quick glances before he returned his attention to the large man.

"Nah, Abaddon. A couple of wise cracks but nothing to get worked up about," Pito said.

The man called Abaddon looked at Carolina. "Is that right? You like to tell jokes?"

She looked up at him but didn't respond immediately,

deciding to let the question hang in the air. She looked Abaddon in the eyes, hoping he hadn't noticed her knees shaking. She didn't want to give any of them the satisfaction of seeing her scared.

"Jokes? No, I don't tell jokes. I just make observations that may seem funny to some people. Like you wearing black leather pants in this heat, for example. I think it's a bold choice, but someone else might think it's hilariously ridiculous," she said.

Abaddon licked his lips before curling them into a sinister smile that made her blood run cold. "That's actually pretty funny." He turned around and walked a few steps. Carolina noticed some sort of handle sticking out of his waistband, near the small of his back. "Is that how you normally deal with stressful situations? With humor?"

"Who says this is a stressful situation?"

"If you say so." Abaddon's voice was low and even, almost monotone.

As scared as Carolina was, she was equally tired and not in any mood for banter. "Why am I here?"

"Money," Abaddon said.

"That much has been made clear. What I mean is, why am I *here*? In this room?" Carolina extended her arms out, as if she were presenting a home for sale.

"I wanted to see a real-life billionaire with my own eyes."

"Bullshit. I've seen the camera. I know you've been watching me. You didn't need to bring me out of the room. So, I'll ask you again—why am I here?"

Abaddon turned and faced her. "Have you ever been outside of Manhattan, Carol?" He reached behind his back with his right hand, and when he brought it back around, he was holding a large knife.

She swallowed hard at the sight of the imposing weapon. "It's Carolina. Of course, I have."

He shook his head and smirked. "I'm sure you have. The French Riviera is pretty far from New York. No, I meant have you ever been to any place in this city that didn't have a gold-plated address?"

She didn't respond. Abaddon held the knife loosely in his hand, staring down at it as he used its point to trace over the lines on his left palm. The handle was wrapped in brown leather, and the dark blade was about seven inches long and wide. One side of the blade was serrated, while the other was smooth and had a curved, sharp edge.

"I didn't think so. Don't worry, you haven't missed much. The whole city is pretty much a shithole. Miles upon miles of some of the worst living conditions in the world. Entire communities of people living in poverty and fighting to survive. Hell, it might as well not be in America."

"Wait, I'm a bit confused. Are you saying this is a political statement? That kidnapping me is supposed to send some sort of message to New York's rich and powerful? Am I supposed to be Patty Hearst in this Symbionese Liberation Army role-playing game of yours?"

Abaddon raised his head. "No, not at all. See, I'm not trying to change anything. I love what you people created with your greed and indifference. Out here, where no one is paying attention, it's survival of the fittest—adapt or die. Social Darwinism at its finest. There're no laws accept the ones I make. I'm the king."

"Surely, you're not serious? What, exactly are you king of? Who *are* you people?"

"We're the beginning and the end," Abaddon said.

"What? What does that even mean?" He smiled but didn't respond. The silence added frustration to the growing list of unpleasant emotions Carolina was feeling. "Stop playing games and just answer me. Who are you?"

"We're just like you and yours, Carolina—we create and destroy." Abaddon twirled the knife in his hand as he spoke. "We are people with wants and needs who'll do whatever it takes to satisfy those wants and needs. We take, we kill, we loot, we plunder."

"Why?"

"Because we can."

"Very poetic," Carolina said sarcastically. "So, what happens now? How much longer are you going to hold me here?"

"I sent a message to your father telling him how much it would cost to get you back. He has twenty-four hours left to get me my money."

"He'll pay whatever it is you've demanded."

"I'm sure he will." Abaddon walked up to her, so close she felt his warm breath on her forehead. He brought the knife up and ran its point gently along the side of her face. "You wanted to know why I had you brought to this room? It's because I wanted you to see my face and remember it in your nightmares. Because regardless of whether your father pays, you're going to die tomorrow."

Abaddon spoke softly, as if he was telling secrets to a lover. "I'll wait till I have my money, but after that I'm going to fuck you in every hole in your body. And when I'm done, I'm going to carve new holes and fuck you in those till the life drains from your eyes. I wanted you to know what's coming, so you can live with that knowledge for the last hours of your life."

He glanced at Pito and nodded, signaling him the meeting was over. Pito placed the blindfold over her eyes and Carolina felt light-headed as the world went dark.

***

Hemlock Gardens Houses was located on 158th Avenue in Howard Beach, between Eighty-Second and Eighty-Third Street and extended north to 157th Avenue, almost directly under the Belt Parkway. The apartment buildings were just one small part of the Howard Beach neighborhood and were about a mile from the nearest inlet leading out to the Atlantic Ocean. It was one of the many low-income apartment communities overseen by the New York City Housing Authority.

After a few minutes searching for the right spot, Vic had parked the GTO on a section of grass off the Belt's main roadway. He and Teri stood by a six-foot-high chain-link fence meant to stop people from walking onto the Belt. From where they stood, they had a clear view down into Hemlock Gardens.

"It's weird, from up here it looks like any other community. There're even kids running around," Teri said.

"What were you expecting to see?"

"I don't know. Armed guards and barbed wire, like East Berlin or something."

"Yeah well, it's a little different when you get closer. Especially at night."

"You've been here before?"

"Here? No. But I've been to a lot of places like it. Even grew up in one. They can be pretty bad. It's a shame too. There are a lot of good people living in these communities. Shuttered in their homes, too scared to walk around. Shit, even the front doors on every apartment are made of heavy steel."

"So, are the steel doors meant to keep people out or in?"

"I don't know if there's a difference."

Vic used his binoculars to look over the entire community. Hemlock Gardens consisted of six ten-story apartment buildings that'd been arranged in a square, one north, one south, and two each on the east and west. Based on what Gabriel had told them, the Kings were keeping the girl in the south tower on 158th Avenue. In between the buildings were pedestrian-only roads, a playground, and what looked like a large recreation center. There was no fencing or barriers around the property, so the interior grounds were easily accessible.

The kids Teri had mentioned, along with several adults who looked like civilians, were hanging around the playground. Vic spotted a few Savage Kings milling about, easily identifiable by the artwork and patches on the back of their denim vests. The large art piece, a black crown surrounded by red flames, was at the center of two rockers. "Savage Kings" was embroidered on the top rocker, while "New York" had been spelled out on the bottom rocker.

"Well, we're definitely in the right place," Vic said, handing the binoculars to Teri.

She looked through the binoculars. "So much for discreet."

"Most of these guys couldn't spell inconspicuous, let alone practice it."

"Aren't they worried about attracting attention? What about the cops?"

"Attention is what they want. And cops are like Bigfoot out here—something everyone has heard about, but no one has ever actually seen."

"That makes zero sense."

"Yeah well, making sense isn't a huge priority in The Fear."

"What now?"

"This is as close as we're going to get to this place for now, so we're done here. Let's head back to the office and get cleaned up."

eleven

KUBRICK'S HEAD darted back and forth between the large bowl of dog food and Vic. It'd been a few minutes since Vic had put the bowl down in front of Kubrick, so a comically large pool of the dog's saliva had formed on the floor beneath him. Making Kubrick wait until he'd been given permission to eat had been a new thing. Vic had found an article on how to teach dogs to wait and decided to give it a try. It had been a bumpy start, but after practicing for a couple of days, Kubrick had it down.

"Okay." Kubrick pounced when he heard the command and devoured the entire bowl of food in less than a minute.

After he'd dropped Teri off at Sugar Hill, Vic had gone home to clean up and take care of Kubrick before his meeting with Oran. After everything he'd been through, he had been tempted to take a long, hot shower. But it'd felt like a hundred degrees in his small, one-bedroom apartment, so he'd decided a hot shower wasn't the best idea. After a quick, cold shower, Vic rummaged through his fridge and found the rest of a chopped cheese sandwich he'd forgotten about. He stood in the kitchen and devoured the sandwich in a few bites, wearing nothing but a bath towel.

By the time he'd finished getting dressed, the sun was setting on the city. Vic wanted some quiet time to think about everything he'd learned before his sit-down with Oran, so he decided to take a cab to Leviathan Security. Vic had been in the cab for about thirty seconds when he'd realized he wasn't going to get the quiet time he'd wanted.

The cabbie had the radio turned to 97.1 WNWS where the news update was all about the so-called Son of Sam killer. A maniac that'd been using a .44 caliber handgun to kill young couples all over the city for almost a year now. The tabloids had really hit pay dirt with this one. It'd turned out when the wacko wasn't stalking and murdering kids, he liked to mail taunting letters to the cops and newspapers.

The most recent letter had been sent to a columnist for the *Daily News*, which the newspaper of course had published, along with a composite sketch and profile of the killer. The ensuing panic could have been predicted by anyone with an IQ above fifty. It'd gotten so bad, women were cutting and dying their hair because the newspaper's profile had mentioned the killer targeted women with long, dark hair.

Vic watched the scene outside his window with trepidation. A sweltering heat wave was suffocating every New Yorker, and paranoia was spreading like wildfire. Trash and debris flooded the streets, filling the air with an almost unbearable stench. Abandoned buildings, like the ancient ruins of Pompeii, stood as reminders of a once-great city. It was surreal and frightening, and Vic felt as if he was living inside a Hieronymus Bosch painting.

He was a New Yorker, born and raised, so Vic was used to the oddities that made the city unique. But everything that had been going on around him, including what he'd experienced in Chinatown, had Vic thinking the city might be at a tipping point. Like maybe they were close to crossing the threshold into a world where madness was the norm and sane people were the outcasts.

"That's some crazy stuff, huh?"

Vic heard the cabbie speak but had been distracted by his own thoughts and wasn't quite sure what he'd said. "What was that?"

"I said that's some crazy stuff. The Son of Sam psycho."

"Oh. Yeah, that guy is a maniac."

"So, you think it's a guy?"

"You don't?"

"No. I mean yeah. It probably is, but they don't know for sure. It could be anyone."

"They've had some eyewitnesses that described a guy."

"I know that, but who's to say they're right? All I'm saying is that the cops shouldn't rule anything out. I mean they ain't got dick now, and we're coming up on the psycho's anniversary. Who knows what's going to happen?"

"That's a good point." Vic thought the guy's point was anything but good, but he wanted the conversation to end.

The cabbie seemed incapable of taking a hint and continued speaking. "Well, at least the Yanks are moving up in the standings. What do ya think? We got a shot at catching the Sox?"

Vic had always thought fans' use of the word "we" when discussing their favorite teams was strange. He was about to ask the cabbie what position he played for the Yankees when they pulled up in front of the building on East Sixty-Seventh Street.

Pito heard "Funk Funk" by Cameo playing loudly on someone's radio and tapped his feet on the aluminum bleacher. He'd been watching everyone from his spot on the top row and thought the crowd was extra rowdy tonight. Already loaded on uppers and cocaine, most of the Kings had been drinking freely from either one-liter bottles of whiskey or forty-ounce bottles of beer. The mixture of testosterone, booze, and drugs had combined to form an adrenaline-fueled ticking time bomb.

It was fight night and three matches had been scheduled. Space inside the gym was limited, so Kings had started filing in early, throwing punches and elbows at each other to secure a spot close to the ring. The temperature had risen quickly in the already hot gym, and it smelled like cigarette smoke and burned marijuana.

Havoc and Frankie Hi-Life were standing in the Savage Kings' version of a boxing ring—four traffic cones and white nylon rope forming a ten-by-ten square—preparing for battle. Most of the money was on Havoc. Six feet of sinewy muscle, the former Golden Gloves boxer hadn't lost a fight yet. But Pito had put his last five dollars on Frankie Hi-Life and his two hundred and eighty pounds of steroid-filled rage. He was unskilled and not very smart, but with no referee and no rules, Pito figured mindless brute strength was a safe bet.

Someone yelled for the fight to start and the combatants, shirtless and with no hand protection, circled each other. Everyone was standing, yelling, and stomping their feet. The noise in the room was deafening. Pito was about to try and make his way closer to the ring when the gym's entrance doors were pushed open.

He looked up expecting to see Abaddon, but Machai walked through the doors instead. He strolled toward Abaddon's chair with his chest out and head up as if he were the big man himself. He glanced around the room, seeming to check if any of the cheers were directed at him. Everyone's attention was on the fight, so he sat down and stared absently ahead.

Pito wasn't too surprised Abaddon was a no-show. He had a habit of disappearing for days at a time and returning without explanation. Not that Abaddon needed to explain anything—he was the supreme president, after all. Everyone figured he just locked himself in his room with a couple of chicks and a pound of cocaine. Pito never asked of course and chalked up the missing time to the man's moodiness.

Pito decided to stay where he was but remained standing, his attention split between the fight and Machai. Havoc was throwing quick jabs straight out from the shoulder, being careful not to overcommit. Frankie Hi-Life moved his head from side to side and stayed low, negating the impact of most of Havoc's punches. Then Frankie Hi-Life pushed forward, stalking his opponent like a hungry beast.

Machai was the only person in the room who hadn't reacted to any of the fight action. He sat expressionless on Abaddon's high-backed chair, two skanks kneeling at his feet, playing the big shot with the supreme president not around. Pito was getting angry and wasn't exactly sure why. After staring at Machai and the clueless women at his feet for a few seconds, Pito realized he was still bothered by the way Abaddon had treated Carolina earlier.

The big man had ordered them to bring her to him, even kicked Pito in the chest when he'd asked why. At first, he had figured Abaddon wanted to scare her a little, but Pito realized right away that wasn't the case. Abaddon had murder and lust in his eyes when he looked at Carolina. He would bide his time till they got the money, but after that all bets were off, and Abaddon would follow through on his threats. Pito winced when he thought about what the supreme president had said to her.

The crowd roared with excitement and Pito looked back at the ring in time to see Frankie Hi-Life pick Havoc up in a bearhug. He threw him to the ground and straddled him. Frankie Hi-Life straightened up, balanced himself, and rained hammer fists down on Havoc's face, like some sort of Silverback gorilla. Havoc seemed to go limp, but no one intervened, and the beating only stopped after Frankie Hi-Life was too tired to throw any more blows.

Covered in blood and sweat, Frankie Hi-Life rolled off Havoc and walked exhaustedly to the other side of the ring. Two junior Kings carried Havoc's lifeless body out of the ring while another mopped the blood off the floor in preparation for the next fight.

It was almost nine p.m. by the time Vic knocked on the door at Leviathan Security. He could hear laughter on the other side and had to wait a minute or so before Oran opened the door.

"Vic, my man. Come on in, brother," Oran said with a warm smile. Vic stepped inside and they embraced in a quick hug. "Come on, I want you to meet the rest of the team."

Vic followed Oran into the reception area. Three people were seated around the conference table talking amongst themselves. Glossy eight-by-ten black-and-white photos of the kidnapping scene outside the building lay on the table, along with an empty pizza box.

"Listen up, fellas. This here is Vic Espada, the guy I've been telling you about. We did our last tour together...shit, when was that? 'sixty-eight?"

Vic nodded. "Yeah. Till we rotated out in 'seventy."

Oran kept the introduction short, leaving out the part where he'd been Vic's team leader. It was just like Oran to keep the "getting to know you" stuff to a minimum. Besides, Vic figured if these guys were in the room, then Oran had worked with them before, and it was probably a good bet they were familiar with Oran's resume.

"That's Walter Herrmann," Oran said pointing to a man seated on the far side of the table.

He had wavy, light brown hair and a thick, handlebar mustache that covered his entire upper lip. Even sitting down, Walter looked to be at least a foot taller than the other men at the table. Vic took a few steps toward him, extending his hand for a shake. Walter wrapped his very large hand around Vic's, swallowing it whole like a Python would a mouse. He was wearing a long-sleeve shirt, which, considering the heat, Vic found odd.

"Nice to meet you," Walter said.

"Walter is retired Air Force. Seventh Air Force Mobile EOD Team," Oran said.

"Explosives disposal, huh? You guys were attached to the 377th Supply Squadron in Saigon, right?"

Walter released Vic's hand and leaned back in his chair. "Yeah, how'd you know that?"

Vic noticed he had a southern accent, more Florida Panhandle than Texas. "Met a lot of people over there, heard a lot of stories. Some stuff just stuck in here." Vic pointed at his own head.

"This big man right here is Tremaine Pope." Oran was standing behind a seated Tremaine with his hands on the guy's shoulders, as if he were giving him a massage.

Tremaine flashed a wide, friendly grin and nodded. "Just call me Tre. How ya doing brother."

"Old Tre here was a member of Tiger Force in Nam." Vic and Tre shook hands as Oran took a step back.

"Really?" Vic tried to mask his surprise, but knew he'd done a bad job when Tre gave him a "yes, really, motherfucker" face.

Tiger Force had been the nickname of an elite long-range reconnaissance patrol unit of the First Battalion, 327th Infantry Regiment, attached to the 101st Airborne Division, and had been responsible for counterinsurgency operations against the North Vietnamese Army and Viet Cong. The guy sitting in front of him was ten years and forty pounds past his prime, wore thick eyeglasses, and had the slumped shoulders of a preteen with social-anxiety disorder. He didn't look like he could have ever been a member of a special operations unit.

"And last but not least, David Kavanaugh," Oran said.

Vic looked over at the man sitting at the end of the table. He nodded but made no effort to get up and shake hands. He looked to be about average height and was solidly built. With long, full, salt-and-pepper hair blown out Bee Gees style, he was clean shaven and Hollywood handsome.

"David's retired Army, Fifth Special Forces Group."

"Green Beret, huh?" Vic said.

"All day, every day," David said.

The guy had a strange, almost aggressive smirk and intense stare that Vic decided was his lame attempt at establishing alpha status. After the events in Chinatown earlier, Vic was too tired to engage and took a seat at the table.

Oran sat down in a reclining chair and leaned back. "All right Vic, what do you have for us?"

Vic looked around the table, impressed with the team Oran had put together. They were all former military and, more importantly, had been members of special operations units. Presumably, they all had the experience needed for what was being planned.

Vic spent the next twenty minutes filling them in on what Gabriel had told him and what he'd learned from his recon of Hemlock Gardens. He left out the parts about being forced to escape from a burning building and what Gabriel had said about the mission not ending well.

"Savage Kings? Emerald Tigers? What in the hell is going on in this city?" Walter said.

"They're street gangs, the city is full of them. They're young and unorganized. Violent and without conscience for sure, but unorganized. Even the kidnapping was a shitshow," Oran said.

"Yeah, but they pulled it off," Tre said.

"Yeah well, even a limp dick can get hard every once in a while," David said, looking directly at Vic.

Oran placed a creased and dirty piece of torn notebook paper on the table. "So, we finally heard from the kidnappers. One of them handed this to Mr. Lynch's doorman a few hours ago."

Vic grabbed the note and read it silently.

ONE MILLION DOLLARS

UNMARKED MONEY IN 100 DOLLAR BILLS

PUT MONEY IN BLACK DUFFEL BAG

SEND ONE PERSON WITH MONEY TO 86 AND SHORE

10 PM ON WEDNESDAY NIGHT

GIRL WILL BE RETURNED AFTER WE HAVE MONEY

It'd been sloppily printed, as if a right-handed person had written it using their left hand. He passed the note to Tre, and it made its way around the table.

Tre glanced at Oran. "That's tomorrow. Your client going to be able to put together that kind of scratch?"

"Money isn't a problem," Oran said.

David let out a frustrated sigh and walked away from the table. "Well, that's a bunch of bullshit. If they get the money before giving up the girl, she's not going to make it back. You can bank on that shit."

"It's not going to matter. We're going in and getting her well before the deadline." Oran walked over to a map of New York City on the wall behind the table.

"How? They took over an entire housing project. Which means they've probably got a lot of people carrying a lot of weapons," Tre said.

"By doing what we do best," Oran said. He used a red marker to circle locations on the map as he spoke. "Hemlock Gardens is right here, on One Hundred and Fifty-Eighth near Eighty-Third Street. We can go in on foot, dressed like people from the neighborhood. It'll be dark by eight, so we'll have some concealment. We know they're keeping Carolina on the tenth floor of the south tower, which should be about here." He circled a spot on the map. "We move stealthily, neutralizing any obstacles as we go. Once we have her, we can evac out through here, Spring Creek Park. I'll have a boat waiting for us. They won't be able to follow on the water. We ride Jamaica Bay all the way to the East River, have her home by midnight."

"Oran, that all sounds really good, but we don't know dick about these guys. What kind of firepower do they have? What are their numbers?" Tre said.

"Vic?" Oran nodded at him.

"The Kings are the biggest gang in the city, with about two to three hundred bangers. Bold and violent as hell, they're a direct reflection of their leader—a guy named Abaddon."

"Abaddon? More fucking comic book names. Je-sus Christ," Walter said.

"Yeah, well, this guy is not a character in a comic. He's very real and he's serious business. Most bangers are kids, no older than twenty-one or twenty-two. But supposedly this guy is in his thirties and connected. The word is the Savage Kings are packing more artillery than some third-world countries."

"How do you know all this?" David asked.

"Finding people is what I do. Being familiar with the world they live in is just smart business."

He could feel David's suspicious gaze, but Vic didn't care what David thought, or how he felt. He was being paid to provide a service, and as far as Vic was concerned, this ass clown didn't need to know that he'd grown up in that world and knew it intimately.

"All right," Oran said, breaking the tense silence. "It looks like this is as much intel as we're going to get, so let's start prepping gear. We'll be moving quick, so we're going in light. I want to be on the road by eighteen hundred tomorrow."

Vic said his goodbyes and headed downstairs. He stepped out of the building into the warm evening and looked up at the starless night sky. He checked the time on his watch and saw it was close to eleven. Exhausted and energized at the same time, Vic decided he wanted some company, so he took a cab to the 118th Street Rose.

"I don't trust him Oran," David said.

Oran rolled his eyes and breathed a sigh of frustration. He was standing in the small kitchen, out of sight of the men in the other room. He poured himself four fingers of whiskey and took a long drink from the glass before walking back into the conference room. "Really? And why is that exactly?"

The question was semi-rhetorical. The bad vibes between David and Vic had been obvious right away. Oran had chalked it up to too much testosterone, and maybe a little elbow nudging for the role of the group's resident heartthrob.

David was leaning back in the chair, with his feet on top of the table. "First, I don't know him. The four of us have worked a lot of jobs together and it's been going fine, so we don't need a new face. And second—he just looks soft to me."

"Well, those are certainly two reasons. Both stupid as fuck, but reasons nonetheless." Oran took another sip of his drink. "We don't know that part of the city and Vic does. We're going to need him to point us in the right direction. And those places are full of people who will want to kill us. We're going to be outnumbered ten to one—at least. If we have to engage, we're going to need as many guns in the fight as possible.

Oran put his drink down on the table and stared down at the other three men. "And just to put this to bed once and for all, let me educate you on Vic Espada. When we were in Nam, he was our team's point man. Back then Recon was about scouting, not combat missions. Emphasis was placed on stealth, infiltration, and communication. We never went in heavy, but we trained like a raid company.

"Vic was smart and moved with surgical precision. His last name literally means sword, which was fitting because he was the tip of the sword for us when we were in Indian country. Anywhere we needed to go, he was first in and effective at eliminating targets." Oran picked up his drink and finished it in one gulp. "Believe me, my friend, Vicente Espada is anything but soft."

twelve

Wednesday, July 13

CAROLINA SAT on the corner of the bed with her back pressed against the wall, holding her knees close to her chest as she stared at the door. She was exhausted and trying to stop from shaking.

The wall-mounted light was turned off, but the room was dimly lit by thin rays of sunlight that snuck in through the edges of the boarded-up window. After she'd been taken to see that horrible monster Abaddon, Carolina had stayed awake all night waiting for his followers to walk in the room and drag her to him so he could carry out his threats. She'd tried to put up a brave front, but after her face-to-face with the madman, Carolina felt nothing but terror.

They'd brought her back to the room after the meeting, and she hadn't seen or heard from any of them till this morning. That was when the little guy called Pito dropped off the bowl of sludge they had been passing off as food. She'd assumed it was oatmeal and had initially decided against finding out. But after her meeting with their leader, she knew she had to keep her strength up, so she ate the food.

She'd spent her sleepless night thinking about what Abaddon had said and trying to figure a way out of this horrific situation. Carolina was confident her father would pay the ransom, but now she knew Abaddon still planned to torture her, then kill her. And as for the police, she assumed the lunatic had made "no police involvement" a stipulation of the ransom. If that was the case, she knew her father wouldn't risk her life by calling them.

But Josiah Lynch was a tough man with unlimited resources and connections around the world. He wouldn't just follow their directions like a stupid mule. She trusted he was doing everything necessary to get her back home safe, but she couldn't wait around to be rescued. She was on her own out here and it was up to her to save herself.

Vic figured it was a waste of time, but he couldn't help himself. He was trying to unwind after spending his first hour in the office going over his plans for tonight. He sat with his feet on top of his desk scanning today's edition of the *New York Times* for the box score from last night's Yankee game but couldn't find one. He'd been a die-hard Yankees fan since he was a kid, so checking the paper for results and box scores had been a part of his daily routine during baseball season since he could remember.

Vic never read the *Times*. He felt like a lot of the writers were pedantic and talked down to their readers rather than to them. But it was the only paper Chris had delivered to the office. And since he hadn't stopped to pick up a copy of *The Daily News* on his way into the office, his options were limited.

He had woken up late after staying at The Rose longer than he'd planned. He'd started rapping with the waitress Brandy and decided to wait for her till the end of her shift. She'd gone home with him, but he was exhausted and had fallen asleep while she was in the shower. He'd woken up three hours later to an empty apartment. He took Kubrick for a walk and fell back to sleep watching *The Honeymooners*. He was a lot more tired than he'd realized because he ended up oversleeping.

Vic was surprised to find the *Times* had a sports section. He was less surprised to see it was only one page long and had been combined with the business section. At least it had the box score for the game. His favorite player, Reggie Jackson, had gone hitless in four at bats, but the Yanks beat Milwaukee five to two. They were half a game out of first and surging. All was right in the world.

He had been there for twenty minutes, waiting for Chris to get back so they could have their meeting, when an annoyed-looking Teri walked in the office. She confirmed his suspicions when she threw her purse on top of her desk and plopped heavily into her chair. The last time he'd spoken with Teri she'd briefly mentioned being nervous about a blind date she would be going on. A friend of hers had hooked her up with the drummer for a punk rock band that unironically called themselves The Provokers. Teri couldn't explain who they were provoking, so Vic had lost interest within thirty seconds.

"So, am I safe in assuming things didn't go well with Mr. poor man's Joey Ramone?"

Teri looked at him and rolled her eyes. "First of all, Joey Ramone *is* the poor man's Joey Ramone. And second, no it didn't go well. Not. At. All."

"So, what happened? Did you find out the Jack Daniels bottle he carried around all night was full of warm tea?"

"Actually, finding out he was a poser would have improved the date."

"Do tell."

"Where do I start? How about this—his breath smelled like old hot dog water."

Vic chuckled. "What?"

"His breath smelled like old hot dog water," Teri repeated. She went into the kitchen and poured herself a glass of apple juice. "We met at a club in the Village. I should have known right away it was going to be a bad night when he walked in ahead of me and beelined it straight past the door girl. Fuckface stuck me with the six-bucks-a-head entrance fee."

She took a long sip of water as she walked back to her desk and sat down. "If that wasn't bad enough, the bands sucked so we were only there for an hour. We ended up sitting shoulder to shoulder at some crappy little pizza spot he chose near Washington Square Park. We're a few blocks away from Little Italy, mind you. A place filled with restaurants serving some of the best pizza anywhere."

"Save me the gory details. How did it end?"

"With me pushing his face into a concrete wall. Even after all that, the dumbass made a move. Can you believe that shit?" Teri let out an exasperated sigh.

"Well, at least now I know who he's trying to provoke."

Teri laughed. "Fuck you, Vic. Where's my uncle?"

"He went upstairs to take a shower."

"In the middle of the day?"

"In case you haven't noticed, *senorita*, it's hot as hell today. Ninety-three degrees the last time I checked."

Ten minutes passed without either of them speaking. Vic smiled when he heard "Living in the Life" by the Isley Brothers come on the small radio Chris kept in the office. The song was a badass Funk track with lyrics about calling out people for passing judgement on others. He started bopping his head and shoulders in rhythm with the song.

"So, you going to get up and dance or what?" Teri asked.

He looked over at her and smiled. She was sitting at her desk, holding a hardcover copy of *Song of Solomon* by Teri Morrison. "I was thinking about it."

"And?"

"It's too goddamn hot."

"It's never too hot to dance." Teri got up and stepped into the space between her desk and his. "Dancing is good for the soul."

She bit her lower lip as she moved her head and shoulders to the music's rhythm. Her movements intensified with the song's drumbeat. So much so, he averted his eyes when the yellow, sleeve-less shirt she was wearing lifted slightly, exposing her naval.

She moved her hips in synch with the music, quickly transitioning to "The Bus Stop." Vic wasn't a fan of the popular disco line dance, but Teri's enthusiasm was infectious. She went through a cycle of movements and was about to start her second when Vic jumped up and joined her.

They stood side by side and were quickly in synch. They were both good dancers, so it looked as if they had spent a lot of time dancing together, rehearsing for their appearance on *Soul Train*. The only thing missing was Don Cornelius.

"What in the holy hell?" Chris said from the front door. They both stopped dancing and laughed at his surprised, and somewhat disgusted, expression. "I didn't know we were doing so well we had time for goofing off."

"Come on, Uncle Chris, we were just dancing a little," Teri said.

"I don't know what you two were doing, but it certainly wasn't dancing."

"Oh really? What would you call it then?" Vic asked.

"Synchronized fucking off," Chris said. He took a seat opposite Vic's desk. "Let's get started with this meeting."

Teri and Vic returned to their seats and Vic went over everything, beginning with what had gone down in Chinatown. He then filled them in on the meeting at Leviathan Security, including the rescue plan details.

"Wouldn't it be easier to have a helicopter waiting nearby? Instead of trying to beat feet to the beach?" Chris asked.

"A bird would be ideal, but there's nowhere to land one. And, we'd have to worry about timing. If the chopper comes in before we have the girl, then we run the risk of letting everyone know we're there."

"I guess it makes sense then."

"It's a solid plan, Chris. Oran was always good at this part. He kept us alive in Nam. But there's something else we need to discuss." Vic stood up and pulled out a folded map of Brooklyn from his top desk drawer. He unfolded it and placed it on top of his desk. "I'm thinking this will take us three hours max. Two hours on the infiltration and extraction, and an hour on the boat ride back in. The first thing I plan to do when I get off that boat is call you. If you don't hear from me by nine tonight, something went wrong. At that point, all bets are off and you call the cops. If something happens and I got to try and get out on foot, this is the route I plan to take."

Vic used a black pen to chart out his alternative escape route, a northwest track back home, using any means available. "I'll stay street side till Ozone Park. It's almost impossible to find a cab in that neighborhood, so I'll probably take the A train across the river. Once I'm back in Manhattan, it should be easier to catch a cab home. There are pay phones everywhere, so I should be able to call you guys at some point along the way to let you know where I am. Does everything make sense?"

Chris and Teri nodded in unison.

"So when do we leave?" Teri asked.

"*I'm* leaving here in an hour. I'm supposed to meet Oran and his team at Leviathan, and we'll drive in from there."

"What are you talking about, Vic? I'm going with you."

"No, you're not. Oran's guys are highly trained operators. They'll be moving fast and taking out anything and anyone that gets in their way. You're not ready to be in that type of environment."

"Fuck you, Vic. I can take care of myself, you know I can."

"Calm down, Teri, he's right. You're not ready for what might go down out there," Chris said.

Teri looked at them with screaming eyes but didn't say anything. After several seconds she got up and stormed out of the office, slamming the door behind her.

Chris looked at Vic. "You can't be mad at her for wanting to go with you. She wants to help."

"I'm not mad at her, Chris. I'm actually kind of proud that she's so freaking tough. But you know she can't go out on this. She's not ready, and I can't be worrying about her and do my job at the same time. You understand, right?"

"You ain't got to convince me, youngblood. That's my only niece and I love her like she's one of my own kids. If anything, I appreciate you telling her, so I didn't have to. Allows me to keep playing the part of the great uncle." Chris smiled paternally but there was melancholy in his eyes. "I know why you're doing this, Vic. And I love you for it, but this is a world not even the cops go into anymore. A world you haven't been a real part of in a long time. I just want you to know that if you don't feel right about this, you don't have to do it. We've made it this far —we can make it the rest of the way without these people's money."

"I appreciate that, Chris, but ain't nothing to it. I'm just going to lead Oran's team in and point out the main attractions—like a tour guide at an amusement park." Vic hoped his eyes didn't betray the false certainty of his words.

"All right then, I said my piece. You be careful out there, youngblood. The city is out for blood right now, and mercy will be hard to come by."

Chris stood up and walked to his office. Vic looked down at the map and thought about what Chris had just said. The truth was, Vic had considered pulling out of the operation. Tell Oran thanks, but no thanks. Even after meeting Oran's team and being convinced they were more than capable of pulling off the rescue, something didn't feel right. The problem was, Vic couldn't put his finger on what was bothering him.

Vic felt a familiar feeling in his stomach, a strange sort of tightness like he'd feel right before a fight. When him and his boys would venture into enemy territory to settle a beef with a rival gang, or when Ariadne would infiltrate enemy base camps in Nam.

The difference was, back then, the feeling in his stomach would be offset by the knowledge he'd have people he loved and trusted watching his back. Tonight, he'd be going into the lion's den with Oran being the only person Vic knew he could trust. For some reason, he doubted that would be enough.

Oracle Boxing Gym was located on the southwest corner of 155th Street and Eighth Avenue, directly across the street from Rucker Park, world-famous for its pickup basketball games that'd attracted participants like NBA greats Dr. J and Kareem Abdul Jabbar. Although she was a hoops fanatic and there were a few games going on, Teri ran past the park without giving the players a second look.

She'd been angry when she stalked out of Sugar Hill, so she'd decided to jog the two blocks from the office to the gym. Teri figured she could get in some roadwork while burning off some of the frustration she was feeling. The sounds of the city and rhythm of her heartbeat helped to clear her head.

When she walked into the gym, Teri was relieved to find it was almost completely empty. There were two fighters sparring in the ring, and another working on one of the speed bags with their trainer looking on. Otherwise, Teri had the space to herself—which was fine with her. She wasn't in the mood to be bothered.

The regulars who knew Teri always wanted to test their skills against hers in a sparring session. Those who were new to the place either hounded her for a date or just ogled her. The sparring she welcomed, the harassment—not so much. Teri frequented Oracle to keep her skills sharp and get centered, not to be leered at like she was the last Coca Cola in the desert.

She had been coming to the gym since she was six years old. Initially, Uncle Chris would bring her when he was babysitting, so he could get in a few rounds of sparring while keeping an eye on her. But rather than play with whatever doll he'd put on her lap, Teri started mimicking his movements in the ring. Uncle Chris had noticed and soon he was showing Teri everything he knew.

Oracle was an old place, having first opened during the Harlem Renaissance in the mid-thirties. A time when African Americans developed their own literature, music, and theater. And great artists like Langston Hughes, Billie Holiday, and Louis Armstrong emerged as international celebrities. After forty years of change and turmoil, the gym was a living record of Harlem's past and present. The kind of place that could be smelled before it was seen. Blood, sweat, tears, and aggression permeated the air and filled every crevice.

Except for the small locker room, unisex bathroom, and manager's office, the gym was just one large space, maybe three thousand square feet. It had high ceilings and two large windows, both of which were on the same side of the room. This unfortunate architectural design had resulted in little to no air circulation, which made the gym one big hotbox during the summer.

The place looked like it'd been frozen in time. The walls, coated with stained and scratched light gray paint, were covered in old fight promotion posters. A large bulletin board, filled with handwritten ads offering various services ranging from fight management to housecleaning, was mounted on the wall next to the manager's office.

The gym's well-used ten-by-ten-foot ring was in the center of the room. Three heavy bags hung from the ceiling to the left of the ring, and two speed bags were attached to the back wall. Rusty free weights rested against the back wall by the speed bag section.

Teri grabbed her gym bag out of the manager's office, an allowance Kirby the manager had made for her since she was the only woman who worked out in the gym. She changed in the bathroom and then made her way to the ring where the fighters were still sparring. Teri sat on a small plastic chair outside the ring and snuck glances at the sparring match as she wrapped her own hands.

The two fighters looked to be in their early teens and although they weren't very skilled, they moved well.

After her hands were wrapped, Teri decided to get started with some rope work and made her way to an open space near the speed bag section. She unwound the rope and started jumping. Within thirty seconds, beads of sweat formed on her forehead, and after ten minutes, she looked like she had just stepped out of a swimming pool.

Teri felt loose and warmed up, so she moved over to one of the speed bags. She worked the bag for three two-minute rounds, with thirty-second breaks in between rounds. Finally, Teri transitioned to one of the heavy bags and decided to go for twenty minutes. She punched and moved for five three-minute rounds, with one-minute breaks in between rounds.

The only thing she thought about during her workout was the meeting with Vic and her uncle. Teri used every movement and punch to try and work through her frustration. Vic had put the kibosh on her going with him and Teri didn't understand why.

He had taken her under his wing and had been showing her what it took to be a Fugitive Apprehension Agent. Teri appreciated his help, but she'd felt like she had proven herself when she chased down Santini, and when she'd stood tall in Chinatown. And now she was supposed to accept being treated like some sort of damsel in distress. A helpless little girl who needed to be protected. Fuck that.

"Teri," a familiar voice yelled.

She stopped working the heavy bag and looked around the gym. She spotted Kirby standing by her office door.

"Yeah?"

"Come see me when you're done."

Teri nodded and turned her attention back to the heavy bag, throwing a few more combinations before ending her session. She grabbed a towel out of her bag and dried her face as she walked into Kirby's very small office.

"What's up, Kirby?"

"Have a seat." Kirby was busy writing notes on her desktop calendar and didn't look up. Teri glanced at the calendar as she sat down. Kirby was writing down names, so Teri figured she was scheduling boxing matches. After a few seconds she turned her attention to Teri. "So, how've you been? I haven't seen you in here in a while."

Stella Kirby was a middle-aged, half Black, half Dominican woman with short dark hair and umber skin. Her once-attractive face, after years of sparring and unsanctioned fights for cash in alleys and abandoned buildings, was now plain at best. Her thrice-broken nose was crooked, and scar tissue had formed on the corners of both eyes.

Despite all the blows she had taken over the years, Kirby was lucid and very intelligent. She had inherited the gym from her father, Dennis Kirby, an ex-fighter who'd fought three years too long and died not being able to remember his kids' names.

She'd worked hard and had managed to turn the gym into a respectable business. A place where a lot of local up-and-coming fighters had started and still came to her for counsel. Teri had known Kirby since she'd first started coming to the gym with her uncle, and she respected and admired her.

"I've been busy. Been working for my uncle. learning the ropes from Vic."

"Vic? I haven't seen him in a long time. How is his fine Puerto Rican ass?"

Teri hesitated for a split second. She was aware Vic was a good-looking man who attracted a lot of attention, but Teri saw him differently and felt awkward whenever someone spoke about him as Kirby had just done.

Kirby seemed to sense Teri's unease. "Apologies, sister, I didn't mean to make it weird."

"No, girl, it ain't like that at all. I'm just a little preoccupied with some things."

"Well, all right then, let's hear it. You know this is a safe place, right? I got you. No matter what."

Teri felt better after her workout, but she still wanted to vent. She was a private person, but she trusted Kirby and considered her a friend. "It's just...fucking Vic and my Uncle Chris. They keep treating me like I need protecting. Vic's got this thing coming up. A job for the shop that could be a little dangerous. But he won't let me go with him. To watch his back."

"Well Vic and Chris—especially Chris—have been around. They know their job and they understand this world. Maybe they're not wrong about keeping you out of this thing."

"Don't do that, Kirby. Just don't, please. You sound like them. I don't need protecting." Teri felt herself getting angry again and was worried she'd just wasted a workout.

"No, that's not what I'm saying. Not at all. I know you don't need protecting. But what if it's not about that. Chances are, there's shit going on you don't have a clue about, but they do. And that's what they're worried about."

"But don't you see, Kirby, it's the same thing. They're still trying to shield me from something. Treating me like a child."

"Is Chris going too?"

"No. And that's what I'm worried about. Vic will be out there alone."

Kirby leaned back in her chair and was quiet for a few seconds. "All right listen. I'm just going to say this one thing and then I'm done. Vic is a tough man who's more than capable of handling himself in any situation." Teri rolled her eyes. "Hold on a second now, let me finish what I got to say before you shake me off."

"I'm listening," Teri said.

Kirby leaned forward in her chair and put her elbow on top of her desk. "What I was getting at was, just because Vic can handle himself doesn't mean you're wrong. Men, especially men like Vic, are sometimes blinded by their own ambition. If it's like I think and he's taking this risk to help the people he loves, then maybe he's the one that needs protecting. So, what I'm saying is this—you're a smart, strong woman, and I suggest you trust your instincts."

Teri smiled, got up, and left the office without saying another word. She'd heard what she needed so why press her luck. Teri grabbed her gym bag, exited the building, and jogged back to her apartment, thinking about her next move.

thirteen

VIC WAS STANDING by the garage stairwell when he noticed Tre trip himself up getting out of the 1970 GMC Vandura. The large man had pulled the van into the underground parking garage of Leviathan Security's office building and had caught his foot on the bottom of the A-frame as he exited the vehicle. Based on the less than graceful way he'd regained his balance, Vic didn't think Tre was much of an athlete. Not wanting to embarrass the man, Vic turned away as if he hadn't seen the clumsy exhibition.

He waited a few seconds before making his way over to where Tre had parked. Vic circled the van, looking it over. He was unimpressed but figured it would suit their needs. The van looked like it had been manufactured a lot earlier than 1970. The light brown paint was covered in scratches and dents, and there were rusty holes on the rear doors and bumper. The windows on the rear doors were boarded up, and its interior was gutted so there was plenty of room for everyone and any equipment they were bringing.

"How long have you guys had this thing?" Vic asked.

"A few hours," Tre said. He lifted the van's hood and inspected the engine. He glanced at Vic quickly and then returned to checking the engine. "Don't worry. We only need it to get from here to there. We're going to dump it at the marina anyway."

Vic was about to respond with some more small talk when Walter exited the elevator carrying two green military-style duffel bags, one in each hand, with a light brown canvas satchel hanging off his shoulder by its strap. Despite the man's considerable size, he seemed to be struggling with the duffel bags' weight. Vic pulled open the back doors of the van and moved aside.

Walter placed the bags inside the van and climbed in. He kneeled, placed the satchel on the van floor, and opened one of the duffel bags. Inside it were five AKS-47 rifles, along with rifle magazines and boxes of ammunition. The rifle, a modified version of the famous AK-47 assault rifle, had been outfitted with a foldable stock and had been specifically developed for Russian paratroopers.

Vic was a bit surprised to see the weapon. It was manufactured in the Soviet Union, a country where Americans usually didn't have access to weapons.

"You know, buying American keeps manufacturing jobs at home," Vic said.

Walter didn't crack a smile at Vic's apparently bad attempt at levity. "For a job like this, we need to be ghosts. Like we were never there. It's a lot easier to get guns in the States, but the stuff from the Eastern Bloc is pretty much untraceable. And with Oran's connections, we can get almost any weapon we want from over there." Walter kept his focus on the contents inside the bag and seemed to be taking a mental inventory. "What'd you bring?"

Vic didn't have anything with him. The way he figured it, he'd been hired to locate and direct—nothing more. His role today was to drive the team to Hemlock Gardens, wait in the van till they brought the girl down, then drive everyone to the extraction site. And besides, he had spent more than four years hauling heavy equipment in some of the worst places on this planet. After he got back to the States and settled into civilian life, Vic had always made it a point to travel light.

"Just this." Vic pulled his hair pick out of his back pocket and held it up.

Walter glanced at it briefly and flashed a small grin before returning his gaze to the bag. He grabbed a black and silver handgun from inside the bag and extended it toward Vic. "Here, take this. You might be able to hide that somewhere in those tight pants."

The sleeve on Walter's too small windbreaker wasn't long enough to cover his fully extended arm, so Vic immediately spotted the track marks on the inside of his forearm.

Walter glanced down at his scarred arm. "Don't worry about it, they're old. I'm good." Walter extended his arm closer toward Vic, offering the gun.

Walter's dark, swollen veins were lined with small puncture wounds that appeared red, irritated, and freshly scabbed over. Vic doubted the track marks were old, but Walter's eyes were clear, and he didn't seem high. Still, Vic found it strange Oran would hire a junkie for an extraction job, no matter what skills he brought with him.

"All right man." Vic nodded subtly as he grabbed the handgun, a SIG Sauer P230.

It was a smaller handgun and easily concealable. Vic thought about the pants comment and smiled. Despite Walter's apparent taste for brown sugar, Vic was relieved someone in the group had a sense of humor, however droll it might be. He ejected the magazine from the gun and inspected it. After verifying the gun was functional and the magazine was fully loaded, Vic reinserted the magazine, pulled the slide back to chamber a round, and placed the gun in his waistband, under his T-shirt at the small of his back.

"What's in the other bag?"

"That's my goody bag," Walter said. He looked up at Vic with a deadpan expression. "Not those kinds of goodies."

Vic suppressed a smile and focused on the bag, curious about its contents. Walter had been an explosive disposal operator in Nam, so Vic figured the bag was full of stuff that could blow things up. As if sensing Vic's curiosity, Walter reached into the bag and pulled out one of the devices. He held it out toward Vic.

"What? You want me to take that?"

"Go ahead, man, it's safe to handle. Just don't go throwing it around like a football or some shit."

Vic grabbed the device, surprised at how soft it felt, almost like a water balloon. It was about six inches long, bulky, and wrapped in gray duct tape. A long, stiff cord hung out one end, making the whole thing look like a giant rat.

"It's a water impulse charge. I put these together in Nam. We never got a chance to use them, but it was fun putting the recipe together."

"What is it?" Vic asked, handing the explosive device back to him.

Walter put it back in the bag. "It's basically a few feet of detonation cord sandwiched between two bags of saline, all held together with duct tape. The detonation cord alone would shred any metal door, but that would send pieces of metal exploding everywhere. Considering how close we'll be to any door we blow, that's not ideal.

"The saline bags create a more controlled explosion. We can be within a few feet of it when it's detonated and be perfectly fine. So will anyone on the other end of it. Unless of course, they're pressed up next to the door when it goes off."

"But everything's indoors. Won't the explosion disorient you guys?"

"Nah, I just tweaked the formula, used a little less det cord. It'll be loud but nothing that will put us out of commission."

"Pretty impressive."

"Yeah, I have my moments."

Vic heard the elevator chime and stepped away from the van

just as David and Oran came out of the elevator. Something about the two of them caught Vic's attention. He looked to his left at Walter and thought about what Tre had been wearing when he did his Jerry Lewis bit outside the van. Vic realized they were all wearing variations of the same outfit—black boots, black pants or jeans, and black windbreakers over dark gray shirts.

He looked himself over and realized he hadn't gotten the memo about matching outfits. His clothing, navy straight-leg jeans, a fitted black T-shirt, and black-and-white Puma Clyde sneakers, made him the odd man out. It also made one thing crystal clear for him—he was part of today's game, but he wasn't a member of the team.

"So, I'm guessing the theme of the day is monochromatic," Vic said.

David stopped a foot away from Vic, about six inches past too close, and stared at him like Vic stole his last candy bar. David was breathing heavy, and the area around his nose was red and irritated. He was sweaty and his pupils were dilated. Vic figured David had inhaled a few lines of cocaine before coming downstairs. "How's that?"

"I thought the idea was to try and blend in with the people from the neighborhood. We don't want them thinking something is up before we're ready. Do we?"

"Fuck those bottom feeders," David said. He ran his tongue along his lower lip and leaned in closer to Vic. "I could care less what they think."

Vic was at the end of his rope with this clown and decided to poke the bear a little. Maybe he could get a rise out of him, and David would make a move so they could settle the bullshit.

"Couldn't."

"What?"

"I believe what you meant to say was you *couldn't* care less. By using the word 'could' you're implying you still care a little. I'm just saying, you might want to be clear on what you mean. I wouldn't want you to confuse the bottom feeders." Vic's mouth curved into an antagonizing smirk, and he held David's eyes with his own. He could see David was trying hard to play the tough guy part but behind the phony grin and hard stare, there was confusion and hesitation—maybe even fear.

He decided to push a little more. "You know, you're not very good at the whole crazy-veteran routine. You should practice some more, then come back and play again when you're better at it."

"That's pretty funny for a tour guide. But I don't put much stock in anything overpaid taxi drivers have to say, so just get in the van and start the engine, bitch."

"See, now you're just being rude. And here I thought we were going to be friends."

"So, are you two going to fight or fuck? It's usually one or the other." Oran said. He was standing behind David, his body language letting them know he was fed up with the macho posturing. "You two need to cut the crap. It's time to go to work."

David sniffed and squeezed his nostrils aggressively as he backed away. "I'll see you on the other side of this, pretty boy."

"You missed a spot." Vic pointed at his own right nostril. He watched David rub his nose and was disappointed and embarrassed with himself. Vic thought he had done a good job of burying the side of him that longed for a fight and could be sucked into juvenile confrontations. He turned away and tried to center himself by focusing on his natural breathing.

"All right, fellas, round up," Oran said.

Vic joined the group at the front of the van. Walter and Tre were both smoking cigarettes and David was chewing a piece of gum as if it was made of rubber. Oran was almost expressionless, and his eyes were both steely and compassionate, evoking feelings of confidence and security from the people he led. It was a look Vic had seen dozens of times and was glad to see again.

"We went over the mission plan upstairs. So unless there's something that needs clearing up..." Oran let the question hang in the air and made eye contact with each of them, giving every man a chance to respond. "All right, then. Walter, we good on weapons check?"

"Good to go."

"Okay, let's get a final comms check and get rolling," Oran said.

Vic walked away from the group and checked his watch. It was almost six thirty in the evening. The plan was to take the Brooklyn Bridge off the island and then traverse the main thoroughfares through Brooklyn, all the way to Howard Beach. They would park the van on 158th Avenue, directly behind the south tower, and walk in on foot. Vic hadn't been inside the building, but based on past experiences, he assumed the apartment was outfitted with a steel front door—hence, Walter's bag of explosives.

Vic estimated they'd be at Hemlock Gardens by seven thirty at the latest. With it still being early evening, he didn't think there'd be very many Kings out and about, so they should be able to walk into the building with minimal interference. Walter would set a small charge on the apartment door Gabriel had identified. The team would use the noise, smoke, and violence of their actions to get in and overwhelm the enemy. Find the girl and get out before the Savage Kings could collect themselves and react.

The only problem with the plan was it was the only one they had. There was no plan B. They had emergency egress and escape plans for themselves but as far as rescuing the girl, they had one shot and if it didn't work, she would more than likely be executed.

***

As Pito watched Carolina on the screen, he was starting to get worried. It was a little after seven p.m. and the ten o'clock deadline was coming up fast. He was pretty sure they'd get the money. Her rich daddy wouldn't risk his daughter's life for what they'd demanded, which Pito figured was chump change for the cloud people. No, he was worried about Abaddon.

Abaddon had always been someone to steer clear of, even when they were younger. He started out killing dogs and shit. Hanging them from fences by their neck and throwing rocks at them till they stopped moving. All the fellas were doing crazy shit back then, so no one had given it a second thought. Hell, it hadn't even been that big a deal when Abaddon started beating people to death for fun.

They were all a little older by then and had started robbing chumps in the park. Except Abaddon hadn't stopped when suckers handed over their bread. He'd put a beating on them and didn't stop till he was punched out or they were dead. Yeah, as far back as Pito could remember, Abaddon had always been serious business.

Pito didn't doubt Abaddon had meant every word he'd said to Carolina yesterday. But he wondered if he could talk the big man out of what he had planned. Maybe convince Abaddon to let him have her. Pito thought he deserved something nice, after the good work he'd been putting in all these years. He'd wait till after Abaddon had his money and was in a good mood. Pito would ask about keeping her, maybe remind Abaddon that he'd been there in the beginning and had been loyal.

The more Pito thought about his idea, the more he believed it would work. He ran his finger along the screen, tracing the outline of Carolina's body. He sat back in the chair and checked his watch again.

It was almost seven-thirty.

fourteen

"WE'RE HERE," Vic said.

He parked the van along the curb on 158th Avenue as planned. Traffic had been bad, so it was close to eight p.m. by the time they arrived. David, Walter, and Tre had spent the drive in the back, checking equipment and loading bullets into the banana-shaped magazines of their AKS-47 rifles.

There'd been some small talk when the drive started, mostly between Oran and Vic. Topics ranging from the exotic cuisine of occupied Saigon to Muhammed Ali's upcoming fight with Ernie Shavers at Madison Square Garden. The conversation had grown sparser the closer they'd gotten to their destination and had altogether stopped by the time they'd arrived.

The silence was anything but uncomfortable and nothing new for people who had been in combat. Small talk and jokes in the beginning to break the tension, followed by the silence they'd needed to get themselves centered and ready to accomplish their mission.

"Target location is north of us," Oran said, scanning their surroundings. "The back door is at nine o'clock—about fifteen feet out. There are two women standing at eleven o'clock, at the end of the block. They look like civilians. I don't see any tangos. You see anything on your side, Vic?"

They were all former military, so it made sense that Oran used military shorthand to communicate. It was quick and concise, and cut down on extraneous information. Still, it had been a while since Vic had heard or used the jargon, so it sounded a bit strange to him. He was especially amused by Oran's use of the term "tango." It was what they'd called enemy combatants in Nam. And considering how much gang members liked nicknames, he'd bet money there was at least one person calling themselves Tango in this complex.

Vic didn't see anyone standing around but took note of how imposing the building looked from where he sat. It was ten stories of brick and steel, and like the other five buildings, had been painted a dark shade of brown.

"No, I don't see anyone."

"Is that it? Just the two chicks?" David asked.

"Looks like it," Oran said. He checked his sideview mirror. "Yeah, I don't see anyone else. All right, let's get to it."

No more words were exchanged. Vic watched the guys in the back through the rearview mirror. Walter reached into one of the duffel bags, pulled out a crowbar and a water charge, and placed both items inside his satchel. David grabbed a rifle, folded its stock, and placed it under his windbreaker. He looked at Walter, nodded, and they both exited out the van's back doors. Tre pulled the doors shut behind them.

Vic watched as the two men headed calmly but quickly toward the back door. It was painted red, and Vic guessed that it, like most doors in the housing projects around the city, was made of steel. Walter reached the door first and pulled out the crowbar as David took a position behind him. They stood back-to-back, so David was watching the street with his hand on the rifle under his jacket. Walter hesitated, staring at the door as if he was solving a math problem. After a few seconds, he grabbed the doorknob and pulled the door open.

"Well, what do you know," Oran said. He turned and looked at Tre sitting in the back. "The fucking door was unlocked. Let's move."

Oran didn't check on the rest of his team till he reached the fifth floor. They'd been moving quickly when they'd first entered the building, only stopping to ready their rifles for engagement by extending the stocks and chambering rounds. He'd been taking the stairs two at a time and felt good. His breathing was even, and his heartbeat was steady, so he thought they could make it to the tenth floor without stopping.

Oran felt a soft pat on the back of his thigh, so he glanced down at the rest of his team. David and Walter were right on his heels and looked steady, but Tre was lagging. He was almost a full flight of stairs behind and struggling to keep up. Tre was a big man, almost as tall as Walter but at least fifty pounds heavier. His size, age, and nervous energy had combined to attach a one-hundred-pound weight to his backside.

Oran stopped on the fifth-floor landing. "Let's hold up a second."

David and Walter leaned their backs against the wall. Although they stood straight up and were doing a fair job at controlling their breathing, their sweat-covered faces were beet red. Tre trudged up the stairs and bent over at the waist with his hands on his knees. He was breathing hard and making no effort to conceal his discomfort. Oran had been employing this group of men on and off for the past few years, but this was the first time he realized how far past their prime they all were.

It'd always been the plan to take the stairs to the tenth floor. Elevators could be dangerous and unreliable, especially in old buildings like this one. The narrow stairwell was barely wide enough for two average size men to climb it shoulder to shoulder. Its dark gray concrete walls were covered in graffiti and dirt, and it smelled of trash and human waste.

Oran waited two minutes. "All right, let's move."

He started back up the stairs but slowed his pace, taking the stairs one at a time the rest of the way. When the team reached the tenth-floor landing, they stopped in front of a red steel door leading to the hallway. David handed Oran an expandable metal pole with a small, round mirror attached to one end. Oran crouched down and opened the door just wide enough to slide the mirror into the hallway.

After using the mirror to check both sides of the hallway, Oran pulled it back and glanced at the rest of his team. "It's clear. It looks like there are apartments on both sides of us." Oran whispered, but it was eerily silent inside the building, so he felt as if his words were being broadcast over a loudspeaker. "I don't know which side 10-B is, so we have to make a decision which way to move. We're going to lose time if we make the wrong choice."

"The building's planners probably designed the apartments to line up like the alphabet, left to right," Walter said.

Oran nodded. "That makes sense."

"Yeah, but which way were they facing when they decided to start on their left?" Tre said.

"Goddammit. He's right," David said.

Oran used the mirror to check the hallway again. He turned back to his team and mouthed the word "empty." He used hand signals to inform them he would be opening the door and they should go left when they stepped into the hallway.

Tre flashed a thumbs up while the other two men nodded. Oran stood up, repositioned his body so the team had room to move past him, and grabbed the doorknob. He pulled the door open, and the team moved quickly and quietly past him and into the long hallway. Oran stepped in line behind Tre, quietly easing the door closed.

They stopped to ready themselves. Fluorescent ceiling lights reflected brightly off the shiny walls. There were six apartments, three in each direction. The apartments' steel doors lined the hallway, alternating from one side to the other.

After a few seconds Oran pointed at David, signaling for him to start moving. The team crept in one line. They moved tactically, every step incorporating the entire foot, heel to toe. David reached the first apartment, checked the number, and looked back at Oran. He mouthed the letter F, informing Oran they'd moved in the wrong direction. Oran signaled with his hand for them to head the other way. He turned and was now the point man, with the rest of his team lined up behind him.

He was about to take his first step when all the apartment doors opened at once and the hallway was flooded with Kings. Dozens of armed bangers poured out of the apartments, pointing handguns, cursing, and yelling commands. Oran heard David, Tre, and Walter raise their rifles behind him, readying themselves for battle. They were surrounded by an ocean of killers with empty, soulless eyes.

Oran leaned over and put his rifle on the floor. He glanced back at his three guys. "Stand down, gentlemen." Within seconds, all their faces ran a gamut of emotions—fear, anger, confusion, and finally acceptance. Oran turned around and heard a chorus of metal and wood rifles landing heavy on the hard tile floor.

Vic was sitting back in the driver's seat, trying to appear casual as he stared at the south tower in front of him. The gun Walter had given him was on the seat under his right thigh. The sun was setting behind him and the sky had turned a deep shade of orange. Vic checked his wristwatch—eight fifteen.

It had only been about ten minutes since Oran and the others had entered the building, but it'd felt a lot longer. Vic scanned the entire area, using the sideview mirrors to check behind the van. The two women who'd been standing on the sidewalk when they'd first arrived were gone, and Vic hadn't seen any other activity—no people walking around or cars driving by—since Oran and his team had entered the building.

He turned his attention back to the south tower. The song "*El Dia de Mi Suerte*" by Willie Colon and Hector Lavoe started playing on the radio and Vic sang along silently. He thought it was funny that a song about some poor schmo believing his bad luck would change for the better before he died would be playing right at this moment.

Vic heard what sounded like an aluminum can rolling on the pavement to his right and turned his head. He was startled upright when the reflection of a person standing by the rear of the van appeared in the passenger sideview mirror. Backlit by the setting sun, the silhouette looked like an apparition warning of a coming storm. The specter was big, with broad shoulders, and looked to be holding a baseball bat in his hand.

Vic pulled the gun out from under his leg and watched the ominous, dark figure in the mirror. Suddenly, he heard loud banging on the back of the van, and it started rocking from side to side. In his side mirror, he saw a group of people pushing the back half of the van. They yelled curses and taunts, and the shaking grew more violent with every passing second.

Vic glanced down at the keys hanging in the ignition and tried to formulate a plan. Driving away was out of the question. Oran and his team were still in the building, and he wasn't about to leave them behind. He just needed some space between himself and the mob of Kings. If he created some distance, he would have a better chance in the fight. He grabbed the key but before he could turn it, two loud pops were followed by the sound of escaping air, and the rear of the vehicle dropped. *Shit. Now what?*

He grabbed the door handle with his left hand and tightened his grip on the gun, taking deep breaths as he readied himself. There was a loud crashing noise to his right, and he turned just in time to see the windshield splinter and crack.

The ominous silhouette had moved to the front of the van and was using a baseball bat to smash in the windshield. The once shadowy figure was close now, so Vic had a clear view of the fury that covered his face. The man swung the bat over and over, with so much violent force the entire windshield collapsed into the van.

With his heart pounding and his mind racing, Vic dodged flying glass shards. The Kings were outside his door now, beating on it and yelling. He raised his gun to fire, but the large man moved out of Vic's line of sight. Suddenly, the noise and shaking stopped and it was completely quiet. Vic looked to his left. The mob, armed with bats and heavy metal chains, had backed away from the van and were watching him.

"We got your guys," a deep, male voice said.

Vic turned toward the voice and saw the big man through the passenger window, standing on the street.

"We just want to talk to you. There's no way out of this if you don't put that gun down and come out," he said.

"I can think of a few ways I like a lot better than what you just suggested."

"It wasn't a suggestion." He lowered his head slightly and smiled. "Let me put it another way. Put the gun down and come out, or we throw your guys off the roof and then burn you alive inside the van."

Vic's hands shook with anger and an overwhelming fear he hadn't felt since Nam. When he'd been alone on scout missions, so close to the enemy any false move would have ended him. Here he was again, alone and surrounded by hostile forces. And just like he'd done in Nam, he had to stay alive long enough to figure a way out of this mess. Vic tossed the gun on the passenger seat and exited the van with his hands above his head.

Two Kings stepped up, grabbed him by his arms, and turned him around so he was facing away from them. The guy who'd destroyed the windshield walked around the van and stood in front of Vic. He was wearing a denim vest covered with tags and patches and Vic read the name embroidered on the tag.

The sun was nearly gone, and it was almost completely dark, but in the last remnants of daylight Vic was able to make out the name Machai.

fifteen

"YOU GETTING OUT OR WHAT, honey? The meter's running."

Teri heard the cabbie but didn't respond. She'd been sitting in the back seat of the cab staring at the giant YELLOW SPRINGS COMPANY sign, contemplating how she should approach Gabriel. Teri had been thinking about it the entire cab ride over and still didn't have a solid plan.

She'd had a bad feeling about what Vic was headed into and thought it was stupid to wait around for him *not* to call. Teri had decided to go into The Fear after him, but she needed help and her options were limited. She knew her Uncle Chris was a no go. He'd try to lock her in the office if she told him what she was planning, so that only left Gabriel.

It was probably a risk going to Gabriel for help. Despite his physical beauty and charming personality, she'd sensed a sort of darkness in him. He hid it well, and it was almost imperceptible, but it'd been there. An aura of danger and violence simmering just beneath the surface—just like she'd sensed in Vic.

She was aware that Vic and Gabriel's similar pasts, growing up in the streets and running with gangs, played a role in the indescribable energy the two projected. But while it'd been clear Vic had fought to rid himself of his demons, Gabriel seemed to embrace his.

She stared up at the bright yellow sign, its edges lit by silver neon lights, and bit her lower lip. She'd wasted a lot of time sitting in the office hoping Vic, having come to his senses, would walk through the door. But that didn't happen, so as uneasy as she felt about being here, there wasn't any more time to waste. Teri paid the driver and exited the cab, stepping onto the sidewalk in front of the Yellow Springs Company.

Teri checked her watch. It was almost nine o'clock in the evening. The night sky, completely washed out by the large, bright, neon signs that lined the tops of almost every building, was black and starless.

Teri walked toward the entrance. The bottom of her steel-toed boots clapped loudly against the concrete sidewalk with every step. She was about three feet from the door when it opened and out stepped Kai. Teri stopped in her tracks, hoping his opening the door at that moment was just a coincidence.

"Hello, Teri. Come on in."

She hesitated, searching his face. He didn't seem surprised to see her and was wearing the same cocky grin from the first time they'd met. Without saying a word, she stepped past him into the dimly lit building. She heard the turning of a lock behind her and spun to face him.

"So why do I feel like you were expecting me?"

"Because we were."

"And how's that exactly?"

Kai's sly grin, which she was beginning to think might be painted on, grew a little wider. "Follow me."

He led her back to the same room she'd met Gabriel in yesterday. It was a similar scene from the first meeting. Only this time Roy Scheider's face had been replaced with Robert Redford's. He was sitting in a newsroom speaking into a telephone handset, and

Teri knew right away it was a scene from *All the President's Men*. She heard a click and the image disappeared from the screen. The room lights came on and she saw the back of Gabriel's head on the couch. Kai was standing by the wall behind the projector.

"Beautiful Teresa, welcome back, dear. Come around here and have a seat." Gabriel remained turned away from her, staring at the imageless bed sheet.

Teri walked to the other side of the couch and sat down. Gabriel sat slouched on the sofa with his hands resting on his stomach, fingers interlocked. His hair was perfectly styled, and he was wearing dark blue silk pajamas. An intoxicating floral smell with hints of citrus and wood emitted from him.

"Do you ever go to a movie theater to watch these?" Teri asked.

"Of course not. Why would I do that when I can watch from the comfort of my own place?"

"Have you ever heard of the communal experience?"

"Of course, I have."

"And?"

"It's terribly overrated," Gabriel said. He stood up, walked over to the mini-bar, and poured himself an amber-colored drink. He sat back down without offering her anything. "There's nothing communal about watching a movie in a packed theater. You sit in the dark for two hours. More than likely sandwiched between two foul-smelling people. People shift, scratch, and heckle the two-dimensional actors. It's such a miserable experience, you end up counting every second till the movie ends. Then you get up and leave without having said a single word to any other person in the theater."

Teri was antsy and wanted to speed past the foreplay. But her first impression of Gabriel had been that he was long-winded and enjoyed this part of the conversation, where he plays with the other person's anxiety, like a cat teasing a mouse before it bites its head off. Rather than risk him not helping her by appearing impatient, she decided to stay calm and play along.

"You sound like you've had some really bad experiences in movie theaters," Teri said.

Gabriel smiled. "I've been alive a long time, Teresa. I've had bad experiences in a lot of places." He lifted his glass in a toasting motion and finished the two fingers he'd poured himself in one gulp.

"Thanks for seeing me. How'd you know I was coming?"

"Just a guess."

"That's an impressive guess."

"Not really. So, what can I do for you my dear?"

"I want to go find Vic. I need your help."

"Vic's a big boy." Gabriel's thin lips curled into a patronizing smile. "Why do you think he needs your help?"

Teri wasn't sure she should be honest. While they'd acted friendly, there'd been a weird tension between Gabriel and Vic. Gabriel had behaved like he took pleasure in having Vic navigate his way through a burning building. But he'd also appeared concerned about Vic's safety when he'd warned him about the rescue attempt.

"I don't really have an answer for that question. Look, I don't know why, but I know he needs help. You said yourself that it wasn't going to end well for him."

"Oh that? I was just messing with Vic. Giving him a hard time for being late with his payment."

Teri rolled her eyes and exhaled a frustrated sigh. "That's bullshit, Gabriel. Cut the Bond villain routine and give me a straight answer."

The grin left his face and his eyes fixed on the birthmark on her right forearm.

"That's an interesting beauty mark. The curve on the bottom, topped with the five ovals—it looks like a lotus flower. Has anyone ever told you that before?"

Teri scoffed. "In my neighborhood?" She looked down at her arm. "No. I've heard people say it looks like a crown, flowers, even

Gumby. At this point I think of it more as an ink blot. Like in the Rorschach test—people are going to see what they want to see."

"No, it's definitely a lotus flower. And a fully bloomed one at that. What do you know about the lotus flower?"

"Jesus Christ," Teri mumbled under her breath and rubbed her forehead. She was way past frustration but figured Gabriel was not going to answer her questions until he followed this thread to its conclusion. "Not much."

"The lotus flower grows in the deep mud, far away from the sun. But eventually, it emerges from dirty waters unstained and grows toward the light. The lotus flower represents the journey from darkness."

"Interesting." She leaned forward. "So, what about Vic? Are you going to help me find him?"

"Yes and no."

"Excuse me? What does that mean?"

"I'll point you in the right direction. Provide you some guidance. But that's as much as I'm going to do. I'm not going with you."

"I don't need guidance, I need help. You know what it's like in The Fear."

"Guidance is help."

"Will you stop with the fortune-cookie bullshit? You know what I mean."

"Now Teresa, there's no need for racist tropes. You're better than that." Gabriel leaned forward and stared at her pensively. "I warned Vicente, but he chose to go anyway. This is his journey now and I can't interfere. And it's the same for you. If you choose to go after him, it will be your journey and I cannot get involved."

Teri had heard enough and didn't respond. Gabriel's cryptic way of speaking had reached her last nerve. She ran her hands through her hair and sighed. *Enough of this bullshit.* Teri stood up and started toward the door.

"Vicente is in Howard Beach, but you should head east," Gabriel said.

"Why east? Why not go directly to where he is?"

"Because Howard Beach is the Kings' home turf, and you would almost certainly be killed."

"Has anyone ever told you that you have a real knack for building confidence?"

"Forget Howard Beach, go east. If Vicente makes it out, he'll head toward what he knows. He'll head home."

"You're talking about Bushwick, right? Vic hasn't been back there since he left for Vietnam. That's not home for him anymore. It hasn't been for a long time."

"There are still people there who know him and who love him. If you can find them, they'll help you." Gabriel leaned back. "Trust me, Teresa, if Vic is in trouble, he'll do what we all wish we could do when we need help—he'll go home."

Teri was tempted to say thank you but thought better of it. Except for a lesson on Chinese culture, Gabriel hadn't helped her at all, and coming to see him had been a waste of time. She walked out of the room without saying another word.

Teri had reached the front door when she noticed Kai walking behind her. She turned and faced him.

"Where are you going?" Teri asked.

"With you."

"Why? I thought Gabriel wanted to stay out of this?"

"He does. I don't." He didn't crowd her or try to intimidate her with his size. Soft spoken and resolute, Kai exuded confidence and warmth. "Come on, we'll take my car."

He held the door open for her and Teri stepped out into the waiting night.

sixteen

PITO PRESSED the button for the tenth floor repeatedly. He knew it wouldn't make much difference, but he was in a rush, and it seemed as if the elevator ride was taking longer than usual. The glowing red numbers above the door showed the passing floors ticking by slow as hell, adding to the stress he was already feeling. Abaddon had ordered that Carolina be brought to the rec center, and Pito was worried about what was coming.

The invaders had been taken over there and were going to be part of tonight's entertainment. The assholes had come on Kings' turf and tried to take Carolina without paying the money. Somehow, Abaddon had known they were coming, so he laid out a trap and had everyone waiting. Now the invaders would pay—but so might Carolina.

The digits above the door turned from nine to ten and the elevator came to a jarring stop. Pito squeezed past the half open door and hurried to apartment 10-B.

Carolina's blood ran cold when she'd heard the loud, animalistic screams in the hallway. She had feared they would come for her next. She'd scanned the room but there was nowhere to hide, and nothing to use as a weapon. Defeated and scared, she'd sat on the edge of the bed and waited.

After several minutes, she heard the apartment door open and close, then heavy footsteps walking toward her room. Carolina stood up and walked to the corner of the room farthest away from the door. She stood with her back to the wall and balled her hands into fists. She decided if this was her day to die, then whoever came for her would leave with the scars that would prove she had existed and had fought.

The locks turned and the room door swung open. To her surprise, she was relieved when Pito entered the room. He looked down at her fists and smiled. It was a warm smile that made her wonder if she'd gone mad.

"Don't worry, you'll be alright." Pito stepped to the side and waved her toward the door.

After the Kings had captured Vic at the van, they made him walk to the recreation center at the center of Hemlock Gardens. He'd felt the muzzle of a gun on his lower back and prayed the guy holding it didn't trip over his own feet. They pushed and shoved him up a couple of flights of stairs and into a large room.

There were Kings everywhere, screaming at the top of their lungs and stomping their feet. The noise was deafening. Vic's pulse quickened when he spotted Walter, Tre, and David but didn't see Oran anywhere. The three men were on their knees and their faces looked like they had gone fifteen rounds with Marvin Hagler.

They put him in line next to David and forced him to kneel.

"What happened? Where's Oran?" Vic asked.

"What do you think happened? We got our asses handed to us.

They took Oran," David said.

"What do you mean, 'they took Oran?'"

"They fucking took him. They beat the fuck out of us and dragged him away."

"Is he alive?"

"I don't know, Vic, I've been kind of busy trying not to shit myself."

"Shut the fuck up," a King yelled from behind.

Vic scanned the room. It was a large basketball gymnasium with three big, square windows on one of the walls. Long rows of aluminum bleachers had been arranged stadium style from the wall to the floor in front of the windows. They were near a basketball hoop on one end of the room. In front of them, directly under the basket, was a large chair with a long backrest. It'd been placed on top of a three-foot-high wooden stage, and there was a light brown wooden baseball bat propped up against it, handle up.

Hundreds of Kings were crowded inside the space, standing shoulder to shoulder on the gym floor and on the bleachers. It'd already been loud in the gym when Vic first arrived, but the crowd grew more thunderous with every passing second.

Vic heard the gym's heavy entrance doors being pushed open and gradually, the noise in the gym stopped. He looked toward the doors and, for the first time since Nam, Vic was stunned. Oran, alone and unrestrained, walked through the open doorway with the confidant strut of a man in familiar and comfortable surround- ings. Every banger in the room watched him with reverence as he made his way to the elevated chair.

While Vic and the others were being beaten and tortured, Oran had found time to change his clothes. He'd gone from one monochromatic look to another, this time opting for a too-tight black t-shirt, black leather pants, and black motorcycle boots. But Oran's clothes weren't the only changes. There was something in his eyes. His once warm and soulful eyes had been replaced with an unflinching, cold stare.

Vic felt woozy and thought he might throw up. He turned and looked at the other three members of the failed rescue party. Walter and Tre each wore expressions of shock and horror, while David, true to form, looked angry and defiant.

Vic turned back to Oran, who seemed to be moving in slow motion. His big, bulky boots landing on the wood floor was the only sound in the room. Oran reached the chair and sat down. He beamed as he scanned the room, like a monarch on his throne basking in the adoration of his loyal subjects.

"All right Kings. Are you ready for a good time?" a speaker-amplified voice from behind yelled.

The crowd erupted at the seemingly rhetorical question—yelling, stomping, and shaking the bleachers.

"Man, oh man, have we got a great show lined up for tonight. All courtesy of our supreme president. Everybody give it up for Abaddon," the voice yelled. The theatrical way he delivered his lines reminded Vic of a carnival barker.

The carnival barker, who was holding a megaphone, had moved as he was speaking and was now standing beside an arrogant looking Oran. The last bit of hope Vic had that this was all part of Oran's rescue plan drained from his body. Vic lowered his head at the sickening revelation.

Oran was Abaddon.

The carnival barker stomped around in circles, gyrating his arms above his head, further inciting the already raucous crowd. He wore tight, bright-red shorts that stopped just below his groin, and white high-top sneakers with no laces so the tongues folded forward. He was shirtless and his huge pot belly protruded out from underneath the long tail tuxedo jacket he was wearing. The black top hat he wore completed the absurd ensemble, and on any other occasion the whole image would have been comical. If Vic hadn't been so worried about dying, he would have laughed.

"But first, let's give a warm King welcome to the guest of honor, the ice princess herself, Carolina Lynch." Vic heard doors being pushed open and The Mad Hatter impersonator pointed to the other side of the room, prompting the audience to look in that direction. The crowd noise rose a decibel as Vic turned and watched the kidnapped woman being led into the gym. Her long, dark hair was disheveled and there was fear in her big hazel green eyes, but she seemed unharmed. She was beautiful and Vic couldn't stop staring at her. He wanted to pull her close and protect her.

The Savage Kings yelled profanities and threats at her. Spit, liquor, and food sprang from their mouths with every vile word. After a few seconds, she was escorted past Vic and the others. Her hands weren't tied, but she was being led by the arm by a short man. They stopped a few feet from Oran. The little guy stepped away and took up a spot near the wall behind Oran.

"This is what the invaders came for, Kings." The barker walked around Carolina with his hands out as if he were presenting a prize, like a television game show host. "This little piece of high society flesh and tits. This is what they trespassed on Kings' property for." The crowd had calmed, so the barker lowered his voice. "So, what now?" He took a few steps closer to Walter, Tre, David, and Vic. "We make them pay for it, that's what the fuck we do!" The crowd erupted when he yelled the last few words.

A young, skinny King walked toward the barker carrying one of the duffle bags Walter had loaded into the van. The barker reached into the bag and pulled out one of the water charges. He extended it out toward the crowd, so they'd have a good look at what he was holding.

"This is what they brought with them. Bombs. These jive ass motherfuckers wanted to blow us up. Can you believe that shit?" He put the water charge back in the bag, then lifted the bag and carried it over to Oran. He placed the bag at Oran's feet and stepped away.

Oran stood up and grabbed the baseball bat that had been leaning against his chair. He stepped off the platform onto the gym floor and walked toward Vic, David, Walter, and Tre. The room had become quiet again, so every step he took thundered on the parquet floor.

Oran stopped and faced the Kings sitting in the bleachers. "Invaders? Intruders? Lame ass motherfuckers? What should we call them?" He projected his deep, raspy voice without yelling. Several Kings shouted out suggestions and Oran smiled. He raised his hand, signaling everyone to quiet down.

"How about interlopers?" He was a master orator, using hand gestures and the cadence of his words to manipulate his followers. They yelled and screamed at the end of every sentence. Oran could have been reciting the Gettysburg Address and the crowd would have been just as enthusiastic. They loved him.

"'People who have trespassed in a place where they don't belong and are not wanted.' Interlopers. Yeah, I think that'll work." Oran turned and sauntered over to Carolina. "Because they don't belong here, and they are most definitely not wanted."

Oran stood close to her, silent and still as he invaded her space. He grabbed Carolina by her hair and pulled her along. Shock and fear covered her face as she reached toward her hair to ease the pain. Oran turned toward the bleachers, holding Carolina out by her hair as if he were presenting prized livestock at a fair.

"It really was a simple arrangement. Just pay the money and I return the bitch. But they go and make things complicated. Come into our home with bombs and guns and try to take without paying. They tried to steal what belongs to me." He pushed her forward, letting go of her hair. "Yes, that's right. The ice princess here belongs to me. Every bit of her." Oran grabbed Carolina roughly by her vagina and threw her on the floor.

She landed with a thud and the crowd went berserk. Vic stared at her, waiting for her to move. After a few seconds, Carolina raised her head and made eye contact with Vic. She looked terrified.

Oran raised the bat above his head and walked toward the

bleachers, eliciting cheers from the crowd. "But this is a zero-sum game and for them to win means I would lose. And I—we—have lost enough. That shit don't fly no more. Because we're smarter than them. We're stronger than they could ever be. We got our money and the prize too. We won." The crowd erupted. Oran ambled over to Vic and the others. "And by the end of the night, I'm gonna have everything else too."

Vic's pulse quickened at the surreal image of Oran inciting the audience. He looked and sounded like his old friend, but it wasn't him. Vic's old sergeant was intense yes, but he was charming and kind as well. The man with the bat and leather pants was crude and evil, and seemed to be taking pleasure in terrorizing and humiliating them.

Oran glared at Vic, Walter, Tre, and David. "I'd ask you guys how it's going, but I think we're a little past any pleasantries."

"Oran, what the fuck, man?" Tre asked.

Oran shook his head subtly. "Around here, people just call me Abaddon." His tone was even, and he spoke soft and low, as if he was whispering secret passwords to childhood friends. "Don't look so glum, fellas. This was always gonna be a one-way trip for you boys."

He knelt beside Carolina and petted her cheek. She tried to pull away, but Oran grabbed her chin and forced her to look at him. "Yes, that includes you, sweetness. You were never gonna make it out of this alive. That's what Josiah wanted. And you know as well as I do, old Josiah Lynch gets whatever he wants."

"What?" she asked through trembling lips.

Oran brought his face closer to hers. "Your rich daddy arranged this whole thing."

Tears welled up in her eyes. "No! You're a liar."

He used his thumb to wipe a tear from her face, and then licked the tip of his thumb. "That's surprising. I expected it to taste like liquid sugar. I'm afraid it's true, princess. This was all Josiah's idea." He looked at Vic and the guys. "Well, at least most of it was his idea. There's a whole lot of stuff old Daddy Warbucks isn't aware of yet. But he will be."

Oran stood up and looked down at them. "I mean, I'd like to take all the credit, but I can't. Especially when letting the cat out of the bag produces those kinds of expressions. You should see yourselves." He scoffed. "Your father wanted you dead, princess. I mean, I've done some pretty fucked up things, but that shit right there...well, all I can say is, *damn.*" He walked back toward his chair. "Pito. Move that bitch away from there."

The little guy who'd escorted Carolina into the gym earlier scurried to her. He took hold of her arm, helped her up gently, and led her back to where she'd been standing before Oran had decided to humiliate her.

"They brought a whole bag full of treats for us. We're about three months from Halloween, but what the hell, we'll take them." Oran projected his comments out to his Kings. He stood by the duffel bag, using the bat to poke around inside. "What do you think we should do with this stuff?"

Comments and suggestions sprang forth from the crowd. Vic's head was spinning with disbelief from everything he'd just heard Oran say. He glanced down the line. Walter and Tre both stared straight ahead, but David was looking down at the floor.

Oran stared at Vic and the others. "I'm talking to you guys." None of them responded. "Well, don't all speak at once." He walked back and forth in front of them, spinning the bat in his left hand. He stopped in front of David after a couple of laps. "Nothing? Well, I guess I'm just going to have to make it up as I go along. What'd ya think, David? Are my improvisational skills up to snuff?"

David didn't say anything. Oran crouched close to him and put the bat under his chin. Oran pulled up, forcing David to look at him.

"Goddamn, you are a pretty motherfucker, aren't you? But that's about all you have going for you. Once you get past the blow-dried hair and phony bravado, there isn't much else. Isn't that right, David? In the end, you're nothing but a coward." Oran slipped the bat away from David's chin and stood up. "Fuck it. Let's start with you. Fellas, pick Mr. Strong Silent Type here up."

Two Kings grabbed hold of David, one on each arm, and tried to pull him up, but David struggled against their efforts.

"Fuck you, Oran. You know I built them, so why don't you start over here," Walter yelled.

Oran turned his attention to Walter. "Hold on, fellas, it looks like someone finally decided to speak up. You can put the coward down."

The two Kings pushed David to the ground. He buried his head in his chest and started weeping.

"Falco," Oran said.

The carnival barker stepped out from the crowd. "Yeah, Abaddon?"

"How many of these interlopers were you planning to put up against Frankie Hi-Life tonight?"

"Two at the most. We got a long weekend ahead of us, so I didn't want to overwork him."

Oran gripped the bat's handle with two hands and in one fluid motion, lifted it high above his head and brought it crashing down on top of David's head. There was a loud cracking sound as David's head splintered open. David fell forward onto his face, and Oran hit him with the bat six more times.

Every swing came crashing down on top of David's head with startling speed and violence. Blood and skull fragments exploded outward. When Oran was done, the room was eerily quiet, and David lay lifeless in a pool of his own blood. Oran dropped the bat on the floor, walked back to his throne, and sat down.

"Take the bomb maker outside and get him ready for the fireworks show." Oran didn't sound winded. "Falco, after we're done outside, you can feed the last two to Frankie."

The crowd erupted in cheers.

seventeen

PITO WATCHED some of the fellas drag the tall guy out of the gym. The invader fought a little at first, but Talon kicked him in the gut and the blow took the fight right out of him. A few Kings had filed outside to see the fireworks, but most decided to stay inside and check it out through the windows. Everyone knew Frankie Hi-Life would be coming next, and there didn't seem to be very many Kings willing to risk losing their spot up close for that show.

He wanted to go outside, but he didn't want to leave Carolina alone. Pito knew he needed to stick close to her until he'd had a chance to speak with Abaddon about keeping her. It'd pissed him off something fierce when Abaddon roughed her up. Enough that Pito had considered stepping in and pulling her away. But a move like that would have really set Abaddon off, and Pito needed the man calm and thinking straight.

When he'd helped Carolina up off the floor, Pito had been impressed to see she wasn't crying. She'd looked scared, maybe even a little shocked, but she wasn't crying. Pito wanted to hold Carolina's hand and comfort her. But he figured that wouldn't go over well with the supreme president, and the last thing Pito needed was for Abaddon to freak out and send him away. He needed to stay close to protect her, so he'd decided to keep his hands to himself.

But Pito didn't want to miss what was about to go down outside. He'd peeped out a spot where he'd have a good view of the fireworks from inside. He tried to guide her toward the windows, but Carolina wouldn't move. He nudged her on her shoulder, but she resisted until he'd applied a little pressure.

Finally, Carolina got the picture and started moving slowly toward the window, a little too slowly for his taste. They'd have to move faster if he didn't want to lose the spot he'd picked out. So, he pushed a little harder and she sped up her pace.

They got there just in time. A half a second more and Charlie Crumbs would have squeezed his fat ass into the spot. As it was, he'd given Pito a hard look but seemed to think better of trying anything more. He waddled away cursing under his breath.

"We'll be able to see real good from here," Pito said.

Carolina didn't say anything. He tried to read her face but couldn't get a feel for what she was thinking. She just stared expressionless at the activity outside the window. He turned his attention to the scene out front, excited by what he was seeing.

A small group of Kings, including his boy Talon, were standing around the tall invader taping the funny looking bombs to his head and hands. The tall guy was on his knees, and judging by the pained look on his face, Pito knew they'd broken his ankles. It was usually the first thing they'd do so the entertainment couldn't run away.

Seeing as how he was so good at working with explosives, Talon was running the show. After being drafted into the Army in 1970, working with bombs was just one of the things Talon had learned while he was over in Nam. By the time he'd made it back to the neighborhood, Talon had developed a taste for booze, underage girls, and blowing up King rivals.

People were crowded around the invader, making it hard to see everything. After a few minutes everyone moved away from the tall invader, scattering in different directions. Talon and two other Kings stepped away from the tall man together, extending three wires behind them as they backed away. Each wire was attached to one of the bombs that'd been taped to the invader.

After about fifty feet, Talon and the others stopped and turned. Talon looked to his left and nodded. Falco emerged from a blind spot underneath the window. He walked out into the open and stood near the invader.

A tall streetlight overlooked the circle shaped space they occupied, illuminating it in a dim, amber light. Falco spun around twice, the tails of his black jacket extending out and away from his body.

"We're getting close, Kings. Soon Frankie Hi-Life will make his appearance, and things will get really exciting. But first, what's any great fight without an explosive preshow," Falco yelled into the megaphone. He jogged a lap around the invader, high-stepping the whole time. The crowd laughed hysterically at his show and burst out in cheers when he stopped. "So, my dear Savage Kings. Guy Kings, lady Kings, young and old. Without any more delay or further ado—it's showtime!" Falco screamed the last few words as he sprinted away.

When Falco was at a safe distance, Talon set off the bomb that'd been attached to the invader's right hand. A suppressed blast was accompanied by a bright orange flash, and the invader's hand exploded in a dark mist. His pained scream excited Pito, and he was smiling when he looked over at Carolina.

He heard the bomb that'd been taped to the invader's left hand go off, and the light from the fireball lit Carolina's beautiful face in a bright orange glow. His heart beat a little faster when he saw her eyes well up with tears. He turned back just in time to see the invader's head evaporate when Talon set off the last explosion.

"That makes zero sense," Kai said.

"It makes perfect sense, you're just not thinking it through," Teri said from the front passenger seat of Kai's Mercury Marauder.

After Teri and Kai left the Yellow Springs Company, he drove them to his apartment on Church Street. He'd told Teri he needed to get some things, so she'd waited in the car while he went upstairs. Twenty long minutes later, Kai returned carrying a duffel bag and wearing a green leather vest with his gang markings emblazoned on the back.

The sound of clanging metal emanated from the bag. He was leaned slightly to his left and the veins in his arm and hand had bulged as he managed the bag's weight. He'd tossed the bag in the backseat, and they were on their way.

"People are Strange" by The Doors was playing on the radio when Kai started the car and pulled away from the parking space. Already upset he'd taken so long upstairs and never a big fan of The Doors' music to begin with, Teri had let out a big, dramatic sigh. Kai must have been intrigued because he'd asked her if she was okay and soon, they were debating celebrity versus art.

"So, your argument is that Jim Morrison wouldn't be Jim Morrison if he hadn't died. Am I getting that right?" Kai said.

"Yes. Well, sort of. I'm saying he wouldn't have been considered a rock titan if he'd lived longer."

"That's bullshit. It's about the music."

"It is, but it isn't. I mean, The Doors were okay—"

"Okay?"

"Yes, they were okay. But that's just my opinion. I know old timers like you revere them. Regardless, it's more than whether you think the music is good or not. He's an iconic figure because of the image of this sexy, dangerous, unpredictable music god. Morrison, Hendrix, Joplin, Redding—they all died too young. Before they had a chance to become irrelevant or had to rely on nostalgia to make a living. I mean, is there anything sadder than watching fat Elvis sweat his way through a rendition of 'Love Me Tender?'"

"Yeah, but Elvis's music is still great. I don't think it matters how he looks now."

"Yes, his music is good to a certain demographic. But he's not cool anymore—at least not to anyone who doesn't need three layers of makeup to hide wrinkles. And he's only important to people who fell in love with him when he *was* cool. To anyone who consumes pop culture, he's only interesting as an Andy Warhol silkscreen—like Marylin Monroe. People buy those things because they want to own a Warhol or they think the art is cool, not because they're fans of *The Seven Year Itch*. It's all about celebrity."

"Didn't he make one of Mick Jagger? The Stones are still considered cool, aren't they?"

"Man, you're old. No, The Rolling Stones are not cool."

"You just say that cause you're into that punk rock stuff."

"Yeah, probably. But that's the point. Mick Jagger and Elvis Presley are famous, but most people couldn't tell you why they're famous. Young people know them because their faces are on lunchboxes and weird paintings, not because of their music."

Kai let the last few words hang in the air and seemed to be thinking about what she'd said. Teri imagined he was envisioning the last image he'd seen of Elvis Presley—overweight and sweaty, in a strange white jumpsuit on the cover of some supermarket tabloid.

"Maybe you have a point," Kai said.

He didn't say anything more and they fell into a strange sort of silence. Familiar and uncomfortable at the same time. Like a couple's first date after a long time apart.

They were travelling north on Church Street, toward Walker Street. She looked at Kai's green vest, with its Emerald Tiger patches, and was a bit surprised. They were headed into Brooklyn. To Vic's old neighborhood in Bushwick to find someone who'd known him and would help them. There was more than a good chance anyone they'd find who fit the description would be a member of Vic's old gang, the Ruthless Ones. She figured Kai had to know flying his colors would antagonize anyone they'd meet.

"You sure that's the best choice?" Teri asked.

Kai kept his eyes on the road. "What?"

"Wearing your colors in enemy territory."

"It'd be a mistake if I didn't."

"Uh huh. And how exactly would it be a mistake?"

"Anyone we find is going to suspect I'm affiliated. They'll think I'm scared if I try to hide it. Can't afford to show weakness. Ever."

"That might be one of the dumbest things I've ever heard. Why not be covert about it? Go in as a civilian and see what happens?"

He glanced over at her and scoffed. "That's not how this shit works. When you're part of something, you stand tall all the time. No matter what."

Teri rolled her eyes. "Je-sus Christ. I am officially convinced testosterone is the nectar of the terminally stupid."

Kai chuckled but didn't respond. As the Marauder turned north onto Essex Street, Teri thought about the meeting with Gabriel.

"Can I ask you a question?" Teri asked.

"I doubt there's anything I can say that would stop you, so go ahead."

"What was with Gabriel and all the lotus flower stuff? He was acting really strange."

Kai didn't say anything, and Teri wasn't sure if he didn't hear her question or was just ignoring her. Teri felt the car slow down and she glanced out the window just as they were merging onto Canal Street. She turned her attention back to Kai and waited silently for a response.

"Gabriel just talks like that. He puts a lot of stock in symbols and old legends for some reason. I think they're dumb myself. Old tales best used as bedtime stories," Kai said.

"What does that have to do with my birthmark? Gabriel seemed really interested in it."

"Who knows. Gabriel's always going on about one thing or another." Kai glanced at her and seemed to notice she wasn't buying what he was trying to sell. He turned his attention back to the road and sighed. "For a lot of people, the lotus flower symbolizes purity and spiritual awakening."

"So, that's why Gabriel wouldn't offer me a drink." Teri was relieved to learn the charming and beautiful Gabriel wasn't simply a rude snob.

"Maybe. Who knows? It could be he just didn't want to share his booze with a kid."

"Doubtful. I'm not a kid, and there aren't many guys who wouldn't want to have a drink with me. Have you seen what I look like?" She smiled but was disappointed when Kai didn't react to her joke. "Anyway, go ahead with what you were saying."

"Look, it's nothing. Just folklore. Every culture has theirs. For believers, the lotus flower represents a lot of different things, all of them good—love, compassion, wisdom...the achievement of complete enlightenment. It's a totem."

"Hence, Gabriel's interest in my birthmark."

She leaned back in her seat and pondered what Kai had said. Under normal circumstances, Teri wouldn't have given any of it a second thought. Every culture had its own mythology. Stories created to explain the unexplainable or to provide comfort in the face of harsh realities. But Gabriel was an obviously dangerous man who, now it would seem, was also a zealot. Teri was a bit uneasy at the idea Gabriel found a skin irregularity she'd been born with at all significant.

Kai shifted in his seat. "Look, it's all bullshit. Just stories only Gabriel and some of the old timers from the neighborhood take seriously. Like you said, he looked at your birthmark and saw what he wanted to see."

"What do you see when you look at it?"

Kai glanced at her arm. "Honestly? It looks kind of like a bad artist's sketch of lit candles or something."

She smiled at the remark and figured her theory the birthmark was nothing more than an organic Rorschach test was sound. Teri fell into a silence and looked out at the star-filled night sky.

They had just driven onto the Manhattan Bridge when the city lights went out and the world fell into darkness.

eighteen

A FEW OF the Kings dragged Vic and Tre over to one of the large windows where they had a clear view of the insanity going on outside. Gang members had strapped bombs to Walter's body as the idiot Falco pranced around like a buffoon. Vic guessed what was coming and tried to look away, but one of the Kings grabbed the back of his neck and forced him to face the vile spectacle.

He closed his eyes after the first explosion but flinched at the sound of Walter's blood-curdling screams. Despite having just met Walter and not knowing him very well, every inch of Vic's body pulsated with anger. He could only imagine how Tre was feeling.

After they were done cheering and applauding Walter's murder, two Kings escorted Vic to where Oran was sitting while a few others dragged Tre to the ring. He could feel Oran watching him, but Vic kept his focus on Tre.

"You're not supposed to be here, Vic," Oran said.

Vic glared at him. "What the fuck does that mean?"

"My people had instructions to let you go. They were going to screw with you, sure, but once you stepped on the gas, they were told to let you leave. I even left the money I owe you inside your apartment."

"You really thought I would leave you guys?"

"I hoped you would, but I should have known better. It doesn't matter now anyway. You took too long, and Machai got a little overzealous. Now you're here and you can't leave."

"Why even bring me? Why bring any of the guys? You had the lady, and you were already close to Lynch. Why not convince him to pay, return his daughter, and leave us out of it?"

"Because I'm going to kill Josiah Lynch, but first he's got to suffer. He's going to watch the destruction of everything he loves before he dies. For that to happen, I need him to trust me and keep me close. He's got to believe he got everything he wanted, including a bullshit rescue attempt." Vic's confusion must have shown because Oran smirked. "Yup, that's right, it was all bullshit. All this so the old fuck can sell the story that he did everything he could to save his little princess from the mean old poor people. That's why I needed you guys. Lynch wanted a rescue team, so I gave him one. Truth is, that bitch was never gonna leave here alive."

"But why?"

"Is this the part of the movie where the villain reveals his master plan?" Oran smiled. "All right Vic, I'll play along. I know how much you love your movies. It's the oldest reason in the book, brother."

"Money."

"Revenge." Oran gazed at Carolina, who was standing by the wall with the little King. "That bitch's father owes me a lot more than money."

"What does that mean?"

"Let's just say Josiah Lynch has ruined a lot of lives—caused lifetimes of pain."

"You're talking, but you're not saying anything. I still don't understand why you're doing this."

"What the fuck do you think, Vic? That I sprang forth fully grown out of the soil of Vietnam? I'm from somewhere. I have a past full of people I've loved. And the rotten motherfucker that cunt calls Daddy killed them. Burned them alive because they couldn't afford to move." Oran leaned forward in his chair. "You want to know how this ends?"

"Well, we're this far down the rabbit hole. We might as well see what's on the other side."

"That's pretty funny, Vic. Not very original, but your delivery was spot on." He glared at Carolina. "It ends with me burning everything down. Starting with her right there."

"Jesus Christ."

"Don't bother. He's not coming."

"But why kill your team?"

"It's all part of the charade. Imagine the headline, 'Heartbroken billionaire sends elite team after daughter. Rescue attempt ends in disaster when merciless gang members murder everyone.'" Oran chuckled. "The shit practically writes itself."

"But they didn't have anything to do with what you say Lynch did. Hell, I bet they never even met the man. They're innocent."

"Innocent? Really? Come on, Vic, listen to yourself. They may not have been involved with Josiah, but they're definitely not innocent." Oran stood up and put his arm around Vic's shoulders. "I can see you still need some convincing. How about this: Besides being a junkie, Walter spent his time in Nam blowing up villages full of civilians. And as for Tre, him and the rest of his crew in Nam spent the better part of 1967 raping and murdering villagers in the Song Ve Valley. Crazy fucks even scalped their victims and wore necklaces made of human ears."

"And David?"

"David? Well, he was just an asshole."

"We did some bad shit over there too, Oran."

Oran lifted his arm off Vic's shoulders and took a step away from him. "That's true. But absolution comes in many forms. This is theirs."

"What will yours be?"

"What? My absolution? There won't be one. I don't feel any guilt for anything I've ever done, so I'm not seeking forgiveness."

Oran had just orchestrated and carried out a kidnapping and at least two murders, yet he sounded self-righteous.

"So, what happens now?"

"Now, I'm going to watch Frankie Hi-Life kill Tre and then you. Then I'm going to spend the rest of the night doing whatever I want to the ice princess. When I'm done, I'm going to cut off her head and have it delivered to dear old dad."

"But—"

"No Vic, we're done. You're done." He nodded at the two Kings and Vic was escorted away.

They led Vic close to the ring. Tre was standing inside the ring, barefoot and shirtless. He seemed even less like an ex-special forces soldier than he had when Vic first laid eyes on him. He was pigeon-toed and his huge, stretch-mark-covered stomach protruded out over his pants.

Kings surrounded the ring, careful not to block Oran's view. There was a clear pathway from where Vic was to where Oran was sitting. Carolina and the little King had moved and were now standing beside Oran.

Vic heard the double doors open and looked toward them. The clown Falco entered the gym, doing his exaggerated version of the walk made famous by the actor Sherman Hemsley on the TV show *The Jeffersons*.

"Was that a show or was that a show?" Falco yelled into his megaphone. He strutted and danced in front of the makeshift ring, playing to the crowd. "Are you ready for the main event of the evening? Coming to the ring—the beast of the east, the annihilator like no other, the killer of killers. Kings, get on your feet and make some noise for Frankie Hiii-Liiiife!" Falco yelled every word, putting extra emphasis on the man's name, and the crowd went berserk.

The double doors nearest the ring swung open and crashed

violently against the walls. Frankie Hi-Life walked in and ambled to the ring, taking his time to enjoy the cheers from the crowd. He wore thigh-length cut-off jeans, and he was barefoot and shirtless. His face was covered in strange paint markings, which Vic guessed was Frankie Hi-Life's version of tribal war paint.

He stepped over the rope and into the ring. Standing across from Tre, a large man himself, the size difference between the two was shocking. Frankie Hi-Life towered over Tre and was twice as wide—neither fat nor muscular, the man was just plain old big. Drenched in sweat, the giant paced back and forth, and the crowd was unhinged. The room shook from the noise of their blood-thirsty screams. Vic stared at Tre's face, covered in fear and sweat, and worried about what was to come.

⁂

Carolina had still been trying to recover from the sight of a man being tortured and blown up when the giant made his entrance. Even from across the room, the man's size was imposing. He dwarfed every other person in the gymnasium.

Pito had brought her closer to Abaddon. Close enough that she could smell the sweat on his skin. She turned and found him staring at her with dark, hate-filled eyes.

According to this monster, her father had arranged her kidnapping and possibly her murder. She didn't want to believe it was true. It couldn't be true. Her father loved her—didn't he?

He had never been an affectionate man, but like any good father, he'd provided for her. He'd paid for the best tutors and educators and had sent her to the best schools. Her father had done everything to prepare Carolina for her role as heir to his empire.

Josiah Lynch wasn't on his deathbed or anything, but he was getting older and there was no one else to replace him. As far as Carolina knew, she didn't have any siblings, and her father didn't trust anyone else. No, it didn't make sense that he'd arranged the predicament Carolina was in now. Only a truly evil person would arrange for their child to be tortured and executed.

But was it that far-fetched? Her father was brutal and merciless when it came to his business. He'd acquire and dismantle businesses like he was taking apart a plastic train set. Lay off entire workforces while he was having breakfast—destroy thousands of lives while complaining his poached eggs were overcooked.

But that was business, and those had been nameless, faceless people. She was his daughter and there was a difference. Wasn't there?

She looked at Abaddon and trembled.

Pito watched as Abaddon stared at Carolina with a weird mix of lust and hate. Pito worried he wouldn't be able to convince Abaddon to let him have her. At least not before the supreme president followed through on his threats from yesterday.

Carolina's hands were clenched, and her shoulders were hunched up into her neck. Pito figured she was thinking about what Abaddon had said he would do to her and was freaking out inside. Maybe moving her away from Abaddon and closer to the ring would relax her. Frankie Hi-Life was getting ready to destroy the last two invaders, and everyone loved the shows he put on.

Pito stepped up to Carolina and gently took her elbow. She flinched and peered at him through wide, glossy eyes, as if he'd woken her from a deep sleep. He nudged her lightly and she moved without hesitation, like she was eager to be going with him.

"Where the fuck are you going?"

Pito turned and faced Abaddon. "I figured she might want to see Frankie fight. So, I'm taking her up close, seeing as how I'm watching her and all."

"Are you fucking stupid or what? Who gives a fuck what she

wants?" Abaddon sneered. He sat up straight and beckoned for them to come back. "Bring that bitch over here."

Falco started the fight by yelling "ding, ding" into his megaphone, and Frankie Hi-Life was all over Tre. He rushed in from his side of the ring, throwing four consecutive roundhouse punches. Tre brought both his arms up to his face and covered up so only one of the punches landed cleanly. Unfortunately, the one that made it through was a huge right hand that landed flush on the side of Tre's face, sending him stumbling.

Tre recovered quickly and circled to his right, throwing jabs with his left hand to keep some distance between himself and Frankie Hi-Life. Even though it looked like he'd had some hand-to-hand combat training, Tre was old and out of shape. Especially when compared to his opponent's youth and brute strength. Even if Tre had been in his prime, Vic doubted he would've lasted two minutes with the giant man.

Tre tried to take the offensive and threw a left-jab, right-hook combination, but Frankie Hi-Life ignored the punches as if he was passing through a swarm of gnats. He lifted Tre in a bear hug and tossed him across the ring as he would a sack of potatoes. Vic tried to stand up, but someone grasped his shoulders and forced him back into his chair.

He glanced over his shoulder. Machai was staring down at him.

"Turn the fuck around." Machai pointed at the silver .32 revolver tucked into the waistband of his jeans. Before he could turn, something across the room caught Vic's attention. He looked past Machai at Carolina and the little King walking toward Oran.

"I said turn around, bitch." Machai barked the command and slapped Vic across the face.

Vic's first instinct was to pounce on Machai and beat him to death. But he was inside the hornets' nest and the odds of it just being he and Machai going mano a mano were zero, so he complied. Vic turned around just as Tre was landing a right hook on the side of Frankie Hi-Life's head.

Carolina shivered as she stared down at the floor. It was hot inside the gym, so Pito figured she was petrified.

Abaddon tilted his head and scowled. "I said bring her over here. You deaf or what?"

Pito had no choice. He realized his plan was not going to work, and that Carolina was not going to survive the night. He took a hold of her elbow and led her back to Abaddon, who reached out and grabbed Carolina by her arm. He glared at Pito as he pulled Carolina to him, forcing her to sit on his lap. Pito lowered his head and made his way to the back wall.

Abaddon was so close to her Carolina could hear him breathing. He ran his hand along her leg, on top of her jeans, resting it between her thighs. He used the tip of his thumb to rub the outside of her vagina. She couldn't stop shaking. She tried to push his hand away, but he ignored her as he would a piece of stray lint.

"You enjoying that, princess?" Abaddon whispered. His warm, foul breath, a mix of stale coffee and plaque, nearly made her gag. She felt his erect penis through his jeans on the back of her upper thigh. "You can feel that, can't you? That's all for you."

He licked the left side of her face and stuck his tongue in her ear. She was startled and pulled her head away from him.

"You don't have to do this. You got your money. Just let me go."

"That's not how this works, sweetheart. I was compensated for a service. Part of the service was making sure you never made it back. What kind of businessman would I be if I reneged on a deal? Why, it would ruin my reputation. Seriously impact my future earnings potential."

"I don't believe you."

"It doesn't matter what you believe. You belong to me now, and I can do whatever I want to you. So enjoy the rest of the fight. It's not the last time you're going to see blood tonight."

Carolina's heart was in her throat. She'd been thinking about everything that'd happened. Her father's insistence she attend the fundraiser. The men who were waiting outside the hotel, and how they'd known exactly when to step out of the shadows and enact their plan. As much as she didn't want it to be true, Abaddon's story seemed plausible. Her limbs shook uncontrollably as she questioned everything.

Frankie Hi-Life was on top of Tre now, raining down thunderous blows on his face and head. It was only a matter of time before the fight was over and Tre was dead. Vic tried to work it out in his head, but he couldn't envision a scenario that didn't end with him being beaten to death by two hundred Kings.

He could feel Machai hovering behind him, close enough Vic could probably press his back against the man's stomach.

"Only a matter of time now," Machai said. Vic heard the revolver's hammer being cocked. "Then it's lights out for you."

Tre covered up as best he could, using his arms to protect his head and face. But most of Frankie Hi-Life's strikes were penetrating Tre's defense. The sound of pounding flesh and cracking bones accompanied every blow.

Tre managed to muster some energy and thrust his hips up off the floor, causing his opponent to fall forward. Tre reached up and wrapped his arms around the big man's torso, pressing his face against Frankie Hi-Life's pelvis. He pushed down on Tre's face, but Tre spun to his right, causing the big man to slip slightly. Tre used the small opening to rotate onto his hands and knees.

Tre was about to push himself to a standing position when Frankie Hi-Life jumped on his back and wrapped his right arm around Tre's neck. The giant placed the crook of his left elbow over his right hand, creating the leverage he needed to choke Tre. He stared at Vic, his eyes pleading for help.

Vic needed to make his move now. He scanned the room quickly. The noise was overwhelming. Every single King was banging sticks and pipes, stomping their feet, and chanting "kill him" over and over.

He glanced back at Tre. His face was fire-engine red and the veins on his forehead were bulging out horrifically. Tre reached up behind his head, feeling for Frankie Hi-Life's face but he couldn't locate his target.

Vic watched as the life drained from Tre's eyes, his body went limp, and the room went black.

nineteen

PITO WINCED as he watched them. His throat was dry, and he felt the heat rising in his neck and face. Carolina grimaced when Abaddon rubbed her and licked her face. She was sitting sideways on his lap and tried to lean away from his mouth, but Abaddon pulled her close.

Come on man. Just let her go. Pito took a step toward them, but there wasn't much he could do to stop Abaddon. He was big and vicious, and every King followed him like he was a god. They had grown up together and Pito had always done what he was told, but Abaddon was going too far with Carolina.

The crowd roared, so he figured Frankie Hi-Life had finished off the fat invader. Pito scanned the room. Everyone was looking toward the ring. When he turned back to Carolina, Abaddon was fondling her breasts. She tried to fend him off, pushing at his hands.

He had to get her away from Abaddon, at least long enough for the man to calm down. Maybe with Carolina out of sight, Abaddon wouldn't be as worked up. Then it'd be a good time for Pito to ask about keeping her.

It wouldn't be a big loss for Abaddon, he could have any

woman he wanted. He would probably be mad at first. But once he heard Pito out, and remembered all the stuff they'd been through together, maybe Abaddon would let him have Carolina.

Pito inched his way toward them. When he was close enough, he reached out, grabbed Carolina, and pulled her off Abaddon's lap.

"What the fuck are you doing?" Abaddon hissed. Surprise and anger battled for space on his face and in his voice.

Pito stepped in front of Carolina. "I need to talk to you."

"What the fuck you mean, you 'need to talk to me?' Now's not the time, Pito. Bring that bitch back here."

Pito backed up a few steps. He could feel her behind him, moving as he moved. "Hold on a second, man. I need to talk to you about Carolina."

Abaddon laughed. "Oh, it's Carolina now. Man, bring that cum catcher back here and get lost."

Pito swallowed hard. "No."

Abaddon stood up and charged at them. "What'd you say, you little motherfucker?"

"I just want to talk—"

Abaddon threw a quick and explosive punch that landed on Pito's forehead. A bright flash filled his vision and Pito tumbled to the floor. He regained his focus as Abaddon stood over him, pointing his knife at Pito menacingly.

Pito recoiled, shielding his face with his hands and arms. "Bro, what the fuck you doing?"

"Guess."

In one motion, Abaddon dropped to one knee and plunged the knife into Pito's neck. When he pulled it out, blood shot out from the wound like water through a geyser. Pito brought his hands to his neck and covered the large wound, trying to keep the blood inside his body. Through blurry vision he watched Abaddon stand up.

Then all the lights in the room went out.

Except for some moonlight creeping in through the windows, the room was dark. Somehow the power had gone out and Vic had a few seconds to take advantage of the confusion. From his seated position, he planted his feet on the floor, sprang up, and arched back with as much speed and strength as he could muster.

The sound of cartilage crunching filled his ears when the back of his head smashed into Machai's nose. He let out a loud groan and stumbled back. Metal clanged against wood as the gun landed on the floor.

Vic knelt, feeling around on the floor for the gun. After a few seconds he felt the gun's cold muzzle and picked it up in a shooter's grip. He stood up, hearing Machai cursing in front of him. Vic reached out with his free hand, feeling for Machai.

"Get your fucking hands off me!" Machai swiped away Vic's hand.

Vic held the gun close to where he thought Machai's head was, pointed it toward the ceiling and squeezed the trigger—careful to close his eyes so he wasn't blinded by the flash from the muzzle. The gunshot sent everyone into a panicked frenzy. Machai flailed at the gun as he let out a pained wail, knocking it out of Vic's hand.

Vic thought about trying to find the gun, but he was out of time. He opened his eyes and looked toward where he'd last seen Carolina. Vic's eyesight had adjusted to the darkness and, with some help from the ambient light from the moon, he spotted her on the other side of the room. Vic sprinted toward her, maneuvering around and through several Kings along the way.

Carolina was moving toward him, and she was alone. *Where's Oran?* As Vic got closer, he spotted him. He was facing away and appeared to be standing over someone.

When Vic reached her, he grabbed her hand and pulled her through the crowd, back toward the double doors. They pushed through the exit, stepping into a long hallway that led off in one direction. Vic ran down the hallway, pulling Carolina by the hand. She tried to yank her hand free, so he tightened his grip and continued forward.

Without slowing, Vic glanced back and said, "Carolina, you need to come with me if you want to survive this." She didn't respond, but there was a flash of recognition in her eyes, and she stopped resisting.

Groping in the dark, feeling for walls, they moved down a flight of stairs as fast as they could. Yelling and banging followed them as the Kings thundered after them. When they reached the first landing Vic inched forward, feeling around for direction. Another bannister. More stairs. They made their way down the staircase to the lobby.

From moonlight sneaking in through some windows, he saw exit doors ahead of them. They jogged to the doors but stopped short of walking through them.

"Come on, think," Vic muttered, scanning the lobby.

The boat. It was docked at Spring Creek Park and if he and Carolina could get to it, they'd be home free. Vic peered outside through the small glass window in one of the doors. He saw shadows moving around about thirty feet in front of them, between them and the park. He angled his head as best as he could, but it was hard to tell how many Kings were over there.

"Fuck," Vic whispered.

Boots clumped down the stairs behind them. They were running out of time. They had to make a move.

Vic remembered the Hemlock Gardens layout from when he'd scouted it with Teri. They were on the front side of the recreation center, which meant that 157th Avenue and the Belt Parkway were behind them.

"When I open this door, we're going to go to the left. Stay right behind me and close to the walls," Vic whispered.

"Okay," Carolina muttered nervously.

Vic pushed the door open just enough for them to squeeze their bodies through. They crept out into the open air, moving quickly as they made their way around to the back of the building. They stayed close to the building's walls, using its shadows as concealment. He slowed his pace for a second and surveyed the terrain. Satisfied there wasn't anyone around, he took hold of Carolina's hand and they sprinted toward the tree line in front of the Belt Parkway.

They reached a thick patch of trees and knelt on the ground. Vic glanced back toward the recreation center. Their pursuers still hadn't made it this way, but he could hear them moving around out there. He figured they had a few minutes before the Kings expanded their search area.

He turned back to their escape route. A short chain link fence stood between them and the Belt. They scaled the short fence, stopping on the other side so he could watch the passing vehicles. Traffic was light, one or two cars drove by in both directions every few seconds. He contemplated stopping one and asking for help but didn't want to risk it being full of Kings.

After a few seconds, they dashed across the six-lane roadway and into the tree line on the north side. They made their way over another fence and through a small section of trees and high grass, finally emerging in a clearing on Shore Parkway. They headed north, away from the Belt and into a residential neighborhood filled with old houses and two-story apartment buildings.

"Thank you," Carolina said. She walked fast, trying to keep pace with him. "I'm sorry about your friends."

Vic kept scanning their surroundings. "They weren't my friends."

"Oh." She was quiet for a few steps. "I'm still sorry."

"Yeah, me too."

"What's your name?"

"Vic."

"Okay, Vic..." She looked around. "So, what do we do now?"

"We need to figure out where we are exactly."

Vic peered into the night for a landmark or sign that would help him get oriented. After a few minutes they came upon a tall street post sign. It was hard to read in the dark, so Vic got up close and was able to make out their location: the corner of 156th Avenue and 79th Street.

"Can't you just steal a car?" Carolina asked.

He glanced back at her. "What makes you think I know how to steal a car?" She seemed frazzled and scared, maybe a little shocked, but man oh man, she was beautiful.

"I'm sorry. I just meant...I'm just really tired."

Vic smiled. "Relax, I was just kidding." Even in the dark, her embarrassment was hard to conceal. "I was thinking the same thing myself. Come on."

They headed north on Seventy Ninth Street. As they walked, Vic looked through car windows and pulled on door handles, checking for unlocked vehicles. Back in the day, he and his boys would sometimes get lucky and freshly stolen cars would be abandoned around their neighborhood. They'd find nice rides with screwdrivers sticking out of ignitions or steering columns already busted and wired to go.

So far tonight, he hadn't found either. After checking a few more cars, he located a white 1972 Ford Pinto parked driver's side to the curb with a bag of tools resting on the front passenger seat. He picked up a rock and threw it through the driver's window, shattering the glass. After unlocking the door, he grabbed a sweater that was lying on the passenger seat and wiped glass shards off the seat. He shook the sweater free of stray shards, placed it on the car seat, and sat down.

Vic put the tool bag on his lap and rummaged through it, finally pulling out a flathead screwdriver. He jammed the screwdriver into the ignition lock and pounded it with an open palm till he heard a click. He turned the screwdriver clockwise, but the engine didn't turn over.

"Come on." He turned the screwdriver again and made a quiet plea for help to the god of car thieves, but the Pinto didn't start. Exasperated, Vic leaned forward and pressed his head against the steering wheel for several seconds before finally getting out. He looked across the car roof at Carolina. "So, confession time. I don't know how to steal cars."

Carolina let out a small, tension-releasing laugh. "Okay. What do we do now?"

"We walk to the nearest train station."

"Vic, take a look around. Notice anything strange?"

Vic scanned their surroundings and quickly realized what Carolina was talking about. He'd been a little preoccupied after they'd escaped so he hadn't been paying attention. Everything was dark. Streetlights, traffic lights, buildings—nothing was on. It was as if someone had pressed the off switch on the world.

When the lights had gone out in the recreation center, Vic had just assumed the electrical issues were isolated to that one building or section. Not unusual for an old building in an even older neighborhood. But he checked every direction and as far as he could tell, all of New York City was in a blackout.

***

Abaddon was furious. In the span of two minutes, everything had gone sideways. When the night began, he had his money and Carolina, and was on the verge of tying up all loose ends. Then it all went to shit.

First, Pito had started acting stupid and needed to be put down. The little motherfucker had been asking for it for a while—pouting and complaining to anyone who would listen about what he was owed. Pulling the bitch off his lap had been the last straw—the bill had finally come due. Then Vic put Machai on his ass, something no one's ever done, and got away with Carolina.

The gym was empty now—just Abaddon and two corpses. He

stared out one of the windows, into the dark sky of a powerless city, becoming angrier by the second. He couldn't allow it to go down like this. Having the money was just the first step. For the rest of his plan to work, Carolina had to die, and Josiah Lynch's involvement in her death needed to be made public.

When the shitbag Lynch had first approached Abaddon about his plans to kickstart a purge, he couldn't believe his luck. As Oran, the head of a cutting-edge security company, he'd already infiltrated Lynch's inner circle. He'd just been biding his time up to that point, waiting for the perfect opportunity to destroy Lynch's empire before he killed him. But when Lynch told him Carolina needed to be sacrificed and directed him to get it done, Abaddon knew it was time to move forward.

He had taken care of everything and was even prepared to sacrifice a decent man to accomplish the mission. David was no great loss—the guy had the outsized ego of a rock star. And as for Walter and Tre, they were walking ghosts anyway.

But Vic was different. The two of them went back a long way, had saved each other's lives too many times to count. Vic not leaving when he'd had the chance had been a bit disappointing—but just a bit. As far as Abaddon was concerned, Vic and the others were collateral damage, no more important than the villagers who had died in the bombs they'd set off back in Nam.

But then Vic, Mr. Monkeywrench himself, decided to play hero. He wasn't upset about Machai. The guy had started to believe his own hype and was long overdue for an ass kicking. And if Vic had left it at that and just taken off, Abandon might have let him go. But Vic had made the mistake of taking Carolina with him —a blatant act of disrespect that needed to be remedied.

Vic and Carolina were out there now, and they probably thought they were on their way home. But there was a whole world between here and there. A world full of soldiers of darkness. And while they all wore different colors and ran with different sets, they all bowed down to the Savage Kings. They all bowed down to Abaddon.

He'd heard suckers talk about The Fear and he wondered if they truly understood the words they were parroting. Did they know that *he* was what made The Fear what it was—a living, breathing nightmare with no escape. Well, if they didn't know before, they would soon—He was going after Vic and the girl himself. He wanted to see the blood drain from their faces and the hope disappear from their eyes when they realized there was nowhere left to run.

But the two of them had a head start and he didn't know which direction they'd headed. He decided to send the word out, ten thousand dollars to the gang that served up Carolina and Vic. People were desperate and starving inside The Fear. Putting out a ten-thousand-dollar bounty was like lighting the fuse on a bomb. The two of them would be surrounded by enemies and there'd be no escape.

His heart began to beat faster when he pictured the hunt that was coming.

twenty

TERI WATCHED the scene outside Kai's Marauder with a mixture of awe and trepidation. The ominous darkness and discomforting quiet created an atmosphere of unnerving danger but was also oddly peaceful. She turned in her seat and looked back at the blacked-out Manhattan skyline. Its tall buildings were silhouettes against the glowing night sky, like giant sentinels watching over the city.

She returned her gaze to the view in front of them. Impeded by drivers who were distracted, scared shitless, or both, the Marauder inched forward at a snail's pace. Teri and Kai were on the Manhattan Bridge for an hour before they made it into Brooklyn. By the time they exited onto Flatbush Avenue, any fear or confusion locals may have initially felt seemed to have passed.

There were people everywhere, milling about on the sidewalks and in the streets. Every situation stood side by side with its own contradiction. Men and women scampered about in all directions —to get close to the mayhem or far away from the chaos. People stood in front of mom-and-pop stores or on the front steps of walkups, gossiping peacefully with neighbors or yelling threats at strangers. Lovers were locked in obnoxious public displays of affection, barely six feet away from large groups engaged in violent fisticuffs.

"This is nuts," Kai said.

"It looks like the whole city is blacked out. What do you think happened?"

"I have no clue. But if it stays like this too long, this city will eat itself."

Teri watched the unfolding madness as Kai navigated the Marauder down Flatbush Avenue toward Myrtle Avenue. Kai's words proved prophetic when she spotted a masked person tossing a brick through a storefront window, smashing it open.

A group of people entered the store through the window, careful to avoid the glass shards still embedded in the window frame. After a few seconds another man, his smiling face completely uncovered, exited the store carrying a television. He was soon followed by other members of the group, each holding their own television, stereo, or appliance. The act must have been contagious because within minutes there were groups smashing storefront windows all around them. Their frenzied actions frightened Teri, causing her to double-check that her door was locked.

As the Marauder turned left onto Myrtle Avenue, there were gunshots in the near distance, followed by a loud explosion. Teri was startled farther into her seat. The air was filled with screams—some were pleading for help while others threatened violence. It was a terrifying madness. *Is this how it ends?*

"You see that?" Teri pointed at a bright orange glow in the distance, about half a mile away, lighting up the night sky.

"Yeah," Kai said absently.

They were coming up on Vanderbilt Avenue when the source of the orange glow revealed itself. A four-story walk-up was completely ablaze. Bright orange flames reached out like claws, threatening to capture the surrounding buildings. Black clouds of smoke billowed out from the building, filling the sky with warnings to stay away.

People of all ages were jumping around in front of the inferno, arms raised in jubilation. Faceless silhouettes danced against the backdrop of the bright flames, celebrating the fire as if it were a deity. There weren't any sirens from fire trucks or police cars, and it was quickly evident that help was not coming.

They drove past the fire, stopping abruptly a few times when people ran in front of their car. As they got farther away, Teri turned and watched the fire recede into the distance.

"Why are people destroying their neighborhoods and homes?" she asked.

Kai shrugged. "They're frustrated and angry. Have been for a while. This blackout just provided an outlet. A way to vent without having to worry about spending a few weeks in Rikers."

"I get that. I'm from the same kind of neighborhood. But if people want to vent, why not do it down at City Hall or at one of the Midtown high-rises, where the people who have their foot on their necks live and work. If they're looking to send a message, it makes more sense to do the damage there."

"You ain't got to convince me. We've been going round and round with this since forever, and we always end up destroying our own shit. We don't ever take our gripes to the people responsible for causing the issues. Those people stay cozy and warm up in their ivory towers, watching all this go down on their televisions. Laughing and shaking their heads in judgment.

"After they've seen enough and are tired of traffic jams, they'll make a few phone calls. Then their puppets in City Hall will make empty promises to stop the unrest, but nothing will change. After a few years, the frustration will build until it can't be contained, and we'll go through the same shit again. Except the damage is always limited to our neighborhoods. No one thinks to take the fight where it needs to go because most people from these areas won't leave—no matter what."

After a few minutes, the fire was just a small orange blip in the Marauder's side-view mirror. They'd left some of the craziness behind them and drifted into another level in this bizarre circus. Besides the light from the Marauder's headlights, it was completely dark and there weren't many people on the street.

The few pedestrians that were out walked aimlessly on the sidewalks and roadway, seemingly oblivious to their surroundings. They were glassy eyed and distracted as they passed absently in front of the Marauder, forcing Kai to keep the vehicle's speed low. Teri lowered her window. The only sounds were the Marauder's loud engine and a dog barking in the distance.

She peered down the side streets and into the alleys between buildings as they passed. She felt a presence, as if they were being watched. Teri peered into the darkness, trying desperately to identify who, or what, was standing behind the shadows.

"Kai—"

A large cinder block landed with explosive force on the hood of the Marauder, bending it upwards. The loud sound of crunching metal scared Teri quiet and made her fall back into her seat. The car stopped moving and steam shot up from its engine.

As Teri leaned forward to get a better look at the damaged hood, a second cinder block smashed into the windshield. It came down from above as if it had been dropped from one of the rooftops.

"Fuck!" Teri yelled as she fell back into her seat again. A corner of the block had penetrated the windshield, causing hundreds of cracks to extend out from the hole in a spiderweb pattern.

"I was wondering when these yahoos were gonna show up." Kai was looking into his side-view mirror, toward the back of the car.

She turned in her seat, trying to see what was holding his attention. Ten people stood shoulder to shoulder on the street, their faces hidden in shadows. Teri couldn't make out any details, but they were of all shapes and sizes—tall, short, wide, and slim.

"Who are they?" Teri asked.

Kai kept his eyes on the reflection in the mirror. "Considering where we are, I'm pretty sure they're Renegade Assassins."

"Who?"

"Small set out of Fort Greene, maybe thirty to forty strong."

"I count ten. So where are the rest?"

"Oh, I'm sure they're around somewhere. If they ain't here now, they will be soon."

"Any chance we can talk our way out of this?"

A tall, slender figure emerged from the group and ambled toward the Marauder. He was holding a long, metal pipe in his left hand, dragging it along the ground behind him as he walked. A trail of small orange and white colored sparks danced on the ground beneath the pipe.

The man stopped a few feet from the Marauder and began tapping his pipe on the ground. The clanging of metal on concrete echoed off the buildings. After a few seconds the others joined in —tapping and banging their bats, pipes, and heavy metal chains against any hard surface they could find. It became a deranged cacophony of metal on concrete, steel, or wood. Loud, disturbing clangs that reverberated in the night.

"If I had to guess, I'd say no, we're not talking our way out of this. Excuse me." He reached past her into the backseat and grabbed the duffel bag he'd placed there earlier. Teri sat back in her seat as he pulled the bag onto his lap. "Wait here."

"Kai, why don't we just run?"

He gave her an amused and slightly confused expression. "Why in the world would we do that?"

Kai exited the vehicle and walked to the front of the Marauder. He lifted the bag onto the vehicle's hood, and it landed with a heavy thud. It took Teri all of twenty seconds before she completely disregarded Kai's direction, got out of the car, and walked to where he was standing.

"I told you to wait in the car," Kai said as he reached into the bag.

"Why in the world would I do that?"

He glanced at her and smiled before turning his attention back to whatever was in the bag.

Kai pulled a sword out of the bag and extended its handle toward Teri, presenting it as if he were handing her a bouquet of flowers. "Here, take this."

She reached out and took a hold of the handle. Teri lifted the surprisingly light sword close to her face. The curved blade was about three feet long, and razor sharp. The sword's bright, shiny metal reflected light from the moon. It was beautiful and hypnotic.

The sound of rubbing metal broke the spell. She glanced at Kai who was holding two swords, one in each hand. The blades were shorter and wider than the blade on her sword. She rolled her eyes when he spun each sword one handed, like a majorette twirling a baton during halftime of a high school football game.

"Compensate much?" she asked.

"Just testing the balance."

"Yeah right." Teri looked over at the line of Renegade Assassins, who were still tapping and clanging their weapons. "I'm normally not the biggest fan of guns, but I'd feel a whole lot better if you had brought some."

"Now, where's the fun in that?" Kai said with a wink and a smile. "Let's go."

They walked around the Marauder, one on each side of the vehicle. When they reached the rear of the car, they came together and walked shoulder to shoulder toward the Assassins' emissary. Teri and Kai stopped a few feet from the gang member, and he stepped toward them just as his people were stopping the incessant banging.

He was solidly built and tall, and his spiky hair protruded out from his head in all directions, as if it was trying to get away from his scalp. His pale white skin was covered in cheap, homemade-looking tattoos, and the area around his eyes was painted a dark color. His familiar garb, white sleeveless shirt, black cargo pants, and black combat boots, was the preferred ensemble of most of the kids who frequented the same music clubs as Teri. Wannabe nihilists who'd decided the most important things in life were to act tough and look like Joe Strummer or Johnny Rotten.

"You're trespassing," the spiky-haired Assassin said.

"We're just passing through," Kai said.

"Civilians pass through, bangers trespass. You're wearing colors, so you're trespassing."

Teri glanced at Kai, itching to say she'd told him so, but stayed quiet. Kai tilted his head slightly in her direction, giving her the "don't say it" look.

Kai turned back to the Assassin. "Look, we were just passing through. We wouldn't have stopped if you guys didn't drop bricks on my car."

The man smiled. His teeth were silver and shiny, like they were made of metal. "It almost sounds like you're saying you guys are tourists." He tilted his head to the side slightly. "Is that it? Are you two tourists?"

"If that helps the situation, then yeah, we're tourists," Teri said.

The Assassin made a show of looking at their swords. "It's funny, I don't think I've ever seen tourists carry swords."

"Well, you know, you can't be too careful these days," Teri said.

"All right then, if you're tourists, then you're sightseeing. It costs money to see the sights."

"How mu—"

"We already paid," Kai interrupted Teri.

"How do you figure?"

"You guys fucked up my car. That's more than enough to pay for passage."

"Oh that. That was just to get your attention. Call it an

entrance fee. Now you pay for the ride. Red or green, your choice."

The Assassin's ultimatum made Teri tense up. It wasn't hard to figure out he meant blood or money. Her pockets were empty. And she figured even if he had money, Kai wasn't planning on paying with cash.

"Red," Kai said.

Her eyes were concentrated on the messenger and the people behind him, so she didn't see Kai's face when he'd responded. But the Assassin's eyes had widened, and she imagined Kai had flashed his pirate's grin when he'd announced his choice. The man whistled and the rest of his flock started toward them.

Teri dropped her right leg back and bladed her body, so she was facing the threat at an angle, making herself a smaller target. She raised her sword up and held it in a two-hand grip like the actors she'd seen in Kung Fu movies. The emissary raised his metal pipe, the kind plumbers used, high over his head and lunged forward.

In one lightning-quick motion, Kai stepped toward the emissary and slashed him across his torso with one of his swords. He slid under the emissary's still raised arm and spun to his left. Blood and flesh exploded out from the long, deep gash and the man let out a loud scream as he crumpled to the ground.

A switch had flipped in Kai, and he moved swiftly and mercilessly. Teri stared wide-eyed at the bloodshed. She was shocked by the level of violence and at how easily Kai committed the act. When he stopped his motion, Kai was facing the oncoming Assassins.

With murder in their eyes, they raced toward Kai. He hesitated for a split second, then advanced toward them, one sword in each hand. The first one to reach Kai held a tire iron with two hands and took a long, wild swing at Kai's head. He ducked under it, stepped to his right, and slashed the Assassin across his stomach with the sword in his left hand. Mr. Tire Iron screamed in pain and pawed at his stomach as he fell over. Kai spun and faced the other gang members.

Two Assassins rushed at him. Kai threw a high front kick that landed on the neck of the lead banger. The Assassin fell backward onto the ground. Kai pivoted and slashed down at the guy who was still standing with one of his swords.

Teri heard grunting and cursing to her left, so she turned. A short, bald Assassin was holding a long, thick metal chain and coming straight for her. He swung the chain at her head, but Teri ducked under it and took a step back. He drew back and swung the chain at her again.

She stood up and raised the sword just in time to block the chain from hitting her, but it wrapped around the sword's blade. Baldy used two hands to yank the chain back toward him. Teri maintained her hold of the sword, so she was pulled forward and lost her balance. She fell on the ground and lost her grip on the sword, which landed in front of the bald Assassin.

He kicked the sword aside and stepped toward Teri, stopping when he was directly above her.

"Now what, bitch?" He flashed a row of rotted teeth as he twirled the chain.

Teri swept her leg out and hooked the back of his ankle. The Assassin fell backward onto the ground. Teri got to her feet, reached into her back pocket, and slid her fingers into her brass knuckles. Baldy was scrambling, trying to get back to his feet, but Teri threw two right hooks in quick succession. Both blows landed flush on the left side of his face, and he was unconscious before his head hit the pavement.

She looked over at Kai, who was engaged with the last three Assassins. They had surrounded him and were keeping their distance, so he had to divide his attention and couldn't engage. Teri picked up a metal pipe and started toward them.

An Assassin behind Kai smashed a lead pipe down on his left shoulder. Kai grimaced in pain and dropped to one knee. The

Assassin who'd landed the blow raised the pipe above his head, preparing to cave in Kai's skull.

At the last second, Kai sprang off the ground and spun to his left. He brought his sword around and slashed the Assassin across his thighs just as he was swinging the pipe down. The Assassin let out a pained wail as he doubled over and fell forward.

When Teri reached the group, Kai was turned away from the last two Assassins. Teri gripped the pipe with two hands and swung at the head of the one closest to her like she was batting cleanup for the Yankees. The pipe landed on the back of his head with a loud crack and sent vibrations up her arms.

Teri spun with her momentum and swung the pipe at the face of the last Assassin. He moved to his right, narrowly avoiding the strike. She balanced herself and squared off with him.

"You fucked up coming here, bitch." His long, unkempt hair covered his face. He tossed the metal pipe from one hand to the other. "I'm gonna beat you to death, you fucking cun—"

Kai brought his sword down onto the wild-haired Assassin from behind, burying it where the neck meets the shoulder. He used so much force the blade penetrated through bone, nearly decapitating the man. Kai pulled his sword free, and the Assassin's lifeless body fell to the ground. Kai stood over the man. He was breathing hard and seemed to be favoring his left shoulder and arm.

"You all right?" Teri asked.

"I've been better."

"Did that go as planned?"

"No. But in my defense, I never really had a plan."

A glass bottle shattered on the ground beside them. Teri barely had time to look at it before another glass object came crashing down from above. She looked up to see dark, faceless figures on the rooftops and in the windows on both sides of the street. The people started yelling, and soon Teri and Kai were in the middle of a monsoon of trash and obscenities.

"I guess that's our cue," Kai said.

He started back toward the Marauder and Teri followed behind. When they reached it, Kai put the swords back inside the bag while trash continued to rain down on them. He grabbed the duffel bag, and they ran east on Myrtle Avenue toward Bushwick.

twenty-one

VIC AND CAROLINA hurried north on Seventy-Eighth Street toward Conduit Avenue. He wanted to cut down on the chances of being spotted by a Kings search party, so he considered staying off the main thoroughfares. But these neighborhoods were a mystery to him, and they'd waste a lot of time trying to find their way through them. Their best option was sticking to the main streets.

They could take Conduit straight up to Atlantic Avenue, which would lead them around Highland Park, a place Vic definitely wanted to avoid. It was one of the few heavily wooded areas in Brooklyn, swarming with lowlifes who used the concealment afforded by the trees to do horrible things.

"Is that a payphone?" Carolina asked, pointing at something across the street.

He followed her finger and spotted the familiar rectangular silhouette of a phone booth.

"Come on," he said.

They sprinted across the street. When they reached the payphone, he pulled the folding door open with so much force, the booth shook. He grabbed the handset and brought it to his ear.

Nothing. No dial tone. No operator. He pressed down on the hook switch a few times but still nothing.

"Damn," Vic said, placing the handset back on its cradle.

"What?" Carolina asked.

"It's not working."

Carolina sighed. "Of course not, why would it work. Being able to call for help would ruin a perfectly terrible evening."

Vic chuckled. "Let's keep moving."

They continued north on Seventy-Eight Street, Vic scanning their surroundings as they walked. They were alone and trying to make their way through enemy territory with the Kings close behind. They were passing through The Hole, a small neighborhood between Howard Beach and Brooklyn that lay thirty feet below the surrounding areas. The neighborhood had an almost nonexistent sewage system, and since everything rolled downhill, the place was perpetually flooded. It was like being on the wrong end of a toilet.

There were empty lots on both sides of the street, filled with rubble and trash, all guarded by eight-foot chain-link fences. The flimsy and weak fences were pretty much a joke. They'd been erected by landowners to satisfy insurance companies rather than to keep people out. But they were topped with rust covered barbed wire, which was more than enough reason to stay on this side of them. Overgrown grass and weeds, almost as tall as Vic, covered the ground on both sides of the street.

"Wow, that's quite a stench." Carolina grimaced at the foul smell in the air.

She had been mostly quiet since Vic's epic failure with the car. But he'd figured it was because she was still in shock from everything she had seen, and not because she thought he was a loser. At least he hoped that was the reason.

"There's no decent sewage system in this neighborhood. Shit gets backed up. Literally."

"That's really disgusting. And we've been walking in it?"

"Look around. There're not many places to step that aren't covered with water."

"I guess." Carolina stepped around puddles, hopping between pieces of dried pavement. She managed to keep it up for half a block before giving up and going back to walking normally. "Remind me again why we came this way?"

"It's kind of hard to plan a route when you're running for your life. And I got turned around in the dark."

"Fair enough."

Music was playing in the far distance, but he couldn't make out the tune at first. He listened intently for several seconds.

"Do you hear that?"

Carolina tilted her head as if she was searching the air for sound waves. "I do now. What is that?"

"Mr. Softee Ice Cream."

"An ice cream truck? At this time?" Carolina checked her wrist for a nonexistent watch. "What time is it, anyway?"

"Around ten."

"Are you sure? You didn't even look at your watch."

"Don't need to. Mr. Softee always shows up around this time during the summer." Even in the limited light Vic spotted the skeptical look on Carolina's face. "But if it makes you feel better," He brought his watch up to his face, "it's a little past ten thirty."

"It feels a lot later."

"Yeah well, you've had a long couple of days."

She strolled past him without responding and he followed behind. They walked silently for several minutes.

"Do you like ice cream?" Carolina asked.

"As much as the next person, I guess. Why?"

"Nothing. It's just when you said, 'Mr. Softee Ice Cream,' there was something in your voice. A sort of reverence."

"I don't know if I would use the word 'reverence.' It's more like nostalgia. That music brings back some good memories."

"Like?"

"Do you really want to hear this?"

"Listen, after what I've been through, I could use some good memories. Even if they're someone else's."

There was a quiet desperation in the request, as if she was pleading for a reprieve. The last week of her life had been a nightmare that maybe a pleasant story might ease.

"Hearing that music reminds me of when I was a kid. Back when we could still have fun without dealing with life-and-death choices. Don't get me wrong, we were doing stupid shit, but we weren't the Mob or anything. It was just kid stuff like fistfights and shoplifting candy bars. We'd get into trouble, maybe get chased by the cops or a pissed-off shop owner. If we got caught, the worst thing that'd happen is we'd catch a beating. Maybe a trip down to juvie.

"But when we heard that music, everyone knew Mr. Softee was coming down the block and everything stopped. Everyone would gather around the truck, waiting to make their order, and everything was cool. Nothing bad ever happened around the ice cream truck. No fighting or worrying about being chased. Shit, even the cops would be out there sometimes. It was only for a short time. Whatever it took for you to get what you ordered and get gone, but it was a break from the craziness. And it was fun."

"Sounds magical."

"What about you?"

"Me? No, unfortunately, Mr. Softee Ice Cream doesn't do anything for me."

"What does?"

"Give me feelings of nostalgia? To be honest, I don't think I've ever experienced nostalgia."

"That doesn't seem possible."

"I grew up attending boarding schools. Cold places filled with distant people. Having experiences that would one day illicit feelings of nostalgia wasn't part of the curriculum."

"That sounds pretty terrible."

"It does, doesn't it?" She let out a deep, rich laugh that made him smile. After she got the laugh out of her system, Carolina lowered her head, as if she were thinking about something. "Do you think he was telling the truth?"

"Who?"

"Abaddon. Do you think he was telling the truth about my father?"

He wasn't sure how to tell her he believed what Oran had said. His head had been spinning since they'd made it out of the gym. It was clear the Oran he knew was either dead or had never existed in the first place. The man he'd dealt with tonight was a complete psychopath, and Vic couldn't wait to kill him, but that didn't mean he'd been lying about Carolina's father. With the benefit of hindsight, it was the only thing that made sense.

Vic was pissed, and the more he thought about everything that'd happened, the angrier he became. He was angry that Carolina was in danger. And he was angry at Oran, and Carolina's piece of shit father. But most of all he was angry at himself. He should have known something was off about this whole deal.

It wasn't like there hadn't been clues: A team of junkies past their primes, not involving the cops or feds, the ambush kidnapping. He'd managed to stay alive a long time by reading people and trusting his gut. Whether out of a sense of loyalty to his old team leader or because he felt like he couldn't say no to his friend, Vic had misread the whole damn thing. Now people were dead, and he and Carolina were on the run.

Vic turned and faced her. "Honestly? Yes, I believe he was telling the truth."

Carolina nodded "So do I." Her lips quivered and her eyes welled with tears.

Vic wanted to hug her. He wanted to reach out and pull her into him but held himself back. They barely knew each other, and Carolina had been through a lot. He figured the last thing she wanted was to be touched by him.

"Caro—"

Vic was interrupted by the sound of hooves clip-clopping on pavement.

"What is that?" Carolina's eyes were wide with concern.

"I'm not sure. It sounds like horses," Vic said. With any luck it was the New York Police Department's Mounted Police. They usually didn't come this far out of Manhattan. But with the blackout going on, their squad being deployed out here wasn't that far-fetched. "It could be the cops. Their Mounted Patrol."

"The police? Let's go find them." Carolina started toward the sound.

"Hold on. We don't know what's going on over there."

He didn't want to go searching for the source because he had a good idea where it was coming from. And if he was right, help was the last thing they would find.

There was a loud neigh near the end of the block, followed by more clip-clopping. Only louder and more distinct. The horses and their riders were close.

"Who else would it be?"

"Carolina, wait—"

Four horses and their riders emerged from the end of the block. Vic could barely make them out in the dark, but one thing was certain—they weren't the NYPD. Carolina stopped short, seeming to sense danger, and backed up to where she was beside Vic again.

"Who are they?" Carolina asked.

The lead horse and its rider trotted into the moonlight. Even with a skewed perspective from the man sitting up high on the horse, it was clear he was a big, powerfully built man. If Vic needed further confirmation as to their identity, which he didn't, the four riders were wearing black cowboy hats.

"Immortal Outlaws."

"Are they good guys or bad guys?"

The question seemed strange at first, but then it made sense. In

Carolina's world everything was binary—black or white, good or evil, right or wrong. She didn't understand that everyone else existed in varying shades of gray, where everything was a little more nuanced, and the only certainty was people would do whatever they needed to survive.

"There's no such thing," Vic said. "They, like everyone else we may meet tonight, shouldn't be trusted."

Vic checked their surroundings for an escape route, but there was nowhere to go. They were standing in the middle of the block with eight-foot fences on both sides of the street, so their only options were straight ahead or back where they'd come from. Either way, the Outlaws would run them down before they made it ten feet.

When Vic turned back toward the riders, he was face to face with the lead horse, so he backed up. Dark brown with white spots near its nose, the horse stared down at him with curious eyes.

"What are you two doing here?" the lead rider asked.

"We were at the beach earlier, but our car broke down on the Belt. We were walking to the train station and got turned around when the lights went out."

Vic glanced past the large man, at the other three riders behind him. Vic couldn't see their faces, but he assumed they were Black like the lead rider.

"Who are you?" The rider leaned forward, his hard eyes fixed on Carolina.

"My name's Vic, that's...Margaret."

The leader sat straight up. "Margaret, huh?" He dismounted his horse and approached Vic and Carolina, petting his horse's muzzle as he walked by. "All right, Vic. You look hip, so I'm just gonna lay it out. You know that even under the best of circumstances, you two would be in a fucked-up situation, don't you?"

"How so?"

He stood close to Vic, silently challenging him with his size. The guy was right about the situation, but Vic wasn't going to concede anything. This was headed in one direction, and showing weakness was a sure way to speed up the trip.

"Come on, Jerrick, hurry this shit up. I'm hungry," one of the riders yelled.

"Shut the fuck up, Jasmine. There's a process to this shit. Where was I? Okay, say we found you out here in the middle of the day. Sun is out and people are everywhere, having a good time. I'd still find a reason to step to you and fuck your shit up. It don't matter that you're Black. You'd still be an outsider and that's all the reason I need."

He took a step toward Carolina but kept his eyes on Vic. "But just in case you didn't know, the Savage Kings put out the word they're looking for a white chick and a brother. Offering ten grand to whoever bags 'em. Now, I'm no Kojak, but I'm willing to guess you two are the ones they're looking for."

"All right man. You're right, the Kings are looking for us. But they were going to kill us, probably rape her first—"

"Save it, blood." Jerrick waved his hands dismissively. "None of that means anything to me. The way I see it, that's the risk you take when you mess with them fools down at the beach." He ambled back to his horse and stood with his back to Vic and Carolina, petting its shoulder area. "Truth is, I can't stand the Kings, and normally I wouldn't help them with shit. But you two are worth some serious green."

"We can pay you," Carolina said.

Jerrick turned and faced them. "You got ten grand on you right now?"

Carolina looked at Vic and then back at Jerrick. "No. But I can get it for you. When we get home. I can have twenty thousand dollars delivered to you tomorrow. I promise."

"Oh, well, since you promised." Jerrick scratched his horse's ear. "Listen, sweetheart, your promises don't mean shit to me. If you had the cash on you, we might've had something to talk about. But you don't—so that's that. Old Abaddon has cash in hand, and we already sent word that we found you. Seeing as how they were already out and about looking for you two, they should be here soon."

"You really think I'm going to let you hand us over to them?" Vic said.

Jerrick's eyes widened, and he let out a big, dramatic laugh. He turned to the other three riders but none of them joined him in the fake laughter bit. "Did you guys hear this motherfucker? He's talking about *letting* us do something." He turned back to Vic and Carolina. "My man—look around you. Where do you think you're at? There is no scenario where you don't end up back with the Kings being ass-raped and murdered, and probably not in that order either."

Jerrick locked eyes with Vic, and they stared at each other. Vic played the angles in his head, but he couldn't think of any way out that didn't involve blood. He took a step to his right, putting himself between Carolina and the Immortal Outlaws.

"Oh, I'm sure there's a scenario you haven't thought about yet." Vic balled his hands into fists and took a step toward Jerrick. "Let's see if we can figure out what it is."

Jerrick didn't budge. He just stayed by his horse, petting its shoulder. After a few seconds his mouth curled into a wide grin.

"Man, you got some balls on you." Jerrick glanced back at Jasmine, who just shrugged. He turned his gaze back to Vic and Carolina. "You ever been hunting, Vic?"

"Not since Nam."

"Nam, huh?" Jerrick seemed to lose himself for a second, as if he was remembering his own experiences.

"Yeah," Vic said.

"I love hunting," Jerrick said, snapping out of his reverie. "But I haven't been for a while. So, since we're here, why don't we have some fun. You and Miss Margaret here run that way really, really fast." He pointed north toward Dumont Avenue. "I'll give you a three-minute head start, and then we're coming for you."

"A-yo, Jerrick," one of the male riders said. He was thinner than Jerrick, with a handlebar mustache and an intense, deadeye stare.

"What's up, Tango?" Jerrick kept his gaze on Vic.

"Why you wanna play games? Them Kings will be here soon with our money. Let's just put these two on ice till they get here."

"Ain't nobody playing games, Tango."

"But—"

"I got this." Jerrick's tone was harsh, but he didn't raise his voice. He turned to Vic. "What's so funny?"

"Huh? Oh, nothing." Vic was smiling as he eyed Tango. "I've just been waiting to meet someone named Tango. I was beginning to think it wasn't going to happen."

"Glad you can find the humor in this whole thing." Jerrick leaned in a bit closer to Vic. "I tried to explain the whole tango thing to him once, but he just looked at me like I was his math teacher or something." He shrugged. "Creativity ain't really a requirement to roll with us, know what I'm saying."

"Yeah well, what are ya gonna do? You were saying something about a head start," Vic said.

"Three minutes." Jerrick held up three fingers. "If we catch you, we hand you over to the Kings and collect the money. But if you get away, I'll trust that you'll be delivering twenty grand tomorrow. What do you think about that?"

"Honestly? I'd rather count the wrinkles on my dog's balls. Why don't you just take the twenty grand and let us walk out of here peacefully?"

"Where's the fun in that? Besides, if you get away, there's more than a good chance I'll never see that twenty grand. But since I'm no Abaddon fan, and the prick might stiff me anyway, I'm willing to take that risk. In the name of good sportsmanship and all. Clock's ticking, Vic. What do ya say?"

Vic glanced over at Carolina, who looked confused. He took ahold of her hand, and they walked past Jerrick.

"See you tomorrow, Jerrick."

"We'll see about that. Your three minutes started five seconds ago."

There was a rumbling of engines as he and Carolina jogged away.

Abaddon muttered curses under his breath as he and his team approached The Hole. Vic had spent the night screwing everything up, so it only made sense he would end up in the one place Abaddon avoided like the plague. With its sewage issues and the Mob using it as their very own body disposal site, the place always smelled like shit and rotting flesh. But since Vic and the Lynch woman were there, he had no choice but to lead his people that way.

And as if the smell and flooding weren't bad enough, dealing with the Black cowboys was another pain in the ass. It was weird enough they rode horses in the middle of the city, but their leader Jerrick was a bottom feeding prick with a big mouth. He liked to talk tough and didn't seem to understand where he and his people were in the pecking order. It made Abaddon's blood boil whenever the spade tipped his hat like he was Roy Rogers.

He had heard the stories about Jerrick and his people being direct descendants of Black cowboys, but Abaddon wasn't buying the bullshit. He'd grown up watching old John Wayne westerns and he had never seen a Black cowboy in any of those movies. But they supposedly had what he wanted, so he planned to play nice—at least for tonight.

They traveled west on Linden Boulevard, toward Seventy-Ninth Street. Abaddon was riding up front on his 1972 Triumph X75 Hurricane motorcycle. A caravan of Savage Kings followed behind him in cars and vans, with some on motorcycles. Every one of them flying King colors like floats at the Thanksgiving Day Parade.

He was always up front when they were on the hunt. Abaddon didn't understand the suckers who hung out in the middle, surrounded by soldiers, and reliant on others for protection. If the shit hit the fan, who was better suited to protect him than himself? And besides, real leaders led from the front—period.

Yeah, being up front was where it was at. All wind, no exhaust fumes, and he didn't have to stare at someone's fat back. He could see everything for himself and didn't have to depend on someone else to warn him of coming danger. But most of all, Abaddon loved being the first face his prey saw before everything ended for them.

When the caravan turned onto Seventy-Ninth Street, Jerrick was standing on the ground by his horse, with three of his people on their horses. Vic and Carolina were nowhere to be seen, so he figured Jerrick was keeping them out of sight till he got his money. Abaddon stopped his Triumph about thirty feet from Jerrick, dismounted, and stood directly across from him, grinning in anticipation of what was to come.

They strolled toward each other. The engines went silent behind Abaddon, and the only sound was the metal heels of their boots landing on the pavement. He peered past Jerrick at the group behind him. It seemed the number of Black cowboys on horses had doubled from the time he and his Kings turned the corner.

"Abaddon," Jerrick said. They stood eye to eye, separated by two feet of air and pavement. Two men of equal height and mass but different hearts and souls. "I see you brought the whole family."

"Yeah, yeah. And you brought your crew. You can skip the preamble, Jerrick. Where are they?"

"Yeah, that. It seems my man Tango may have jumped the gun when he called your people."

"So, what are you saying? You don't have them?"

"No, I'm sorry to say we don't. Somebody somewhere thought they saw something, but it turns out, they didn't see anything." Jerrick flashed a smirk that made Abaddon want to cut off his head.

"You're wasting my time, Jerrick. You and the rest of your horse-riding assholes. I don't like having my time wasted."

"Well, it's a good thing I don't give a fuck what you like." Jerrick checked his watch.

"You late for something or what?"

"Actually I am. I'm missing *Starsky and Hutch*."

Jerrick's voice was low and calm, which made Abaddon even more angry. He felt like killing Jerrick and his entire crew right then and there.

"You want to know something, Jerrick? I'm going to finish up what I got going, then I'm coming back here. And there is no version of this story that doesn't end with you and your buddies buried in that Mob graveyard up the block."

Jerrick's eye twitched subtly, and Abaddon smirked. Jerrick's cool veneer had melted away and his cracks were showing. Abaddon was readying himself for what might spring forth from those cracks when he heard a whistle from above.

He lifted his head up and spotted Dirty on one of the roofs. He was pointing at the street north of them. Dirty was one of the younger Kings. Athletic with a lot of energy, he was perfect for the role of spotter. His job was to stay ahead of the group, often on rooftops, locating threats and targets.

Abaddon glanced back at Jerrick. "Well, Jerrick, my man, it looks like we're gonna have to pick this up later. I have some more pressing business to attend to. Why don't you go and watch that episode of *Starsky and Hutch*. Maybe have yourself a plate of neck-bones, or pickled pigs' feet, or whatever the fuck it is you people eat. We can settle up when I get back."

"I look forward to it." Jerrick turned and headed back to the rest of his Outlaws.

Abaddon faced his Kings and twirled his right index finger in the air, signaling for them to start their vehicles. All the engines roared to life simultaneously. And in an instant, the silence and darkness were gone, replaced with loud motors and bright headlights.

He stared at the spectacle and grinned because they had a track now, and the hunt was on.

twenty-two

TERI AND KAI had trudged for several blocks, making it to
Sumner Avenue, and Kai was laboring. He'd been favoring his left
arm since the fight with the Renegade Assassins, also known as the
"We Just Murdered Everyone Tour."

"Let me take that." Teri reached for the bag of swords.

Kai pulled the bag away. "Nah, I got it."

"Kai, I appreciate the whole chivalry act, but you look like shit.
I can carry it for a while."

"I'm good. I promise you I'm good. Anyway, we're almost
there."

Too tired to pursue the topic, Teri shook her head and threw
her arms up in surrender. "How do you know your way around
here so well? I thought everyone pretty much stuck to their own
neighborhoods."

"I spent a lot of time sneaking in and out of here when I was a
kid. Got chased a lot too. Had to know the neighborhoods pretty
good just to make it out alive."

"Up to no good, I'm sure."

Kai chuckled. "A little bit, yeah. But mostly to see a girl."

"Really?"

"Don't sound so surprised. I do like women."

"No, I'm sure you do. I'm just surprised you'd find someone this far away from where you lived. And that you'd be into her enough to risk major beatdowns to see her."

"Well, I did. And I was."

They were silent for a few steps, and he didn't seem in any hurry to finish the story.

"And?"

"And what?"

"Bro, you're not just going to leave me hanging. I need the whole story. First of all, what was her name?"

"Milagro. Everyone called her Millie."

"Okay, Millie, short for Milagro. Got it, now go on with the rest."

"There isn't much to tell. We were kids, fifteen or sixteen. Met at the Botanical Gardens. It was one of those big trips that schools take poor kids on. To show them there's more to this world than the four corners of their neighborhoods. Anyway, there were a few different schools there and we bumped into each other—literally. She fell, I helped her up and we started talking.

"Before I knew it, we were spending a lot of time together. At least, as much as we could. I lived off Canal Street at the time and she was out here. Her family was Dominican, mine is Chinese. As you can imagine, neither neighborhood was very welcoming."

"Sounds very Tony and Maria." Teri was smiling when she glanced at Kai, who looked puzzled by the reference. "Tony and Maria? *West Side Story*?"

"Never heard of it."

"You've never seen *West Side Story*? I thought it was required viewing for street gang members."

"Not for me, it wasn't."

"Well, check it out, it's a classic. So, what happened?"

"We had some good times. I think about the shit we pulled just to spend ten minutes together. It's interesting the risks people will take to be with someone they like. We made it about eight months before it ended—like most romances do. We were young, so it probably wouldn't have lasted anyway. But everything got too heavy for teenagers from where we lived. The distance...the racial stuff."

He stared ahead absently and was quiet for a few seconds. "She's dead now. Murdered a few years back. Some piece of shit shot her over two dollars in Washington Square Park."

"Kai, I'm so sorry." Her words came out in a whisper, as if she was consoling him while standing over Millie's grave.

"There's no need for that. I hadn't seen her in over fifteen years. Hearing about her passing didn't really affect me." It was subtle, but there was a change in his voice. Kai wasn't being honest when he said Millie's death hadn't affected him. "I'm just sorry there wasn't more of a happy ending to the story."

They glanced at each other, and he forced an awkward smile. A big difference from the cocky grin he often flashed.

"Don't worry about that. I'm used to unhappy endings. Besides, at this point in my life I'm a lot more interested in the beginning of things. And the beginning of your thing with Millie sounds beautiful," Teri said.

They held each other's eyes for a few brief seconds. The experience was neither romantic nor uncomfortable. And she wasn't sure if he was friend, foe, or something in between. The whole thing was a bit strange. Just yesterday he'd try to burn her mentor alive, and now she was sharing an intimate moment with him.

"Look at that," Kai said.

Teri followed his eyes to the aftereffects of a world gone crazy. They were standing about a half a block from the southeast corner of Myrtle Avenue and Bushwick Avenue. Debris and trash covered the streets, and several cars and buildings were burning—filling the air with black smoke and ash. They'd missed the mayhem, so except for some people rummaging through shattered storefront windows in search of leftover goods, the area looked deserted.

Teri turned to Kai. "Now what?"

"Let's head up there." Kai motioned with his head toward Bushwick Avenue. "Whoever we're looking for knows we're here. They'll come to us."

They walked to the corner and waited. Civilians strolled by them, too caught up in their own lives to give Teri and Kai a second look. The last stragglers disappeared into the darkness, and everything was still and silent. It lasted several minutes, just she and Kai alone with their fears and stress.

The silence was replaced with loud banging, shouts, and whistles. Teri and Kai took a few steps and stopped in the middle of the street, scanning their surroundings. Old, dilapidated buildings stood on both sides of them, putting them smack dab in the middle of a concrete and metal valley. The noise went on for several minutes, rising to a deafening crescendo, and then it stopped.

"There they go," Kai said. She followed his eyes to a large group of people standing on the street about a hundred feet from them. It was dark out, the only light coming from the moon and some small fires. The group was bunched together, blocking the entire road ahead. "Vic's old set. The Ruthless Ones."

"That seems like a lot of people for just the two of us."

"Yeah well, they're kids. Restraint isn't really a word they're familiar with. Besides, with this blackout going on, I'm sure they have every one of their members out looting and stealing."

"Do you think any of them will know him?" Teri asked.

"I'm not sure. Vic's been gone awhile, and gangs shed members like snakes shed their skins. Whatever the reason—jail, death, or just plain old age—old members go away. Replaced with new, younger versions. The chances of one of them knowing him, or even remembering him, aren't good."

"So, what do we do now?"

"We wait. Hopefully they're more curious about what we want than offended that we're here. Someone will come looking for answers." Kai unzipped the bag and placed it on the ground between them. "But if we have to fight—we fight."

It was hot and the air was dense with humidity. She glanced over at Kai and her eyes fixed on his injured left arm. He was bent over slightly at the waist and sweat covered his face. He looked bad and she figured this was him doing his best *not* to look hurt.

Teri turned back to the crowd, their numbers hidden by shadows and darkness, and she was worried. Not so much about the possibility they'd have to fight again, she'd spent most of her life fighting in one form or another. She was worried she might fail, and she wouldn't be able to get the help she needed to save Vic.

Out of the corner of her eye, light flashed from the bag at Kai's feet. It was moonlight reflecting off the surface of one of the steel blades that lay inside the bag. She stared at it for a few seconds, mesmerized by the beauty of the lethal weapon. She found the sight oddly serene.

Before Kai could argue or decide for them, Teri took off for the crowd. He called her name, but she ignored him and continued forward. No one said anything while she made the walk over. Her footsteps and the small, crackling fires from some of the buildings were the only sounds. An unexpected gust of wind lifted paper off the ground and blew ash into her face.

Teri stopped a few feet from the crowd and waited. She had a better view of the group now and was able to make out the details of their clothes and faces. There were dozens of them, all different shapes and sizes. Some of them gave hard looks, while others looked relaxed or even stood with their backs to her.

In her limited experience with street gangs, Teri found they were mostly homogenous, usually consisting of one race or sex. But this group seemed to be made up of people of all genders and skin colors. The only thing consistent about them was their inconsistency.

They were all dressed like most kids their age, in jeans and t-shirts. And most of them wore cheap-looking denim vests with different variations of the same picture on the back—the Grim Reaper holding its scythe, overlayed on top of two crossed axes.

Teri stared at the crowd, and they returned her glare. Hostility and curiosity beamed from their eyes. It was a weird stalemate where no one made a move. The two minutes of silence and anticipation felt like hours.

A woman stepped out of the group and sauntered toward Teri. She was tall and young, probably about the same age as Teri. She had long, wavy, dark hair and wore a fitted black tank top under her denim vest, exposing a large tattoo on her chest and neck. Teri was able to make out a lion and a crown, but it was too dark to make out more details without staring and risking a severe blow to the head.

"What are you doing here?" the woman asked.

"I'm looking for someone," Teri said.

"Oh yeah? Who?"

Teri hesitated. "I don't know."

The woman looked incredulous. "What?"

"I don't know who I'm looking for. Look, I know it sounds strange but I'm trying to find someone who might know someone else."

"Bitch, is you high or what? You come around here with a motherfucker flashing colors from another set," the woman said, glancing at Kai. "Looking for someone you don't know, who might know someone else? Am I getting that right?"

"Yeah well, it made more sense before I said it out loud." The woman didn't crack a smile and Teri realized her attempt at humor had failed miserably. "Look, I'm trying to find someone who knows Vic Espada. He used to be one of you. He used to be a Ruthless One."

"Never heard of him."

"I'm not surprised by that. He was before your time, but I'm trying to find someone who has heard of him or might've known him."

"Listen, lady, I never heard of him and neither has anyone else here. You fucked up coming around here, especially with that motherfucker over there." The woman pointed at Kai. "But we got other shit going down tonight. So I'm gonna give you a chance to get the fuck out of here before you get done up."

The woman gave Teri a hard stare. Teri glared back defiantly, but for the first time in a long time, she was intimidated, and she didn't like the feeling. She was confident in herself and her skills, maybe even too confident. Uncle Chris had called it the hubris of youth. But Teri had worked hard, both in the classroom and in the ring, sharpening her mind and body. Too hard, she thought, to be feeling this way now.

She figured it was just her body's response to fatigue and a week's worth of blood, guts, and violence. For whatever reason, the heavens opened up an all-out assault on her psyche, and Teri was finally feeling the effects of fate's scorched-earth approach to her life. She may have officially reached the end of her rope. After a few seconds, Teri took a step sideways and looked at the crowd behind the woman.

"Vic Espada. I'm looking for someone who knows Vicente Espada," Teri yelled.

"Bitch, I told you don't no one here know who you're talking about."

"What are we waiting for, Sonia? Let's just fuck them up," a voice from the crowd hollered.

Sonia turned her head slightly to her left but kept her eyes on Teri and Kai. "Nah, I got a better idea." She flashed a devious smirk. "Let's put them up against the Box. Let them earn their way out of this."

"Oh, hell yeah. The motherfucking Box," another voice from the crowd shouted.

"Oh damn. Shit just got real," a different voice chimed in.

Sonia set her gaze on Teri and Kai. "What do ya say? You want to go toe to toe with fate?"

"Do we have a choice?" Teri asked.

"Of course, you have a choice. But you're not going to be happy with the options."

Teri turned her head and made eye contact with Kai, who seemed to be thinking the same thing she was—that they were probably screwed. Just then, with their backs against a wall and the deck stacked high against them, the only thing going through her head was something her uncle had said to her once, "Anything worth loving is worth fighting for."

Teri turned back to Sonia. "Fuck it. What do you have in mind?"

twenty-three

"WHY MARGARET?" Carolina asked.

They'd been sprinting down Dumont Avenue when they heard the rumbling of engines. Carolina had lost steam after a few blocks, but Vic had grabbed her hand and pulled her along for another two blocks before she couldn't run anymore. Now they were speed-walking on Eldert Lane, and despite being chased by a psychopath, his gang, and people on horses, Carolina couldn't push the question out of her mind.

"What?"

"Why did you tell the cowboy my name is Margaret? Sounds like a princess."

"Huh? I guess it just seemed like a good name for a society woman. Listen, I'm sorry if you were insulted, but we have to keep moving."

She was disappointed that Vic just thought of her as a "society woman." She was used to it after all—people treating her differently based on their own preconceived notions of her. Even during her boarding school years and then while attending university, surrounded by people who were raised with the same privileges as her, she had been treated differently. Perhaps it was because of who her father was, but everyone in her life had treated her the same way—with cold and distant regard, as if they were admiring a piece of art in the Louvre.

She realized she wanted Vic to see her differently. She didn't want him to treat her like some high-born princess that needed to be protected and kept at an arm's distance. Carolina wanted Vic to want her like she wanted him.

"Vic, I—"

Engines roared loudly behind them. They both glanced over their shoulders.

"Come on," Vic said.

He grabbed her hand, and they made a left onto Sutter Avenue from Eldert Lane. They headed west, quickening their pace to a fast jog, but the noise from the engines grew louder as their pursuers drew closer. The moon was covered with clouds now, its hope-inspiring light diminished and faint. Ahead of them, in the far distance, there was a flash of lightning followed almost immediately by the sound of thunder.

They had run for five blocks, and Carolina was exhausted. Her heart was beating hard and fast in her chest, and she was gasping for breath. But the gang was getting close, so she pressed on despite the pain. By the time the two of them turned north onto Euclid Avenue, the Savage Kings were so close their screams were no longer indiscernible primal howls, but comprehensible taunts and threats.

"In here." Vic led her into a three-story walk-up apartment building.

They stepped into the building's tiny vestibule, and Vic shut the entrance door behind them just as the first headlight beam appeared on the street. The light invaded their space through the square window in the center of the metal door. Vic faced Carolina, backed her gently into the wall behind them, and pressed his body against hers, trying to use a blind spot and some shadows as concealment.

She turned her head sideways and pressed it against his chest. His heartbeat was fast and loud, and her pulse quickened. Lights passed the window in intervals, and footsteps and scheming voices filtered in from the outside.

"They're not leaving," Vic whispered. He leaned backward slightly to try and see outside. Carolina touched his shirt, wanting to pull him close to her again. "We can't stay here."

He grabbed her hand and they sprinted up four flights of stairs, not stopping till they reached the door to the roof. When they stepped out onto the roof, Carolina was winded. She bent over and put her hands on her knees, trying to catch her breath.

"This way," Vic said.

He crept toward the roof's far side, being careful to stay low and out of sight. She crouched down and followed behind, catching up with him when he stopped at the roof's edge. She peered over the side. The neighboring building was so close it may as well have been connected, but it was about a ten-foot drop to its roof.

"What now?" Carolina asked.

Vic was focused on the next building. "We have to get down there, to that roof. We can hide in that pigeon coop till they clear out of here. Then make our way back to the street when they're gone."

The small plywood pigeon coop on the adjoining roof appeared to be just big enough for the two of them to squeeze into, but she was more concerned about how he planned to get there from here.

"That sounds like a great plan. Now how do we get down there?"

Vic gave her a look as if she'd just asked him to describe the color red. "We jump."

"Um, okay, that's one way to go. Here's another—let's not jump and just stay up here till they leave."

"Carolina, look around. There's nothing up here, we're fully exposed. Pretty soon they're going to start checking roofs. But they're moving fast. If we're out of sight inside the coop, there's a chance they'll move on quickly." He looked at her reassuringly. "It's not that far, maybe ten feet or so—like landing on the ground after dunking on a basketball hoop."

"Yes, well, I've never dunked a basketball so that example does nothing for me."

"I've never dunked one either, but guys do it every day and they're fine when they land. We'll hang over the edge, straighten our bodies as much as we can, and then drop. If we do it that way, the drop will only be about five feet or so."

Carolina glanced down at the roof below, trying to gauge the length of the drop. The noise from wild gang members on the street below pierced through any reservations she was having. They had to get out of sight.

"All right Vic, let's—"

She was interrupted by a sharp whistle. Vic turned and scanned their surroundings. After a few seconds he pointed, and she followed his finger to three dark figures on a rooftop across the street. They whistled two more times, and all three motioned excitedly at Carolina and Vic.

"Looks like we're done debating." Vic took her gently by the elbow and led her closer to the edge. "Just sit down and swing your legs over. Turn slowly and hold onto the edge as your legs drop."

He crouched and held onto Carolina's arms. She did as he instructed, holding onto the edge of the roof with her hands as her lower torso hung loosely over the side. There was a ruckus coming from behind Vic as he lay down flat on the roof's surface.

Vic locked eyes with her. "I got you."

He slid his hands along her arms and took a hold of her hands. Vic squeezed her hands reassuringly as he extended his arms as far as he could, getting her closer to the next roof's surface. The shouting and banging seemed to get louder as he let go. Carolina kept her eyes on his till she landed, but he disappeared just as she was stumbling backward, trying to regain her balance. She took a few steps back and searched the roof line above her, the sound of her own breathing loud in her head.

She took a deep breath when Vic lowered his body over the side. He gripped the edge above him and then used his legs to push off the wall. He landed gracefully and jogged toward her without breaking stride.

"You look like you've done that before." Carolina turned to run with him.

"Yeah, I've had a lot of practice jumping off buildings this week."

The gravel-covered roof was almost half a block long. They sprinted toward the far end, every rock-crunching step bringing them closer to the edge. Vic ran ahead and looked over the side.

"Vic, where—"

He walked back toward her. "Get ready to jump."

"What?"

She looked past him, toward the next roof. It was the on the same level as this one, but she couldn't tell how far away.

He grabbed her hand as he turned. "It's only a few feet to the next building. As soon as your foot touches the edge, jump with every bit of strength you have in you."

"Vic, I can't—"

"Yes, you can Carolina. I promise you, you can. Stay with me." He tightened his grip on her hand and started jogging toward the edge.

After a few steps he started running faster. Carolina increased her speed to keep pace. Everything seemed to be moving in slow motion.

Vic's sweaty hand almost came free of hers and she felt him adjust his grip. She stepped on a pile of gravel and almost slipped. She regained her balance quickly and eyeballed the edge, planning to wait till the last possible second before she leapt.

Here it comes. Just a few more steps. Her lead foot reached the edge. She dropped her weight slightly and pressed off her foot with every ounce of strength she could muster and sprang. She raised her head toward the sky and spotted Vic out of the corner of her eye. He was a bit higher than her and slightly ahead.

He stumbled a little but stuck the landing. Carolina lost her balance and fell to her knees. She glanced back at the gap they had just leapt and took a deep breath—relieved and proud that she'd made it across. Carolina was smiling when she turned to Vic, but he had gone over to the door to the building. He tried to pull the door open, but it was locked.

"Fuck," Vic said.

He jogged along the edge of the roof, looking over its sides. When he was done, Vic walked back to Carolina, not bothering to mask his concern.

"What is it?" she asked.

"There's no way off this building."

twenty-four

GABRIEL BROUGHT the glass to his lips and inhaled deeply, his eyes closed. He detected notes of honey and molasses and hints of rose petals as well.

He took a long sip, letting the amber liquid fill his mouth. The five-year-old bourbon's heat warmed his lips and tongue. He closed his eyes and savored the flavors of lemon peel and nutmeg for as long as he could before he allowed it to slide down his throat.

Gabriel lowered the glass and rested his hand on the armchair in his sparsely decorated bedroom. With its overstuffed, suede padding and elevated armrests, it was his favorite chair, perfect for watching them sleep.

Whenever he was feeling particularly good about himself, like tonight, Gabriel would order some entertainment. He'd given the pimp Quinn a call and asked for the cleanest in his stable. Gabriel wasn't overly concerned with how they looked so long as they were born with the vagina they had, and it was clean. Quinn had sent over a redhead tonight. Plain looking and unusually tall, she had big, lopsided breasts and a firm, round butt.

As usual, he couldn't perform at first. She had walked in and immediately took him in her mouth, but his member wouldn't respond. She'd been a true professional and had done what she could to get his penis erect. She'd licked, kissed, caressed softly, jerked roughly, but it had remained flaccid.

He wasn't embarrassed. He had been having the problem for years and was used to it by now. And besides, she was a prostitute after all, so Gabriel didn't care what she thought.

At this point in his life, Gabriel was more amused by the process than anything else. He'd order up a working girl and she'd come in and play the role. After some time spent watching them try every trick in the book to get him going, he'd inhale four lines of Columbian snowflake, which got him erect, and spend the next hour pounding out every ounce of frustration. He'd even pay for the whole night just in case he wanted to go a few more rounds before they did exactly what he paid them to do—leave.

He'd been contemplating waking her up by snorting a line off her vagina and going one more time when the phone rang. Gabriel kept two phones in his bedroom and had staged them side by side on a small round table by his bed. The cream-colored phone was the everyday phone, where he received most of his calls. But the crimson phone, the one that was ringing now, had been reserved for members of The Council.

The Council. Gabriel almost laughed out loud when he thought about the silliness of the name. It'd been what the old farts had settled on after far too much discussion for such an insignificant topic. The long-winded debate, as bad luck would have it, portended of what was to become norm for The Council. It turned out it was a pain trying to get twelve old, wealthy men hell-bent on controlling the world to agree on anything.

Gabriel wasn't so much a member of The Council as he was its fixer. Providing information and taking care of problems was his job, and he was very good at it. One of the members would come up with some half-baked idea and it fell on Gabriel to make it happen, no matter how ridiculous and doomed for failure the idea might've been.

He finished the rest of his bourbon in one gulp and stood up. Buzzed and lightheaded from the chemicals flooding his system, he took a second to steady himself before making his way over to the phone. He sat on the edge of the bed and slapped his cheeks, trying to clear the fogginess from his head. He answered the phone halfway through its fourth ring.

"This better be important." Gabriel concentrated on enunciating every syllable, hoping he sounded sober to whomever was on the other end of the line. But hearing his own thick-tongued words, he knew he'd failed.

"Gabriel. You sound like you've been enjoying yourself," Josiah Lynch said from the other end of the line.

Despite the late hour and his advanced age, Josiah sounded as if he were wide awake. His guttural voice was low, and Gabriel could hear the faint traces of his native Ireland when he spoke.

"Yes. I had a few drinks with a friend. Just celebrating tonight's success."

"Friend? Is that what you're calling them these days? Interesting," Josiah said. The line went silent for a few seconds and Gabriel was unsure if he was expected to respond to the comment. "It seems your celebration may be a bit premature."

"What do you mean?"

"There may be a problem."

Gabriel pulled the phone's handset away from his face and let out a frustrated sigh before bringing it back to his ear. "What makes you think there's a problem?"

"Oran should have made it back by now. At the very least, he should have checked in."

"He's probably out celebrating."

"The boat he was to use for his escape is still sitting in the marina at Spring Creek Park."

Gabriel's eyes widened and he sat up straight. "How do you know that?"

"That's not your concern. What is your concern, however, is

doing whatever is necessary to ensure Carolina does not return alive. Is that understood?"

"I don't answer to you, Josiah. I was asked to facilitate. That's it."

"Your job, Gabriel, in case you've forgotten, is to minimize complications. In other words, keep things simple. I suggest you get up, get dressed, and do your job."

Gabriel didn't respond and the phone went silent. He figured Josiah had hung up but waited for a dial tone before he put the receiver down. He rubbed his temples, laid back in the bed, and thought about what Josiah had just told him. He didn't know how any of this fell on his shoulders and wasn't all that concerned. Josiah wasn't his boss—Gabriel didn't have any bosses.

Besides, Josiah had chosen his so-called security expert Oran for this deal. It'd only been Gabriel's job to help move pieces around. To make sure the right people received the information necessary to keep the charade moving forward. As far as Gabriel was concerned, any failures fell directly on Josiah Lynch's shoulders.

"Goddammit, Vicente," Gabriel whispered.

It was just a guess on his part, but Gabriel figured if anyone was going to throw a monkey wrench in this whole thing, it was going to be Vicente Espada. If the girl had made it out alive, the only person with the skills and self-righteous motivation to help her would've been him.

Gabriel had tried to warn him off. More out of concern Vicente would get killed than believing he'd screw everything up. Gabriel even used his "I can see things you can't see" voice to try and sell it, but Vicente hadn't bought it and now he was screwing with their plans.

He had to admit he was a bit surprised. He knew there was a time when Vicente escaping from a human viper pit filled with over two hundred sociopaths was a possibility. But that was a long time ago.

Now, Vicente was just like him. A used-to-be-tough guy who was pushing thirty, and probably suffering from the same emasculating sicknesses as Gabriel. All the fancy Special Forces training in the world didn't mean anything if you spent your nights covered in sweat from nightmares and couldn't get it up for a naked woman.

Gabriel felt his eyes getting heavy and all he wanted to do was sleep. He considered getting up and trying to fix this mess, but he was exhausted, and high as the Goodyear Blimp. It made more sense to wait till morning, see how everything shook out. If it worked out as he thought it would and Vicente and the girl ended up as ghosts, then everything would move forward as planned.

If not, then he would get more directly involved and set everything on its correct course. Either way, Gabriel would wait till the sun was out and the world made more sense. He closed his eyes and allowed himself to drift off to sleep.

Josiah placed the handset back on the switch hook and turned his gaze to the view outside his window. The dark skyscrapers, backlit by the fires that had overtaken the city, loomed large, like fallen titans. He was seated in a high-back leather chair in his den, and despite not having any plans, Josiah was fully dressed in one of his tailored suits.

He brought the Montecristo A cigar up to his lips and sucked in a mouthful of its silky-smooth smoke. Josiah held the smoke in his mouth for several seconds, savoring its rich nutty flavors of almond and hazelnut. It was dark in the room, the only light coming from the end of the lit cigar. He drew in another mouthful of smoke from the Cuban cigar and thought about the mistakes that had been made.

More specifically, he thought about the mistakes that had been made by Oran. Josiah had plans, and whether those plans moved forward relied heavily on what was supposed to happen tonight.

Oran had been tasked with putting everything in motion. Igniting the fuse, so to speak. Had he failed?

Joe Renfrow was the perfect candidate. He was handsome, charismatic, and although he was a Democrat, he leaned far enough to the right to run on a law-and-order platform. The city was a powder keg, full of miscreants waiting for the opportunity to be who they were—thieves and vandals. So, Josiah had provided for that opportunity by arranging for a city-wide blackout. Now, the bottom feeders would spend the next twenty-four hours tearing the city apart.

Afterwards, the city's rich and civilized would be outraged, and Josiah would have the public sentiment he needed to push Renfrow over the top. His "law and order" candidate would win the election in a landslide.

Josiah had been confident his plan would work. Unless of course incompetence reared its ugly head. He had always made it a point to hire the cream of the crop. It was one of the few expenditures he didn't mind. Surrounding himself with the best people had helped get him to the top and had made staying there easier. He'd thought that was what he was paying for when he'd hired Leviathan Security.

Oran had used a shadow network of assassins and thugs to reach out to Abaddon and propose an opportunity he couldn't ignore. Kidnap and kill a beautiful heiress for a cool million dollars. Once she was dead, Josiah's bought-and-paid-for media empire would report the news. How the kidnapped socialite had been taken against her will to a lawless land ruled by Godless criminals. And how, despite her loving father's best attempts, she had been brutally raped and murdered. The world would be outraged, and it would demand action. Actions that he was more than ready to take.

But whether out of incompetence or betrayal, Oran had failed. And now it seemed Carolina may have gotten away. Josiah had built his empire on being able to read the terrain and stay three steps ahead of everyone else. But now, as the world stood on the precipice of madness, he had no idea what might happen next.

The horde was barreling toward them. Vic had checked every corner of the roof but didn't see a way to get them both off it without breaking a bone or two. They were about thirty feet above the ground and the metal door leading inside the building had been bolted shut. Vic had found what was left of the building's fire escape on the far side of the building—one flight of stairs with no landing and no rail, hanging loosely from the building's exterior wall.

"What do we do now?" Carolina asked.

He glanced at her but didn't respond. He tried to come up with something clever or reassuring to say, but the sounds of the Kings clomping toward them from other rooftops, combined with their lack of escape options, left him at a loss for words. He was confident he could make it off the roof in one piece, but he wasn't as certain about Carolina. Out of time and options, Vic decided the only choice was to face whoever was coming for them and go down swinging.

He swallowed nervously as he stared across at the roof they'd jumped from. *Alright, this is it. Calm down, breathe, and get ready.* A soft whistle followed by a horse's neigh emanated from the alley below.

"Did you hear that?" Carolina sounded as surprised as he felt.

"Yeah."

They stepped to the roof's edge and peered over. Jerrick, Jasmine, Tango, and two other Outlaws were sitting proud and strong on top of their horses. Vic took a deep breath, allowing himself a small feeling of hope.

"Thought you two could use a ride," Jerrick said with a wink and smile.

"Be right down." Vic turned to Carolina. "All right, same thing as before, just a little more of a drop. I'm going to lower you down as much as I can, then you'll drop down onto the horse."

Carolina nodded and lowered herself over the edge just as she had done on the other roof, this time quicker and sure-footed. He took a hold of her arms and lowered her a few more feet. He waited for Jerrick to bring his horse closer, but he didn't move.

Jerrick was leaning forward in his saddle, his arms resting on the horn. He nonchalantly pointed toward the bottom of the building, directly underneath Carolina. Vic followed Jerrick's finger to the large pile of full trash bags stacked against the building. He felt foolish for not having seen them earlier.

Vic released his grip on her arms and Carolina landed in the pile of trash-filled plastic bags. He lowered himself over the roof's edge and waited for Carolina to clear out. She scrambled out of the way, and he let go.

He landed in the trash pile with his legs slightly above his head. He grabbed one of the bags and pulled himself up to a standing position. When he got to his feet, Carolina was sitting on Jerrick's horse, with her arms wrapped tightly around his waist.

"You coming or what?" Jasmine asked.

He turned to his right and was slightly startled when he came face to face with Jasmine's horse. The animal's black eyes looked down at Vic with curiosity. Its ears were pointed at Vic, and it moved its head in small circles as if it was trying to gain a sense of him. Vic lost himself for a second, hypnotized by the horse's beauty and tranquil nature.

"I think she's pretty too, but it's time to go," Jerrick said.

He took hold of Jasmine's hand and lifted himself onto the horse. They were in a dead-end alley, so the only way in or out was through Euclid Avenue. Vic looked toward their escape route. There were lights from the Kings' vehicles shining on the dark asphalt. The lights grew larger as the vehicles got closer.

"Tango," Jerrick said.

"On it," Tango said.

He dug his heels into his horse's side and his horse trotted toward the lights and noise, with the other two Outlaws close behind. Jerrick made a clicking sound with his mouth and his horse inched forward, Jasmine's horse followed behind. Tango and the two Outlaws slowed their pace as they neared the alley entrance. When Jerrick and Jasmine got close to them, Tango and the two Outlaws' horses raced off toward the Savage Kings search party.

Jerrick turned onto Euclid Avenue and headed in the opposite direction. Jasmine leaned forward, snapped the lead, and her horse went into a full gallop close behind Jerrick's horse.

Shouting and cursing from the Savage Kings trailed close behind them. Vic turned his head toward the noise and saw silhouettes of Tango and the two other Outlaws sitting atop their horses. They moved back and forth in front of a wall of bright headlights for a few seconds before heading toward Vic and the others. He faced the road ahead just as they were turning onto Pitkin Avenue.

"Don't worry, they'll be alright. Them fools have cars, but this is our neighborhood. Don't nobody know their way around these streets like us," Jasmine said.

"Uh huh." Vic could hardly hear her over the horse's hooves landing heavy on the street and his own heart beating loudly in his chest.

"What were you waiting for back there?" Jasmine asked.

"Huh?" He'd heard her over the noise but was surprised by the seeming randomness of the question. And considering their current predicament, her eerily calm demeanor threw him off a bit as well. "What are you talking about?"

"On the roof. What were you waiting for?"

"I don't know."

They had created some distance, so it was dark for a few seconds. But then the mob turned the corner behind them, filling the night with bright lights and loud noises. Tango and the two other Outlaws turned down a side street. Vic figured they were trying to get the mob to follow them.

"Did you think we were going to bring the horses to you? So, you could jump on them like in one of those corny old Westerns?"

"No. Well, maybe. Shit, I don't know."

"Ha. You did, didn't you? That. Is. Hi-la-ri-ous."

"I think it's great that you're having such a good time, but maybe we can talk about this later."

"It's a date."

They headed north on Crystal Street, made a quick turn into an alley, and continued traveling west between buildings. Vic's arms were wrapped tightly around Jasmine's waist, and his body was pressed close to hers. She snapped the lead and kicked her heels into her horse's sides, willing the animal to gallop even faster.

When they reached the intersection at Montauk Avenue they were met by a wall of buildings, so the alleyway that had provided them some cover was at an end. Fortunately, the lights that had blanketed them were gone, and the once overwhelming sounds were now a bit fainter.

Vic glanced behind them when they turned back onto Pitkin Avenue and saw their pursuers were nowhere in sight. He was about to crack a smile when he felt Jasmine's body tense up. Vic turned his head to the front. Four or five cars, fully engulfed in flames and lined up bumper to bumper, blocked the roadway ahead. Jasmine slowed her horse to a trot and pulled up alongside Jerrick who was stopped and checking the area.

"This is as far as we go," Jerrick said.

"What do you mean? Can't we go around?" Carolina asked.

Vic and Jerrick locked eyes and Vic nodded. They both knew this wouldn't be the last obstacle. Although there were three or four other directions they could go, the Kings were after them and dead set on bringing them to Oran. Vic figured there would be blockades everywhere.

"We can go the rest of the way on foot." Vic dismounted Jasmine's horse.

"What do you mean? It'd be faster and safer if we stay on the horses and in a group," Carolina said.

Vic walked over to Jerrick's horse and extended his hand to help Carolina down. "They've helped as much as they can. We can make it the rest of the way on our own. Hurry up, we have to go."

Carolina's head darted frantically between Jerrick and Jasmine. When her eyes returned to Vic, her expression had changed from confusion to understanding. Jerrick, Jasmine, and the other Outlaws had risked a lot by helping them, but they would only go so far, and they had reached that limit.

Carolina took Vic's hand and he helped her off the horse. He took a step back and glanced up at Jerrick. "Thanks for the ride."

"Ain't nothing to it." Jerrick didn't look at Vic. He was focused on the road behind them, watching for Kings. "Here they come. If I were you, I'd make like Harriet Tubman—follow the underground railroad to safety." Jerrick nodded to his left toward the subway entrance on Shepherd Avenue.

It was a risk to try and walk the tunnels. It wasn't that Vic was afraid—he'd been in them dozens of times when he was a kid. Either out of boredom, stupidity, or a dangerous combination of the two, he and his friends would walk the tunnels. They'd make their way from platform to platform, staying ahead of the train and the transit cops who followed behind.

But going into an enclosed space in complete darkness with only one way out didn't seem like the best idea. If the Kings followed them into the tunnels, Vic and Carolina would be in a literal race for their lives. It would take every bit of speed and stamina in their bodies to stay ahead.

On the other hand, maybe the Kings wouldn't follow. If they were too stupid to consider that Vic and Carolina would try to escape through the subway tunnels, maybe they'd continue searching for them topside. The Kings might waste time spinning their wheels on a fruitless search while Vic and Carolina made their way to a safe place. Either way, their options were less than ideal.

Vic looked back at Jerrick. "I owe you."

"Yeah, you do. And you can count on me collecting sometime soon." Jerrick snapped his horse's lead and it galloped away. Jasmine and her horse took off behind him.

Vic and Carolina sprinted toward the subway entrance. They raced down the steps, into the underground station unsure what waited for them.

twenty-five

TERI AND KAI followed Sonia into a four-story abandoned and decrepit building, with the rest of her Ruthless Ones trailing behind. The interior of the building was almost completely dark, and the acrid mix of smoke and sulfur, the remnants of a past fire, filled Teri's nostrils. She figured the building's owner, in a soulless attempt to either collect insurance or run off unwanted tenants, had taken a match to this place. Whether for mayhem or money, arson had become a common occurrence in The Fear, resulting in neighborhoods filled with detritus and uninhabitable structures.

Footsteps, a combination of rubber soles and wooden heels, echoed off the concrete walls as gang members scampered around in the shadows. Water dripped from somewhere high. The sound of striking matches filled the emptiness, and after a few seconds candlelight illuminated the area around them, revealing the large empty room they were standing in. Several long metal beams stood floor to ceiling in various locations, and there didn't appear to be any doors or walls in the large, industrial space.

Teri and Kai walked side by side behind Sonia. She stared at the Grim Reaper on the back of Sonia's denim vest. It had been painted in the gang's colors, metallic blue and white, and looked homemade and cheap. There were obvious flaws in the sloppily drawn eyes and the uneven shape of the scythe blades. Regardless of its artistic quality, the image was dark and threatening, which she assumed was the point. The menacing character bounced in rhythm with Sonia's steps and its toothy grin made it seem as if it was taunting them.

Sonia walked slowly, seemingly doing her part to prolong the event. Everything about the situation, from the lit candles to the whispers floating out from the shadows, seemed ritualistic and ceremonial. It reminded Teri of scenes from books she had read like *Heart of Darkness* and *The Most Dangerous Game*. Stories where man, as a species, had devolved to its most primal form, and preying on each other was more about sport than survival.

After a few minutes they came to a stop at a large wall. Sonia turned and stared at them but didn't speak. Taunts and laughter sprang forth from the blackness.

"I appreciate the whole haunted house thing you guys have going on here, but really—what the fuck?" Teri took a few steps toward Sonia. "We came here for help. Vic might be in serious trouble, and you want to waste time with this bullshit?"

Sonia's face was expressionless. She lit a cigarette, inhaled deeply, and turned away from Teri. "You keep mentioning this person Vic as if you expect his name to mean something here."

"Well, that *was* sort of the plan," Kai said.

"I know the lighting is dim in here but take a look around." Sonia extended her hand and motioned around the room as if she were presenting a prize, like one of the models on *The Price is Right*. "This Vic guy you keep mentioning, if he ever was a part of what we got going here, has been gone a long time. This is a whole new generation of Ruthless Ones, and none of us know who the fuck you're talking about."

Teri scanned the room. The faces staring back at her, now slightly more visible in the candlelight, were young and completely indifferent. Perhaps Sonia was right, and Teri had wasted her time coming here. Shit, even Teri wasn't quite sure what she'd expected to find.

Maybe on some level she thought it would play like a scene from a fairytale. She would say Vic's name, as if she was whispering the name of a legendary king returning from a far-off land, and it would evoke a call to arms. Hundreds of loyal followers would spring to action in defense of their long-lost leader.

But that wasn't the reality. Vic hadn't been back here in over a decade. In a place where time is measured against the speed of a bullet, it may as well have been a hundred years. A whole generation of Ruthless Ones had come and gone, and Vic's name meant less than zero to this current group.

Teri glared at Sonia. "So, if you're not going to help us, what are we doing in here? What's the point of all this?"

"The *point*, sweetie, is I don't like your ass. And if you remember correctly, I gave you a chance to leave. But you didn't take it, decided to open your big, fucking mouth. So, now you're going to have to take your chances with the Box."

"The what?" Teri asked.

Sonia stepped aside, revealing a large, oval table. Teri had been distracted by her own thoughts, so she hadn't noticed it till now. One of their members emerged from the shadows and placed two lit candles on the table, beside a plywood box. It was rectangular and large, about four feet long, three feet wide, and three feet high, with multiple cup-size holes cut into the top half. Black burn marks spotted the box's lower half.

"It's something one of the OGs came up with back in the day. Shit, it might have even been your boy Vic. A way to test prospects. See if they had any balls. Now we have other ways to check on that, so we don't get a chance to use this as much as we'd like," Sonia said.

Teri figured "other ways" meant the gang had evolved from juvenile methods of initiation for prospective members to other, more challenging tests. She had no idea what those tests included, but she assumed any rite of passage for this group involved some form of mayhem.

"So, what are you using it for now?" Teri asked.

"A little bit of this, a little bit of that." An obnoxious smirk was plastered on Sonia's face.

Teri was about to respond when a sound emitted from the box. The murmuring from the crowd had grown louder so the scratching from inside the box was barely audible. Sonia's lips curled up into a mischievous grin and the room went silent, watching for Teri's reaction.

Teri tilted her ear toward the box. She heard the scratching again, but this time it was accompanied by soft squeaking sounds. Her pulse quickened.

She'd been holding her breath and now felt as if she might faint. She stood straight up and took a deep breath as she stepped away from the box, her eyes fixed on the cup-size holes. *No. Can't be. Rats.* She shuddered.

"I've seen that look before." Sonia laughed. "That's the 'Holy shit, what did I get myself into?' look."

"Nope." Teri glared at Sonia. "I know exactly what you're planning. And I'll tell you what—I ain't playing your fucking games. So, you can just cut the bullshit."

Sonia stopped laughing and a coldness washed over her face. "*Mira a esta pendeja.* What'd you think was gonna happen? That you were just gonna walk into our neighborhood, ask your questions like you're calling the shots, and then walk out with no problems?"

"That's exactly what we're going to do," Teri said.

Sonia stepped toward Teri, invading her space. Teri knew it was juvenile, but she was determined to win her stare-down with Sonia. She'd tried to use her words but that didn't work. Now she figured the only way out of this situation was good old primal aggression.

The two women were a few seconds into their standoff when

Sonia blew out a sharp whistle. Before Teri could react, she heard the hammer being cocked on a revolver behind her. She turned around and saw a man pointing a gun at the back of Kai's head. Two other men grabbed Kai by his arms, one on each side, and forced him to his knees.

"Ain't talking so tough now, are you, bitch?" She felt Sonia's breath on her ear as she whispered the words.

Teri exhaled deeply and turned back to Sonia. "So, what now?"

"It's pretty simple. You circle the Box, sticking your hand in each hole. You can't pull your hand out till I say you can. You make it around once without stopping, we can have another conversation about you and your boyfriend walking out of here."

Teri stared at the box. She pictured dozens of rats crawling around inside it—biting and clawing. Her heart was beating through her chest, and it was hard to breathe. She trembled as childhood memories of the vermin flooded her like nightmares come to life.

Just hearing the sounds emanating from the box made her queasy with terror. Every instinct she had was screaming for her to run. To push past Sonia and take her chances with the crowd. But she glanced at Kai with the gun to his head, and running wasn't an option.

Teri still wasn't sure why he'd done it, but Kai had come out here with her. He could have stayed tucked away in Chinatown, far away from the madness they were dealing with tonight. Instead, Kai chose to come with her. He'd willingly ventured into enemy territory to help Vic, someone she thought he didn't even particularly like, and now he was injured and stuck with her on the wrong side of a loaded gun.

Without saying a word, Teri started toward the table, bumping her shoulder into Sonia's as she passed her. She stopped at the head of the table and faced the crowd. After a brief hesitation, Teri lifted her hand, ready to insert it in the first hole.

"Hold on," Sonia said.

Teri pulled her hand back as two young women approached the table holding lit candles. At first Teri thought they were there to provide more light for the show that was about to start. But then they began moving methodically around the table, holding their candles' lit wicks against the box. The flames massaged the box's wooden sides, leaving behind more black scars.

The faint scratching Teri had been hearing now sounded like violent clawing and gnawing, and the soft squeaking had grown frantic and loud. The rats, already scared and probably starving, had been driven into a rage-filled panic.

"Now you can start." Sonia smirked.

Teri stared down at the box. The crowd's whispers and giggles, once obnoxiously loud, had been quieted. Her own heartbeat reverberated loudly in her ears, like ceremonial drums. The rats' frenzied movements shook the box, and their squeaking now sounded like human screams. The beads of perspiration that had been forming on her brow streamed down her face, stinging her eyes.

Teri wiped the sweat from her eyes with the back of her forearm. She moved her hand from her face down toward the box. She held her hand over the first hole and hesitated. For how long exactly, she wasn't quite sure. Every sound was deafening but indistinguishable and every movement was slow and blurry.

Teri took a deep breath and lowered her hand into the first hole. She kept her hand balled into a fist with her fingers tucked in tight.

"You're gonna have to do better than that," Sonia said.

"What?"

"Lower."

"You said 'stick your hand in each hole.' That's what I'm doing."

"Don't play with me. Lower."

Teri swallowed hard and went lower, till her arm from the elbow down had disappeared into the box. The air felt warm and moist, and she could feel the rats rubbing their bodies and tails against her forearm and hand as they scurried past. Their fur was soft and smooth, and their tails felt like human skin.

Then she felt sharp pricks on her skin. One, maybe two at first, reaching out and exploring her arm. Nothing to get worked up about. Within seconds, the numbers multiplied, and she could feel them all over her hand and forearm, scratching and clawing. Teri's breath caught in her throat, and she made a move to pull her arm free.

"Not yet," Sonia said.

Teri locked eyes with Sonia and silently pleaded with her to end the torture. Sonia flashed a dark grin and shook her head. She had no intention of ending the perverse game.

The rats were all over her arm now and seemed to have grown more ravenous. The clawing and scratching had torn through Teri's skin, and she let out a pained scream as she pulled her arm out of the hole. She brought her arm to her chest and took a step back from the box.

"Bitch, I told you not yet," Sonia yelled.

"Fuck you. They were tearing at my arm like it's a chocolate-covered turkey leg."

Sonia glared at Teri for several seconds. "All right then. One down, twelve to go." Teri stared at the box. *No more. Please.* Sonia rolled her eyes and sighed. "Come on already. Let's get this shit over with."

Teri inched back to the box and stood over the second hole. The back of her head was throbbing, and she felt dizzy. She wiped her sweaty palms on her jeans as she readied herself. Looking at the scratches that had drawn blood from her right forearm, she decided to use her other hand and hope for the best.

"Hold on, Sonia."

The deep, male voice came from the other side of the room, away from the crowd. Teri looked over, searching for the source, and saw the silhouette of a man standing in the threshold of the entrance door. He lit a cigarette and walked toward them.

The shadows retreated as he drew closer, revealing the man behind the voice. Short and thin, his long, dark hair flowed out from the dark baseball cap he was wearing.

"What's going on?" the man asked.

He was speaking to Sonia, but the man's gaze was fixed on Teri. Despite his size, or lack thereof, there was something in his intense eyes and the way he carried himself. He held his head high and he didn't walk so much as he strutted—like John Travolta in *Welcome Back Kotter*. The man exuded confidence.

"It ain't nothing I can't handle, Ray Ray. This chick kept asking about someone called Vic. Wouldn't take no for an answer, so I decided to put her on the Box," Sonia said.

"You decided, huh? Without checking with me first?" Ray Ray's hard stare went back and forth between Sonia and Teri. "So, what's going on with Vic?" He furrowed his brow, and his eyes went from intense to curious.

"Do you know him?" Teri asked.

"Let's just say I *knew* him. What's going on?"

Teri stepped around the table and made her way to Ray Ray and Sonia. "I think he's in trouble. He needs your help." She noticed he was looking past her, so Teri glanced over her shoulder. Kai was kneeling behind her, the gun still pointed at the back of his head. She turned back to Ray Ray. "*We* need your help."

His hard stare and strange mouth twitch made Teri uncomfortable. It was subtle, a slight bouncing of the skin near his right nostril. But it made Ray Ray appear unreasonably angry, as if he was on the edge of exploding. Teri figured it may have been intentional. A premeditated method of intimidation made possible by years of studious practice in front of a broken mirror.

She was too tired to be impressed "Are you going to help us or not?"

"I haven't decided yet." He shifted his gaze back and forth between Teri and Kai.

"Why do you keep looking at him? I'm the one talking to you."

"Because me and Kai go way back." Ray Ray started toward Kai, brushing Teri's shoulder with his own as he passed by her. "And he knows he shouldn't be here."

"Hold on." Teri hurried past Ray Ray, stepping between him and Kai. "He came to help Vic."

"Agreeing to help Vic was his first mistake. Coming here was his second." Ray Ray continued toward Kai and stood over him. He nodded at the three young men standing guard, and they backed away. "What the fuck are you doing here, Kai?"

Kai stood up and, although he tried his best to mask it, grimaced with pain. He stared at Ray Ray defiantly. "Times are tough, so I started a theme tour. Like one of them ghost tours in New Orleans. Except there ain't no ghosts on this tour, just a lot of assholes and dumb bitches." He flashed a pained version of his familiar grin.

"Same old Kai. I've been waiting a long time to cut that tongue out of that smart mouth of yours."

"Well, now I feel kind of bad. I haven't thought about you at all. You should really consider taking up a hobby or something. That kind of obsession can't be good for your mental health."

Teri rolled her eyes at the exchange. She thought the bullshit macho dialogue between Kai and Ray Ray was comical, bordering on sad. It was clear the two had a history. What wasn't as clear was the reason for the bad blood. Teri hoped the tension was the residual effects of years fighting it out as rival gang members. But she feared it had something to do with a woman, and more specifically, Millie. She figured childish gang crap could be worked out, but when it came to love triangles, the only resolution usually involved a lot of blood.

"Can you two cut the shit?" Teri stepped between them. She

turned her gaze from Kai back to Ray Ray. "Are you going to help Vic or not?"

Ray Ray kept his hard stare on Kai, and she assumed Kai was staring right back at him. The right side of Ray Ray's upper lip lifted slightly, and he placed the tip of his tongue between his teeth and upper lip. The act created an obnoxious whistle, sucking sound that made Teri cringe.

He didn't answer immediately, his eyes moving back and forth between her and Kai. Teri tried to read him, but Ray Ray was stone-faced and emotionless.

Finally, his eyes fixed on Teri. "Tell me more."

twenty-six

VIC AND CAROLINA cleared the first flight of stairs quickly, emerging at the fare control area of the subway station's mezzanine. A few overhead fluorescent lights were still on, so he figured they were being powered by an AC power backup connection.

"That's funny," Carolina said.

"What is?"

"There's more light down here than above."

Vic chuckled. "I was thinking the same thing."

They stopped in front of the station's unmanned token booth, and he surveyed their surroundings. The platform was completely empty. The familiar smells of the subway—a mixture of Creosote, steel brake dust, electrical smoke, trash, and human waste—filled the air.

"Do you think they'll follow us down here?" Carolina asked.

"Maybe. Probably."

"So, what do we do now? Can we hide down here?"

"No. There isn't anywhere to hide. We're going to have to follow the tracks."

Carolina looked around. "Okay." She sounded tired and defeated. "It's strange how things work out."

"What do you mean?"

"I've lived in New York for almost ten years, but I've never been in the subway."

"Really?"

"Yes." She thought about Abaddon's words, accusing her of having never left the comfort of her wealthy surroundings in Manhattan, and she was embarrassed. "There wasn't much of a need. There was always a car available. And I was constantly being warned away from using them. You know...with all the muggings and assaults that occur."

He picked up on her embarrassment. "Hey, you're preaching to the choir. If I can avoid it, I don't ride the subway either." He smiled reassuringly. "Come on. This way." Vic started toward the entrance turnstiles.

He eyed the metal turnstile and briefly considered hopping it, as he had done so many times in his youth. Vic figured the trip down memory lane wasn't worth the expended energy and decided to enter through the "Exit Only" gate. He ignored the warning sign on the yellow gate and pulled it toward him, holding it open so Carolina could pass through ahead of him.

They walked quickly through the long, wide mezzanine, toward the stairs leading down to the A train platform. Rows of graffiti covered steel pillars, created walkways. Overhead, a long fluorescent light bulb, running parallel with the steel pillars, lit their way. Its light reflected off the ceramic-tile walls, filling the large space with a soft bluish glow.

Vic and Carolina raced down the steps, stopping when they reached the platform so he could look around. Mosaic signs spelled out SHEPHERD AVE in bold white lettering along the top of the platform wall. The westbound A train was stopped at about the platform's halfway point, so he figured it'd been pulling into the station when the power had gone out. It was quiet and as far as he could tell, they were alone.

The track was completely clear ahead of the train, so they made their way to the end of the platform. Vic walked down the six narrow, yellow steps leading to the tracks, but Carolina didn't follow. He glanced up at her. She was standing on the platform, her eyes fixed on the tracks below.

"What's wrong?" Vic asked.

"Won't we get electrocuted if we step on the wrong thing?"

Too broke and indifferent to pay subway tolls, Vic had walked the tracks a lot when he was a kid. He'd heard from neighborhood kids that the most dangerous part of the track was the third rail. It was where the electricity to power the train was generated and was located near the center divider.

The information had been confirmed when Vic was fourteen years old and Eddie "Doughnut" Dembowski was electrocuted on the L train tracks near Montrose Avenue. Doughnut was being chased by three members of Satan's Soldiers after having just cheated them in a dice game. He tried to avoid his pursuers by running across the tracks, but he tripped and fell face-first on the third rail.

"Not if we stick close to this side. There's a walkway against the wall here." Vic pointed at a narrow dark-gray walkway set at the base of the track wall nearest them. "And besides, I'm pretty sure the power is out everywhere, including the power that runs through the rail. Otherwise, why is that train stopped?"

A two-note whistle echoed behind him. He turned and saw the silhouette of a man about twenty feet in front of him. Two more silhouettes emerged from the shadows and flanked both sides of the first figure.

"Nice night for a walk, huh?" one of the figures said.

"Not bad," Vic said.

"What are you two doing down here?"

"We were on the train when the power went out. We got tired of waiting so we decided to walk. What about you guys?" Even though they were concealed by shadows, Vic didn't think the three people were Kings. He hoped if he kept his tone friendly and played it right, he and Carolina could avoid more complications and move on without too much delay.

"Us? We live here."

For as long as he could remember, Vic had heard stories of New York City's subterranean dwellers. He'd always chalked it up to urban legend, like Area 51 or the Chupacabra. But considering the city's homeless problem, it made sense some of them would find refuge in the hundreds of miles of tunnels the city had been built on.

"Uh huh. Well, it was nice to meet you fellas, but we need to get going."

"Nah, that's not going to work. You two seem to be in an awful hurry to get on these tracks. And seeing as how it'd be much simpler, and safer, to exit through the station, I'm figuring that lynch mob we spotted on the street is looking for you."

So much for avoiding complications. "All right, what do you want to let us pass?"

"What do ya got?"

Settling up with Gabriel had left Vic with twenty dollars. He figured he would need cash for a cab if they ever found one, but decided he'd cross that bridge if they came to it. He reached into his pocket, pulled out the twenty, and presented it to the man.

"That's a start," said the lead figure.

"It's all I have," Vic said.

"What about the princess back there?"

"Nah, that's not going to happen."

The three men inched forward. "You sure about that?"

Vic balled his hands into fists. "Positive."

The lead figure was quiet for a few seconds. "All right, Prince Valiant, how about this—you answer a riddle correctly and we'll let you pass."

"Are you serious?"

"As a heart attack."

"Come on, guys, we don't have time for this." Vic balled up the twenty and tossed it on the ground in front of the lead figure. "Just take the money and let us pass."

"You can always head back through the station, see how that works out for you."

Even if Vic was good at riddles, which he wasn't, they didn't have time to waste trying to solve one. The Savage Kings were on their heels, so going back the way they came was a nonstarter. It seemed the only way forward was through the three silhouettes.

Vic started toward the men. "All right, let's—"

"What's your riddle?" Carolina asked.

Vic stopped and glanced back at her. He turned back to the three men.

"Well, look who decided to join the party." The lead figure chuckled. "Alrighty then: You measure my life in hours, and I serve you by expiring. I'm quick when I'm thin and slow when I'm fat. The wind is my enemy."

After everything that'd gone on the last few hours, Vic's brain was fried. As far as he was concerned, the guy sounded like Charlie Brown's teacher.

"A candle," Carolina said.

The lead figure leaned down and picked up the money. "Godspeed, princess." The three figures receded into the shadows, back through the side tunnels they navigated daily.

Vic looked back at Carolina. She nodded quietly and descended the stairs. Vic waited till she reached the last step and started walking ahead of her, leading her along the narrow pathway.

"I'm impressed," Vic said.

"Don't be. It's an old riddle."

Vic grinned and continued forward. He planned to keep to the tunnels for a little while, till they made it to the Broadway Junction Station. There they could make their way to the J train line, and the rest of their trek would be on elevated tracks, out in the open.

"We should be able to follow the tracks most of the way. We'll have to use the streets again when we get to Flushing Avenue, but we should be good till then. I think we lost them."

Carolina didn't respond and they walked in silence for several minutes.

"You know him, don't you?" He glanced at her but didn't respond. She was dividing her attention between him and the pathway, her arms folded across her chest as if she was cold. "Abaddon. You know him, right?"

Her question surprised him. Not the question itself—Vic figured it would be coming at some point. But Carolina had been withdrawn and quiet for a while so the sudden break in the silence put him a bit off balance.

"Yeah, I know him." Vic returned his gaze back to the path ahead. "He hired me to find you."

Carolina stopped walking. "What?"

Vic turned and faced her. "Relax. It's not what you think. It was after you'd been kidnapped. Oran works for your father. He tracked me down and hired me to find—"

"My father? What are you talking about? And why do you keep calling that freak Oran?"

Even in the darkness, Vic could see the confusion in her eyes. The truth was, he understood exactly how she must have been feeling. His head had been spinning ever since Oran had made his appearance at the gym dressed like he'd just walked out of a Motorhead concert. But he couldn't stop or slow down to explain now.

"Carolina, I know you're confused and scared. I am too. I'll explain everything, but we got to keep moving."

She didn't budge. He understood her hesitation but hoped what they'd been through together would be enough to convince her she could trust him. They stood facing each other, separated by fear and suspicion.

Vic was about to speak again when Carolina started walking. He turned and fell in step beside her, the sound of crunching gravel and dirt beneath their shoes amplified by their silence. Vic spent a few minutes collecting his thoughts, then he started from the beginning and told her everything that had occurred from the moment Oran reentered his life.

Abaddon had arrived in time to watch Jerrick and his Immortals ride off through the blockade of fire. He'd stopped the pursuit after getting word from his rooftop scouts that nobody was riding bitch on any of the Immortals' horses. He planned to catch up with Jerrick another day, make him pay for interfering with his business tonight. But right now, Abaddon's attention was on the rabbits he was chasing. He knew Vic and Carolina were in the tunnels.

Abaddon looked toward the subway entrance and smiled as he thought back to his early days, when he'd finally made peace with what he was. Before making it to Vietnam, he'd spent three months at the Edgewood Arsenal in Maryland playing lab monkey for a bunch of sadists in white lab coats. Part of the Department of Defense's Medical Research Volunteer Program, they'd conducted experiments on him and other guinea pigs to evaluate the impact of low-dose chemical warfare. It would have been bearable except for the fact that he hadn't volunteered, and the members of Mengele's lost tribe were using anything but low doses.

At some point, all hell had broken loose in Nam, and the shot callers decided they needed Marines over there, not tucked away inside a lab in Maryland. By that time, Abaddon had been pumped so full of hallucinogens the whole world seemed like a Lewis Carroll book. Before he knew it, Abaddon found himself assigned to 2nd Battalion, 7th Marines and on the south side of Hill 562 facing the Qui Nhon Airfield. The Two-Seven spent the next few months in one firefight after another, and like pretty much every other outfit stuck in Vietnam, they were finding tunnels built and used by the enemy everywhere they stepped.

In 1946, the Viet Minh had begun digging a network of tunnels under the jungle terrain of South Vietnam during their war for independence from the French. By the time the Vietnam War broke out in the 1960s, the Viet Cong had hundreds of miles of tunnels they'd used to mount surprise attacks on American and South Vietnamese forces. It'd become common practice to send Marines and soldiers into the tunnels looking for enemy combatants. Abaddon, because he was so skinny when he'd first arrived, had been regularly tasked with the job.

It'd been rough going the first time, no doubt about it. Especially having to drag along that spaz Cornelius. But Abaddon had made it through those tunnels without a scratch. And after he'd found and killed the gray goblins, he was hooked, and his thirst grew.

Most of the fellas hated it, and they weren't wrong for feeling that way. Fucking Charlie had set booby traps everywhere. Tripwires attached to grenades or boxes full of scorpions and poisonous snakes designed to turn over onto soldiers and Marines' heads. But not him though—he'd get a rush every time he inserted himself headfirst into one of the spider holes. He loved hunting the goblins and everybody knew it, so after a while he became the go-to guy.

Abaddon closed his eyes and remembered being inside a tunnel with nothing but a flashlight, his .45 pistol, and his K-Bar knife for protection. Crawling face first through the dirt on his belly an inch at a time, his hands buried in the earth ahead of him. Standing here now, Abaddon rubbed his thumbs and fingers together remembering how the dirt had felt surprisingly cold against his skin

Alone, in the infinite blackness where the only sound had been his own breathing, the minutes had felt like hours. Just when he thought there was no end to the darkness and he was inside a tunnel to nowhere, he'd smell them. The stink of gook food and human filth grew more intense as he'd gotten closer to his prey. Pretty soon the orange glow from their fires would light the world around him and he'd find himself in one of their base camps.

Most times he'd find an empty room. But the still-burning fire and pots of boiling water had let him know he'd just missed them. Abaddon would collect anything he thought might be important. Then he'd set the C4 charge and head back the way he'd come before blowing the whole thing to shit.

Occasionally, Abaddon would find them in there. The goblins with their gray skin and big, wide-set eyes—and he'd execute them. He licked his lips as he remembered how he'd rid the world of the little monsters by shooting them in their heads or slashing their throats. He'd spent his last year as a teenager going into tunnels and killing goblins.

Soon, it'd become too difficult to cover up the exterminations and as quickly as it'd started, the goblin hunt was over. Usually, someone like him would have been treated like a rabid dog and put down. The military would have sent a cleaner to inject him with potassium chloride, make it look like his heart had stopped beating while he was sleeping.

But someone high up must have had the epiphany that killers are needed to fight wars, because Abaddon wasn't murdered in his sleep. It'd been decided a change of scenery was in order, and he was sent to Marine Corps Air Station Kaneohe Bay in Hawaii for some rest and relaxation. While Abaddon was away, he dropped the Velez part of his last name and after a while, Oran Burke-Velez was just Oran Burke and on his way to Ranger school. He eventually made his way to Force Recon, where he met his old brother and current adversary, Vicente Espada.

"What now?" he heard Machai ask, pulling him back to the present.

For this whole operation to work, everyone involved, including David, Tre, and Walter, had had to believe everything was on the up and up. They'd needed to think that Abaddon—or Oran to them—had done his part to ensure the mission would be successful. His responsibilities as team leader included locating, scouting, and reconnaissance.

That's where Vic had come in. Once the fellas knew Abaddon had hired one of his old Force Recon buddies to locate the princess, someone from these neighborhoods no less, it'd seemed like he was doing his part, and it was just like any other mission. But therein lay the problem—and the solution.

Having grown up out here, Vic probably thought he could figure out a clear path to safety, a route only he knew about. The only problem with that idea was Abaddon had grown up out here too. He knew the terrain and had the added benefit of over two hundred Kings flooding every corner of the streets from here to the East River. Of course, it didn't hurt that he could draw on almost four years of stories about life back home while sitting in foxholes to predict where Vic was heading.

"They're headed to the Williamsburg. Take some of the fellas ahead to the Broadway Junction station. I'll take the rest into the tunnels." Abaddon stared down into the subway entrance.

There was a ruckus coming from behind the burning cars. Abaddon peered past the flames and spotted Jerrick sitting on top of his horse. They locked eyes, and a smirk came across Jerrick's face. Was it a challenge? Abaddon didn't see any other Black cowboys, but he assumed they were out there too, waiting to rumble.

"Should we go after him?" Machai asked.

Abaddon glared at Jerrick. Every bone in his body was itching to go after the smug prick. But the longer he stood there, the more he realized what Jerrick was doing.

"Nah. We've wasted enough time. We'll settle up with those motherfuckers later. Right now, just do what I told ya."

Machai nodded and took off toward the Williamsburg Bridge. Abaddon glared at Jerrick for a few seconds before heading into the subway station. He sped down the steps and a sense of nostalgia overwhelmed him, like returning home after a long time away.

twenty-seven

WHEN THEY ARRIVED at the Broadway Junction Station, Vic and Carolina made their way out of the tunnel and into the large mezzanine. Aside from a few commuters who seemed to be waiting for the power to return, the station was almost entirely empty. The two had hurried through the large, multi-level station, reaching the deserted J train platform quickly. They'd made their way onto the tracks and were almost to the next station at Halsey Street when the sky opened.

The thunder had been rumbling in the distance for a while, but now the rain had finally come. The drizzle made a soft popping sound as it fell on the dirt and gravel that lay between the train tracks. They were out in the open now, high above the ground on the elevated tracks. Carolina felt soft, warm droplets on her skin, so she looked up and toward the sky, hoping the falling water would mask her tears.

She had listened in silence as Vic told her about his relationship with Abaddon, whom he kept calling Oran, and recounting everything he had experienced in the past few days. He'd told her about the offer from Abaddon to help find her, and of the other men who had joined them on the rescue attempt. Vic even spoke about his protégé Teri and their information-seeking escapade in Chinatown. He'd shared a lot, but except for saying he believed what Abaddon had said about her father's involvement, Vic didn't have any facts regarding Josiah Lynch's role in everything that had happened.

Carolina had listened silently, trying to process everything he'd told her. She had spent most of her time in captivity trying to understand what had happened. The one thing she was certain of was that her kidnapping was not some random act. Abaddon's followers had been waiting for her outside the party that night and seemed to have more than a working knowledge of her schedule and security precautions.

She thought back to the gym and Abaddon's allusions to her father's involvement. Actually, he had more than alluded to it. He had outright said her father had arranged the kidnapping. Carolina didn't believe it at first. But the dots had slowly started to connect, and now she wasn't so sure anymore.

When it came to his business, she knew her father was a ruthless man. And despite her current role within his company, they had never been particularly close. He'd been well into his forties and in the middle of building his empire when she'd been born, so he hadn't had much time for either her or her mother. By the time she was twelve, her father had moved on to his third wife and Carolina was living full time in San Francisco with her mother. Their interactions had been limited to short, awkwardly silent breakfasts once a year, when he'd pass through California on business.

Despite her father's proclivity for marriage and other dalliances, Carolina was his only heir. So, on the day she'd graduated from Columbia University, he'd handed her two things—the keys to her first apartment on the Upper West Side and an executive position within his company. Nepotism aside, Carolina had spent the next ten years working harder than anyone else and doing well at her job. Consequently, the company had grown, and her father's wealth had expanded.

Carolina could be forgiven for believing she was an important part of the company, and of her father's life. The old man had even let his guard down on one occasion and told her as much. She had believed him. She had even thought she'd heard a hint of paternal pride when he'd said the words. But the more she thought about what she had done for that small display of warmth, the more ashamed she felt.

Carolina knew the outer boroughs hadn't always been the desolate landscapes they were today. In the mid-nineteenth century, they'd been thriving communities full of shipyards, warehouses, distilleries, sugar refineries, and manufacturing plants that had attracted German and Italian immigrants with promises of employment and opportunity. Individuals had prospered and communities grew.

But by the 1960s, everything had started to change. Impoverished Southern Black people and Puerto Rican immigrants, looking for their piece of the American dream, started moving into the area. Racist beliefs inherent in most community members emerged, creating ethnic and racial fissures throughout the city. A panic set in amongst white residents, and her father and other unscrupulous speculators took advantage of the irrational fear.

Those men used the paranoia caused by the race riots that'd raged throughout the country during the Civil Rights Movement to frighten white residents into selling their properties for well below their value. And then, using fraudulent appraisals and a corrupt federal mortgage program that insured home loans to low-income buyers, sold them to poor Blacks and Puerto Ricans at unreasonably high prices most families could not afford.

Many of the homeowners defaulted on the loans, so the scheme backfired. Unable to pay their mortgage, people abandoned their homes, which massively depressed property values everywhere. By the end of the decade, most of the buildings her father owned stood empty, investment in the neighborhoods stopped, and a large part of her father's business became worthless.

And as if the mortgage scam hadn't been bad enough, she'd heard rumors of the horrible things her father had done to try and recoup some of the money he'd lost. Like hiring thugs to burn down the buildings he owned to collect on insurance or to rid himself of tenants who couldn't afford the rent.

Carolina didn't have a real role in the company when those things were going on, but she didn't feel any less guilty. She was in her last year of university when she'd heard the rumblings of financial issues within the company. But by the time she'd graduated and started working for her father, the rumblings had stopped.

Over the years, there'd been stories of her father's less-than-ethical business practices, but she'd chosen to ignore them. Choosing instead to reconcile her own feelings of guilt with the idea that one day she'd lead the company and would be able to move it in a different, more ethical direction. It wasn't until the last few hours that she'd felt truly complicit in her father's actions.

Now with Abaddon's accusations still echoing in her mind, and Vic, the one person she believed she could trust, telling her Abaddon had been working for her father the whole time, Carolina wondered if her choices would make her complicit in her own death as well.

"Wait. I still don't understand. You're saying my father hired Abaddon to rescue me...Abaddon?"

Vic shook his head. "No. Yeah. I mean, not exactly." They walked shoulder to shoulder, both staring straight ahead. They had been speaking like that for a while now, neither one making any efforts to look at the other, as if the information being shared made it too awkward for eye contact. "The way Oran explained it to me, he'd been working as the head of your father's security for a while.

When you were kidnapped, his guys lost you, so getting you back was his responsibility. At least that's how he sold it to me."

"But he arranged the whole thing?"

"Yeah, at your father's direction. It makes sense that he would have Oran make all the arrangements. That's what people like Oran do—they make things happen. Technically, he's the head of your father's security, but really Oran is a fixer. One of his jobs is to make problems go away. But it was all bullshit. Oran was playing your father from the beginning. The way Oran was talking back at the gym, it sounds like payback. For what, I don't know."

Carolina shook her head absently. "I need to tell you something."

She spent the next ten minutes explaining the mortgage scam to him, including the part about mass arson. He listened quietly, and when she was done, he didn't say anything for several minutes. Carolina thought about what she'd described to him and thought herself a monster. Every second that passed without him speaking convinced her Vic thought she was a monster as well.

Vic had listened intently as Carolina told her story, and he didn't say anything even after she stopped speaking. Instead, he walked silently as he tried to process everything he'd seen and heard over the past week. Pretty soon things started to make sense.

In his day-to-day job, Vic knew if he'd needed to find someone or something, all he had to do was follow the money. So, he figured it was a safe bet that all the shit that had gone on came down to Josiah Lynch's money problems. Lynch had spent a lot of time and energy devaluing entire communities so he could buy low and sell high. And when that scam had blown up in his face, he'd tried to burn it all down—literally.

But he'd overplayed his hand, and now most of his portfolio wasn't worth the paper it'd been written on. Lynch needed a big influx of cash to get out from under. But where does an over lever-aged pseudo-billionaire get that kind of money when any bank worth its salt would probably take a match to his loan application? Why, the United States government, of course.

But the United States doesn't just hand out loans without a little push. So, Lynch had to create just the right crisis to motivate the people holding the purse strings. New York City, the financial capital of the world, had already been on the cusp of bankruptcy, so it shouldn't have taken much. But the people most affected by the city's financial crisis, the impoverished living in crime-ridden neighborhoods, were the ones without voices. So, it had been easy for the government to ignore the pleas for help.

Lynch needed to create a boogeyman to get what he needed. If a beautiful, white, socialite was kidnapped and murdered by the monsters who inhabited the out-of-control slums, all the people with voices—the rich and powerful—would feel less safe and demand action. That call for action, combined with his puppet Renfrow using his position as mayor to dictate which neighbor-hoods received attention, would be just what Lynch needed.

But it seemed Lynch had done more than create a boogeyman. After what Carolina had told Vic about the arson rumors, what Oran had said to him back at the gym made sense now. Something about Lynch burning people Oran loved alive because they couldn't afford to move.

What if Lynch, in one of his insurance scams, had killed members of Oran's family? It was hard for Vic to think of a bigger reason for Oran wanting revenge than getting back at the person who'd murdered his family. Without knowing it, Josiah Lynch had unleashed a walking, talking nightmare.

"It makes sense if you think about it," Vic said, finally ending the long silence. "With everything you know about your father's business and what he needs to happen so he can get out of what-ever hole he's in, you getting killed out here helps him."

"Yes. I've considered that as well," Carolina said.

Vic wanted to tell her what he thought about Abaddon's real motivation but seeing her glassy-eyed stare and slumped shoulder walk, he decided to keep his suspicions to himself. She'd been through a lot, and it couldn't be easy for Carolina realizing that her father had tried to have her murdered.

Besides, Vic was trying to reconcile what Carolina had revealed with how he felt about her. She hadn't had an active role in what her father had done. She was still in school when Josiah Lynch and his coconspirators decided to play their deranged version of Monopoly. But Carolina knew her father was dirty, and rather than take a stand and risk the life of privilege she'd enjoyed, she'd chosen to go along.

Despite his best efforts to ignore it, Vic was disappointed. He knew he didn't have a right to feel the way he did. Hell, up until a few days ago, he didn't even know who Carolina Lynch was. He couldn't deny the feelings he had for her. But hearing about her father's business, and her role in it, gnawed at his insides.

Josiah Lynch and people like him had caused a lot of damage. And while Carolina hadn't been directly involved, or even known about it when it'd been happening, Vic couldn't help but feel she'd somehow been derelict by staying quiet. He had grown up in these neighborhoods, so he was aware of the anger, pain, and outrage people like Lynch had created with their heartless actions. The overwhelming poverty and defeatist attitudes that permeated his community were big reasons he'd enlisted in the Marines.

It'd been bad out here when Vic was a kid. Hell, he had even contributed to some of the issues back then. Kid stuff mostly, a lot of fist fights and petty thievery. Maybe a stolen car here and there. But by the time Vic got back from Nam, switchblades had been replaced by handguns, and heroin had been substituted in for reefer. Every block was full of old buildings and lost souls—his *barrio* didn't exist anymore. He was resentful and angry and was looking for someone to blame.

Vic glanced at Carolina. Her head was down, and she was

staring at the ground. He figured she was ashamed. And despite being pissed off about the story he'd just heard—deep down, he knew all the shit her father had pulled hadn't been her fault.

"Do you have any thoughts on Abaddon?" Carolina didn't really want to talk about the madman, but she was tired of the long silences and couldn't think of another topic. Their conversations had become stilted and awkward, and it'd upset her. She had become intensely fond of Vic and wanted desperately to rewind time fifteen minutes, to before she'd spoken about her father's dealings.

"Aside from him being fucking nutso? Not really," Vic said.

"You said you knew Abaddon in the war, correct? Was he always...what was the word you used? 'Nutso?'"

Vic let out a small laugh. "To be fair, we were all a little crazy over there. Oran was...intense, maybe even violent. But it was war. You had to be those things to survive. But that was with the enemy. With us he was funny and smart. It was the way he spoke and carried himself, it made you want to follow him. I was a kid, so to be honest with you, I looked up to him. There was some horrific shit going on over there. Oran did crazy stuff, but him being the way he was got most of us back safe."

Carolina let out an exasperated sigh. "Do you mind if we settle on one name for the maniac? You calling him by one name, and my calling him by another is driving me a little *nutso* myself. It feels like we're in that movie *Sybil*."

"The one with Sally Field? Where she has multiple personalities?" Vic asked.

"Yes."

"Yeah, I remember that one. It was a pretty good flick. A little unrealistic, but it was all right."

"It was based on a true story."

"Was it? I always thought Sally..." His voice trailed off and he was quiet for a few seconds. "Whoever it is we're running from, it's definitely not the Oran I knew. So, we might as well call him Abaddon."

Vic's abrupt change in topics was jarring. Carolina felt like he'd wanted to discuss the movie further but then suddenly remembered their situation. Their conversation had, for a moment at least, organically shifted to an enjoyable topic. Almost as if she was on a date with someone she found very interesting and attractive. She thought about pushing forward with the movie topic but reconsidered.

"All right then, Abaddon it is. So, *Abaddon* had been planning this the whole time?"

"Yeah, it seems that way. He's been working for your father for a few years, but you never laid eyes on him. Why do you think that is?" A few silent seconds passed, as if the question was anything but rhetorical. "He was playing the long game. Oran...Abaddon had everything planned out from the beginning."

"But why the games? Why not just kill my father in his office or bedroom? I know that sounds terrible, but the question has to be asked."

"The way he was talking back in the gym, sounds like a whole two-birds, one-stone situation," Vic said.

"What are the two birds?"

Vic turned toward her, and for the first time in a while he looked in her eyes. "You can go all the way back to the Old Testament, and it's always the same two birds—money and revenge. The money part isn't hard to figure out. A million dollars would be reason enough."

"And the revenge portion of the problem?"

"Abaddon wants your father to suffer before he dies. And since your father doesn't seem to care about you or anyone else, the only thing that will cause him any suffering is losing his empire."

"This all seems like more than just revenge for destroying neighborhoods. It all seems so...personal. Like a vendetta."

"Calling it a blood feud is probably right." Vic hesitated and looked away from her. "I think your father may have been responsible for the death of someone Abaddon loved."

"What? How? What do you mean?" Carolina heard the stress in her voice.

"It's just a guess on my part. But Abaddon said something back at the gym about your father murdering people he loved. Something about burning them alive. I thought it was just more rambling, but after what you said about your father hiring people to burn down some of his buildings...well, it's not hard putting two and two together."

"Lord. If that's true, I'm not so sure I can even blame Abaddon for what he's doing."

"Oh yes, you can. However he got there, Abaddon is a permanent resident in crazy town. And his beef is with your father, not you. If Abaddon wants to settle old scores, then he should go directly to the source and leave you out of it."

Vic hadn't missed a beat and Carolina was appreciative of his efforts to make her feel better. She looked in his warm eyes and wanted nothing more than for him to kiss her. As if reading her mind, Vic lowered his head toward hers.

He pressed his lips against hers and time seemed to stop. Carolina's knees were weak, and a warmness filled her. She felt lightheaded and tried to focus on the softness of his mouth. It felt surreal, as if she were watching herself in a dream. But then she felt his hand on her arm and the electricity of his touch reminded her she was awake.

* * *

Vic pressed his body against hers. His heart was beating so loud and heavy he imagined Carolina could hear it through his chest.

He ran his hand gently down her arm. She shivered despite the warm night air, and her skin was covered in goosebumps.

He kept his eyes partially open trying to take in every detail of her face, enjoying every second of this moment. He wasn't sure if he believed in fate or luck, but every breath he took reminded him of what was possible.

She leaned into him, her hands on his lower back. Vic brought his hands up to her face, placing them gently on her cheeks. Just as their kiss was intensifying, Vic heard yelling, so he pulled away from the kiss. The sounds were faint at first, but they grew louder with every passing second.

He looked to his left and saw them. Not their faces of course, it was too dark for that. But their ominous shapes, hurtling toward him like a nightmare come to life.

"Let's go." He took a hold of Carolina's hand and they sprinted away from the approaching mob.

They were coming up on Hewes Street Station and Vic knew they were near the Ninetieth Precinct. He stopped and looked through the chain-link fence down toward the police station. He was tempted to head toward it, but the building was blacked out and looked deserted. He decided not to waste time seeking out nonexistent help and they continued jogging on the tracks.

"Vic, I—"

Carolina didn't finish her sentence, but he heard the exhaustion in her voice. They had been running for a while. Combined with the adrenaline and fear that had undoubtedly flooded her system, he didn't think she could go much longer.

Vic thought they'd be okay if they could make it over the Williamsburg Bridge and back into Manhattan. He didn't think Abaddon would lead his Kings out of Brooklyn. The cops weren't out here so they had to be somewhere. Vic figured they were concentrating their limited resources protecting Manhattan and its millionaire residents. As bad as Abaddon wanted Carolina, Vic didn't think he wanted to take on hundreds of cops to get her—not when he already had his money and what he needed to implicate Josiah Lynch.

But then he spotted the fire ahead and feared getting across the bridge was no longer an option.

twenty-eight

ABADDON and his Kings had been moving fast and were making up ground quickly. He figured it was only a matter of time before he had Vic and Carolina. Vic was good at what he did, and alone he might have gotten away. But he was dragging a useless sack of entitled shit and Abaddon was betting Vic couldn't maintain his pace.

Vic was trying to make it across the bridge, and it wasn't hard to figure out why. As much as he didn't like to admit it, Abaddon wasn't ready to take on the entire NYPD. And tonight, with the city blowing up, most of the cops in New York were on the island of Manhattan. Abaddon needed to keep Vic and Carolina on this side of the river. That's why he'd sent his boys ahead to set the blaze to the tracks near the Williamsburg Bridge.

The glow from the fire ahead lit up the sky. Vic and Carolina had nowhere else to go. He had enjoyed the hunt when he went into the tunnels. It'd reminded him of his early days in Nam—when he first realized who he was and what it took to quiet the beast. But they weren't in the tunnels anymore and he was growing impatient. It was time to end this.

Abaddon was going to kill Carolina—Josiah Lynch had sealed

her fate a long time ago. But Vic was another story. He didn't love Vic, but he had no animosity toward him either. They had shared too many times, both good and bad, for that to be the case. Their history even had him considering a pardon for the man.

He'd interfered with their plans, and for that Abaddon's Kings would expect him to carve Vic up real nice. Anything less could be mistaken for weakness. And for the shot caller of some other outfit, that could be a problem. But Abaddon wasn't worried about being challenged—there wasn't a person around with the balls to try that shit. He was the supreme president, so if Vic didn't put up a fight for the girl, Abaddon planned to let him make it back home.

His plan only worked if Vic wised up and stayed out of their business. The only thing he felt like he owed the man was a choice. If Vic chose wrong, he would die painfully and in the first place he called home.

Vic hoped the fire was an optical illusion. That somehow the flames were coming from the buildings burning on both sides of the tracks, and that their path was not blocked. But when they reached the Marcy Avenue Station a large, impassable fire had engulfed the tracks just past the platform.

His immediate concern was who had set the fire and where they were now. He scanned their surroundings, and although he didn't see anyone, he guessed whoever started the blaze was close.

"Come on," he said.

Vic and Carolina raced up the steps to the platform. They quickly made their way through the station's south exit and down the stairs leading to the street. Like the rest of the elevated train station, the staircase was in the open air, so Vic and Carolina found themselves inside a cloud of ash and dark gray smoke from the burning buildings. Vic could barely see through the thick smoke, so he reached out and grasped one of the steel handrails that book-ended both sides of the staircase. Overhead, the rain landed heavy on the aluminum canopy that covered the staircase.

The smoke was less dense when they reached the street, so he had a clear view of their surroundings. Even if he hadn't been able to see, Vic would have been able to picture every inch of the area. He'd grown up in this neighborhood and spent his formative years doing so much dirt around here, he still had some of it wedged under his fingernails.

They were standing on the southwest corner of Broadway and Marcy Avenue. Broadway was a long, narrow, two-way street that went on for miles in both directions, from the East River to Jamaica Avenue. Old buildings, most of which had been built around the turn of the century, flanked both sides of the street. Small mom-and-pop businesses took up the first floor of most of the buildings, while the rest consisted of walk-up apartments. Directly overhead, the J train tracks ran parallel with Broadway until about Roebling Street, where it veered to the right to cross the Williamsburg Bridge.

The streets were empty now, but it was clear there had been a lot of activity earlier. Most of the businesses that lined the side-walks were either on fire or had been destroyed by looters. Vic and Carolina were headed west on Broadway when he heard breaking glass close by. He glanced over his shoulder in time to see a record store go up in flames.

"What was that?" Carolina sounded panicked and spoke louder than needed.

"Firebomb."

"What?"

"A firebomb. It's a glass bottle filled with alcohol or gas. They stuff one end of a rag inside it, light the other, throw it, and boom. Most of these buildings are so old and dried out, the fire spreads fast."

"Were they aiming for us?"

"I don't—"

He heard glass bottles breaking in the distance, followed by yelling, cursing, and banging metal. He turned and saw a few dozen Kings headed toward them, carrying metal pipes and chains. They filled the street from one side to the other, banging their weapons on the sides of buildings and on the steel train-track pillars that lined the sidewalks. The noise they made echoed loudly in the concrete-and-steel ravine.

"Come on." Vic said, grabbing Carolina's hand.

They ran west on Broadway toward Bedford Avenue, where Vic planned to use the Williamsburg's pedestrian path to cross the bridge. Behind them the noises from their pursuers grew louder as the Kings gained ground on them.

They had just made it across Driggs Avenue when Vic picked up movement out of the corner of his eye. He glanced to his left. A group of Kings were sprinting across an empty lot and headed straight for Vic and Carolina. They were running fast, and from the angle of their approach, the group would be on them quickly.

Vic turned his attention back to the road ahead. They were coming up on Bedford Avenue. His heart was beating hard and fast inside his chest, and the burning sensation in his legs was so intense it felt like they would give out at any moment. Still, Vic tried to speed up, but an exhausted Carolina pulled on his arm, so he fell back into pace with her.

"We're almost there." He barely managed to squeeze out the words between breaths. She responded with a grunt.

Vic wasn't sure why he kept implying that their reaching the bridge would make them safe. Maybe he thought giving her, and himself, something to aim for would provide them the energy to push harder. For some reason, it made sense to identify a safe place.

Like when he'd played Hide and Seek as a kid. Back then, all he had to do was stay out of sight long enough to reach a predetermined spot and he'd be safe. But this wasn't a game and the only kids involved were a bunch of blood-thirsty drones with murder in their eyes.

Vic and Carolina veered to their right, running diagonally across Broadway and onto Bedford Avenue, a wide, one-way street that ran directly under the bridge. Despite the darkness, Vic could make out the silver chain-link fence that marked the entrance to the pedestrian path. It was about half a block ahead of them, on the west side of the roadway.

The Kings he had spotted running across the empty lot were right behind them now, close enough Vic could hear their footsteps and heavy breathing.

"Grab the bitch."

The words rang out from behind just as lights appeared ahead of them. Vic heard the revving motorcycle engines and figured it was the rest of the Kings. Initially, the lights were on the north side of the underpass and pointed westward. But then the Kings turned onto Bedford Avenue, and the blinding lights were directly in front of them, filling the entire space under the bridge.

Vic and Carolina were about to turn onto the pedestrian path, but one of the Kings that had been behind them was already blocking the entrance. Vic tried to back away, but another King stepped out of the shadows and grabbed Carolina's arm.

"Let go!" Carolina yelled, trying to wrench her arm away.

Vic threw a right-handed punch as he pulled Carolina away from her attacker. He was moving fast so the punch was poorly aimed, landing on the top half of the King's ear. Still, the blow had the desired effect and the guy let go of Carolina's arm.

She stepped behind Vic, and as they backed away, the light from the motorcycles revealed the truth of their situation—they were surrounded by dozens of expressionless Kings. Vic took a few deep breaths, readying himself for the coming fight.

The rain intensified, landing heavily on the surrounding street and bridge above them. There was a bright flash of lightning that seemed to last longer than usual, and within seconds it was followed by loud thunder, letting them know the storm was close.

"You never did know when to quit," Abaddon yelled from behind the lights.

Vic looked toward the sea of headlights, but he couldn't see the maniac. "You make it sound like a bad thing."

Abaddon stepped out from behind the lights, his large silhouette advancing slowly on Vic and Carolina.

"Usually it's not." Abaddon stopped a few feet from Vic. "That *Boriqua* tenaciousness served us well in Nam. But tonight, it's just been a big pain in the ass."

"Yeah, well, I guess you got to take the good with the bad." Vic glanced down at Abaddon's hands. He was unarmed. "So, what now?"

Abaddon smirked. "What do you think?"

"I was kind of hoping you'd congratulate us for putting up a good fight and let us be on our way."

"You know that's not going to happen."

"Why not? You got your money."

"It's over, Vic. Give it up," Abaddon said.

Vic hesitated while he considered his options. They were surrounded, so running was out of the question. And throwing blows would more than likely end with him drowning in his own blood. He figured their only salvation hinged on whether he could figure out the answer to one, simple question: How do you rationalize with the irrational? "I know Josiah Lynch was responsible for killing people you love. But Carolina didn't have anything to do with it. If you want to kill the man, go ahead and be my guest. The sick fuck deserves it as far as I'm concerned. But let her go."

"No can do, Vic. She's got to go. First, I plan to have some fun with her, but then she dies."

"They'll come for you. The people with all the money and all the power. Right now, your biggest asset is their indifference. You and your people are protected by their complete lack of interest in anything that happens out here. But if you kill one of them, they'll come for you. And everything you've built will come crumbling down."

"That'll be their first instinct, sure. But once they learn who really put all this in motion, old man Lynch will be done." Abaddon took a step toward Vic. "Now, the only question is, how do you want this to end for you?"

He was close now, so Vic searched his face. Although he looked like Oran, the man in front of him was unrecognizable. The mischievous twinkle that had once shone brightly in his eyes, the one that'd inspired confidence from a group of battle-weary Marines, was gone. In its place was a soulless stare that evoked feelings of dread.

"What do you mean?" Vic asked.

"Walk away and live. You saved my life once, so now I'm willing to save yours, but you got to walk away. But, Vic, this is a onetime offer. What's it gonna be?"

"And if I don't?"

Abaddon made a show of looking around at his Kings. "Look around, brother. It's over. She's done, but you still got a shot. Step away from the bitch and walk across the bridge, back to your sad little life up in Harlem. Otherwise, I'm gonna beat you to death and my Kings will feast on your bones."

Vic didn't say anything. He turned his eyes toward the ground, as if he were considering Abaddon's offer. He wasn't really, but he was buying himself some time to try and figure a way out. He laid it all out in his head, trying to envision a scenario where both he and Carolina walked away from the situation in one piece. It took him a few seconds, but Vic realized there was only one thing left to do.

He dropped his right foot back and took a fighter's stance. "Who's first?"

twenty-nine

TERI, Kai, and the Ruthless Ones had been standing on the Williamsburg Bridge pedestrian path, close to the Brooklyn side, when it'd started raining. After Ray Ray had agreed to help, he'd suggested the Williamsburg would be the best place to wait for Vic and whoever might be chasing him. After he and Kai were done with their macho posturing, Teri had been surprised how easy it'd been to convince Ray Ray to help.

After Sonia's theatrical show of force, Teri would have bet a month's salary he wasn't going to help. Ray Ray had seemed suspicious when she'd mentioned Vic, and he'd been more than a little hostile toward Kai. But Teri had gone through it all, telling him everything they'd been through over the past few days, and the ice had seemed to melt.

The rain felt cold on her skin, and despite the warm temperature, Teri was shivering. She glanced down at her goosebump-covered arms, crossed and pressed against her chest, and noticed the rain had washed away the dried blood from the rat scratches. Soaked and standing in a crowd of Ruthless Ones, smelling their sweat and dirt, Teri couldn't help but wonder how she'd gotten here. Until tonight, the closest she had come to Brooklyn was a Patti Smith show at the Palladium in the Village last year.

Three days ago, the only things she'd cared about were having fun and finishing up school. Those two things were the reasons she wanted to work for her Uncle Chris in the first place. Teri figured she'd have some fun chasing down crooks while making some green to pay for school.

Yeah, Vic had been a little overprotective, so Teri hadn't gotten to do as much as she'd wanted. But she'd gotten used to being under his watchful eye, and she'd learned a lot. Hell, if she was being honest, Teri kind of liked Vic's big-brother routine. For someone who didn't have any family—besides her Uncle Chris of course—having someone she knew she could count on felt good.

Her circumstances growing up hadn't been ideal. But she'd grown up fast and, with a little help from her uncle and Vic, Teri had made sense of the mess. Vic was like family, and she loved him. She knew if it was her out there, Vic would be doing everything he could to bring her home safe.

While a big part of her wanted to be at a club somewhere listening to The Ramones, covered in a warm blanket of anonymity. Teri looked around and realized those days were probably behind her. It was time to stand up and be counted.

She tilted her head toward the sky and whispered a silent prayer.

"You're not going to find any answers up there," Ray Ray said.

Teri lowered her head and when she opened her eyes, he was staring back at her. "What?"

"If you're looking for help from Him." Ray Ray nodded toward the sky. "You can forget it. He left this place a long time ago."

"You really believe that?"

"Look around you, honey. This place is dead, and everything that went into building it is dead too. There are no laws or morality. Nothing we do—nothing we create or love—has any value or meaning at all."

"If you really believe that, why are you here? Why bother helping Vic if you believe that in the end, it doesn't mean anything?"

"Because we're the people out here suffering. We're the lost ones. There was a time when Vic was my brother, and he was lost too. But he decided to leave. Went and found himself something else. I ain't mad at him for that. At least no more I ain't."

"I—" Teri was interrupted by the roar of motorcycle engines, interspersed with yelling and cursing.

Ray Ray tilted his head downward and seemed to be listening to the sounds emitting from the underpass ahead of them. He looked up at her, a dark grin on his face. "But if I'm being honest, I just like wrecking shit. And these motherfuckers need to be wrecked." He turned away from her and started marching toward the noise. Teri, Kai, and dozens of Ruthless Ones fell in step behind him.

***

All the bravado-filled yelling had stopped, and the crowd of Savage Kings had grown quiet. The tension in the air was palpable as they waited anxiously for Abaddon's next move. Vic's knees shook as adrenaline and fear flooded his body. He clenched and unclenched his fist, trying to quiet his nerves.

Abaddon tilted his head upwards and took a long, deep breath. When he returned his gaze to Vic and Carolina, a contemptuous smirk covered his face. "I can't say I'm surprised. You always did take the long way."

"Maybe, but I always got us where we were going," Vic said.

"That you did." The smirk melted from Abaddon's face. "All right, Vic, have it your way."

He turned and sauntered toward the crowd, letting out a sharp whistle as he walked. The mob, seemingly eager to follow the wordless command, started toward Vic and Carolina. Vic guided Carolina behind him and pivoted, so their backs were to the building rather than the crowd.

As the Kings advanced, Vic scanned their hands for weapons. Most of them were carrying metal pipes and chains. And while Vic was sure they were out there, he didn't notice any knives or guns. Vic figured he could hold out for a while if all he had to endure were blows from fists and other blunt force objects. But once the knives and guns came out, it would be game over.

He brought his hands up and readied himself for the coming fight.

"This doesn't seem fair, now does it?" A voice yelled from the shadows.

As if part of a dance company working out a choreographed routine, the Kings stopped advancing and looked around for the source of the voice. Vic noticed cursing and scuffling coming from behind the crowd, near the pedestrian path entrance, but he couldn't make out what was happening.

He thought there might be a chance to get away while everyone was distracted. He looked around for an exit route and noticed Abaddon standing to his right, staring at him. They made eye contact and Abaddon shook his head. Vic took a deep breath and waited for the next surprise.

"Where's your president?" The male voice projected out from behind the crowd. He sounded aggressive, intense, and familiar. Vic peered into the crowd, trying to get a look at the man.

Abaddon took a step toward the ruckus. "Who's asking?"

"I am, motherfucker. Come up here and talk to me." Now there was an unmistakable cockiness in the tone, and Vic smiled.

Abaddon stomped off angrily toward the challenge. When the crowd parted, Vic was both surprised and relieved at the sight. Reinaldo "Ray Ray" Martinez, backed by what seemed like a sea of Ruthless Ones, was the source of the familiar-sounding voice and cause for Vic's feeling of relief. The surprise part came from the sight of Teri and Kai standing alongside Ray Ray, looking just as cocky and defiant as he did.

"What the fuck do you want?" Abaddon stopped a few feet from Ray Ray.

Abaddon towered above Ray Ray and outweighed him by at least fifty pounds. The size difference made the square-off seem almost comical, and if it was anyone else but Ray Ray, Vic would have felt pity for the smaller man. But he'd grown up with Ray Ray and knew better than to bet against him in any situation.

"I'm just wondering how you and your little War-cocks got so lost. Last I checked, Howard Beach was about thirty miles that way." Ray Ray pointed to an imaginary spot behind Abaddon.

"We're not lost, we're just stretching our legs. And you'd be smart to turn around and leave."

Ray Ray took a few steps back. "Maybe so, but there are two problems with that idea, fucko. One, this is my neighborhood, and I call the shots around here. And B, that's my friend your boys are crowding over there." He nodded toward Vic. "How ya doing, Vic?"

Vic nodded and cracked a small smile. "I've been better. How ya been, Ray?"

"Rock solid, baby," Ray Ray said.

"All right, cut the shit." Abaddon tilted his head in Vic and Carolina's direction. "You can take him. I just want the bitch."

Ray Ray didn't answer immediately, as if he was considering the offer. "That's not gonna work. It looks like my man Vic is attached to the young lady, so they're both coming with us. That's the tax you pay for trespassing—and for being an asshole."

"You got a big mouth, little man. I'll tell you what—I'll give you and the rest of your lollipop kids thirty seconds to walk away before it gets bloody."

Ray Ray flashed a devilish grin. "What? Are you gonna have your period?" He took a step toward Abaddon. "Listen, you fucked up by coming into our territory. And you really fucked up by running up on my man and his lady. Under normal circumstances, I'd say let's rumble, cut on cut. But that would leave a lot of bodies—on both sides. What do ya say we settle this one on one?"

"You and me?" Abaddon said with a surprised tone. He looked around at his Kings and belted out an exaggerated laugh. Abaddon was a born prick and trained killer, two things that contributed to his over-the-top display of confidence.

"Me? Nah. I was thinking you and Vic." Abaddon stopped laughing and glanced at Vic before turning his attention back to Ray Ray. "Yeah. You two straight up. Vic and his lady go with the winner. Everybody walks away when it's over. No matter what."

"The only problem with that is Vic won't be walking anywhere when I'm done." Abaddon turned his entire body toward Vic. "What do ya say, Vic? You ready to step into the ring one more time?"

Vic searched Abaddon's face for something recognizable, but the person standing before him was a stranger. He could have guessed it would come to this, and maybe it was inevitable. It seemed, even before their experiences in Nam—a place where death, guilt, and sadness were the norm—that Abaddon had experienced a lifetime of darkness. Vic didn't know what those experiences entailed, and honestly, he didn't need to know. All that really mattered was what'd gone on tonight. And for Vic, the mad acts he'd witnessed tonight where those of an anonymous monster.

Vic looked into Abaddon's eyes and there was nothing familiar in his cold stare. The Oran he knew was gone—if he'd ever existed at all.

"I'd love to," Vic said.

Carolina listened intently to the back and forth between Abaddon and the man Vic called Ray, wondering how it would play out. Most of the dialogue was macho bullshit, stuff she was sure she had heard in a Clint Eastwood movie. And if she hadn't been surrounded by so many violent people, she would have rolled her eyes derisively and laughed out loud.

But the truth of the matter was she was surrounded by violent people, capable of inflicting pain and suffering on whomever they pleased. And while at first, she thought the group led by Ray were there to help, now Carolina wasn't so sure. He'd struck a deal with Abaddon as if he were promoting some sort of boxing match. Abaddon and Vic would engage in a barbaric fist fight, with her and Vic's lives the prizes at the end of the blood-soaked rainbow.

Carolina knew she was being selfish by expecting more help from Ray and his followers. They had risked a lot by even showing up, and at the very least, had bought her and Vic more time. But watching Vic ready himself for the fight, she couldn't help her feelings. The size difference between him and Abaddon, while not as comically unbalanced as that of Abaddon and Ray, clearly favored Abaddon. And while Vic had shown he was more than capable of defending himself, Carolina shuddered to think about what would happen if he lost.

thirty

FROM WHERE SHE WAS STANDING, Teri had a front-row seat to all the happenings. She watched as gang members moved to different sides of Bedford Avenue, using the Williamsburg Bridge overhead as a divider between the two groups. The Ruthless Ones lined up on the south side of the underpass, while the Savage Kings took up position along Fifth Street on the north side. The chain link fences that had been erected on the east and west sidewalks along Bedford Avenue combined with the two lines of raucous gang members to form a crooked square directly under the bridge.

Both sides screamed, yelled, and banged on anything they could find. Teri stared at the surreal scene, which seemed to have been pulled from a Federico Garcia Lorca poem, and realized the two gangs, whether intentional or not, had coordinated their numbers to create a boxing ring—or a gladiator pit, or a field of honor, or a dirt road outside an old saloon. Pretty much anyplace where two testosterone-fueled morons would face off in a life-or-death dick-measuring contest.

Teri gazed over at Vic, waiting on the fringes of the makeshift ring with his back to a crowd of obnoxiously loud Ruthless Ones.

He was standing a few feet from her, motionless and looking calmly determined. Teri pulled her brass knuckles out of her back pocket. Palming the cold, heavy metal in her left hand, she made her way to Vic and stood in front of him. After a few seconds of giving her hardest stare to Abaddon and his band of merry men, Teri turned and faced Vic.

"What are you doing here, Teri?"

"It's the strangest thing. I've never actually been to Brooklyn before, and tonight seemed like as good as time as any." Teri smiled warmly, but Vic stared at her stone-faced. "I came for you, schmuck, what do you think?"

"I appreciate the concern, but I told you to stay out of this."

"Yeah well, if you actually believed I'd listen, you only have yourself to blame."

A small smile crept across Vic's face. "I can't really argue with that."

"So, what do you think? A minute, minute and a half to finish this clown?" Vic looked past her but didn't respond. She wrapped her arms around his waist and pressed her body close to his in a deep hug. "Well, just in case you're too tired for a victory hug later." Teri slid her hands down a few inches, to where they lay on his buttocks. She felt around and slid the brass knuckles into his right back pocket. Teri pulled away from him and they looked at each other knowingly. Vic nodded subtly and walked past her.

She glanced over at an emotionless Kai. He seemed bored, as if he were staring at two ducks in a pond. Kai caught her looking at him and the two locked eyes. He shrugged nonchalantly and flashed his familiar grin. Teri wasn't sure if he was putting on an act for her benefit or if Kai was being sincere, but he seemed unimpressed with the whole spectacle.

She turned her attention back to Vic and the big man standing in the center of the makeshift ring, a little shocked by their differences. The two men stood a few feet apart, and while the size disparity between the two was clear, it was the different energies radiating from them that concerned her. Although Vic was standing tall and seemed confident, the big man looked savage and menacing. And while Vic stood motionless, with a zen-like calm, his adversary paced back and forth, like a predator sizing up its prey.

She wanted to believe Vic could win this thing. Her Uncle Chris, never one to praise a fighter's skills no matter how good they were, had thrown some compliments Vic's way. And although she'd never seen him in a fight herself, she'd heard stories about his victories. But those were just stories and the Vic she knew relied on his charm and smarts to settle problems. Teri eyed the giant man with murder in his eyes and didn't think charm would work on him.

As if remembering a lost loved one, Teri thought about one of the last conversations she'd had with Vic. They'd talked about dreams, and she remembered telling him that she didn't dream anymore. He'd smiled warmly and told her everyone dreams, even if they couldn't remember having them. Vic had said we needed our dreams to protect us and to keep us moving forward, especially in the darkest times.

A flash of lightning snapped Teri out of her reverie. The Savage Kings had been backlit by the light from their vehicle's headlamps, so they'd been mostly anonymous silhouettes. But the lightning provided a brief illumination, revealing dozens of soulless faces. Teri scanned the crowd and noticed that, despite all the histrionics, their eyes were surprisingly lifeless. Like the dark, cold eyes of a reptile.

She thought about her own dreamless existence and wondered if she would survive this night. If Vic winning his fight would be enough to get them through the darkness. Or if when this was all said and done, the reptiles would kill her for not dreaming.

Vic had been watching Abaddon pace back and forth. Even in the limited light from the vehicle headlamps, he spotted the scowl on Abaddon's face. Vic felt a familiar feeling as he tried to visualize the next few minutes. Adrenaline flooded his bloodstream, causing slight trembles in his hands and knees.

Water droplets landed on his back and Vic looked up. He was standing under the bridge's edge, only partially protected from the falling rain. He smiled to himself and thought it'd been the story of his life—it didn't matter what he did, any cover he got only went so far.

"It's time, Vic," Abaddon yelled.

Vic lowered his head and fixed his eyes on the person he had once thought of as a brother. He tried to think of something witty to say, but nothing came to mind. There was nothing left to say. One way or another, it was time for this to end. They both nodded and started toward each other.

Vic brought his hands up to his chin, keeping his fingers loose and unclenched. The two men converged at the center of the makeshift ring, circling each other counterclockwise. Abaddon feinted a lunging movement, as if he was going to rush in, but he gathered himself and the two continued circling. Vic flicked out a left jab that did not connect but helped him to measure the distance between him and his opponent.

Abaddon exploded with a right kick that landed on the outside of Vic's leg. He felt a burning sensation on his thigh and took a few small steps back. He thought about rushing in but decided to be patient and continued circling.

Abaddon feinted again and Vic flinched. Abaddon used the distraction to shorten the distance and threw a straight front kick. Vic hopped back, avoiding the attempt. Like a copperhead snake landing multiple bites in quick succession, Abaddon threw a kick with his other foot that struck Vic on the front of his hip. He staggered backward a few feet, and Abaddon shuffled to his right.

Vic threw a wide, right hook at Abaddon's head. He leaned

back and avoided the blow, but he tripped and almost fell. Vic rushed in, but Abaddon quickly gathered himself and extended a front kick, followed quickly with a straight punch. Vic blocked both blows and continued forward.

Vic ducked under a high kick from Abaddon and threw a quick one-two combination. Abaddon blocked both punches, countering with his own thunderous left hook that landed flush on Vic's jaw. A flash of light followed by a second of dizziness caused him to stumble backward. He shook his head to clear the fuzziness and spotted a blurry Abaddon charging him.

He sidestepped away, trying to give himself some time to get his head right. After a few seconds Vic was still seeing two Abaddons. There was no time left, so Vic chose the one on the left and went after him.

Vic charged in, throwing a one-two combination as he closed the distance. Abaddon easily blocked the two blows and countered with his own straight kick that landed on Vic's stomach. He winced and staggered backward as the sharp pain radiated through his entire torso.

Vic took in a deep, pain-free breath and looked up just as Abaddon was barreling toward him. Vic sidestepped the charging maniac and backed away. Abaddon bounced off the fence, turned, and advanced toward Vic. He threw a straight punch, but Abaddon countered with a lightning-quick high kick that landed with a loud thud on the side of Vic's face. A flash of light. The blinding pain caused Vic to stumble backward several feet.

Abaddon's lips curled up into a taunting smile as he pressed forward, stalking Vic.

"Come on Vic, the fight's over here," he snarled.

Vic's vision was a bit fuzzy, so he waited for Abaddon. When he was close enough, Vic threw two, quick outside leg kicks. Both strikes landed on Abaddon's lead leg, just below his knee.

Seemingly unaffected, Abaddon pressed forward. Vic landed two more leg kicks, but Abaddon ignored them and threw his own punch. Vic ducked beneath the blow and answered with multiple kicks to Abaddon's leg. His face contorted into a pained grimace with every blow, motivating Vic to continue with the attack.

Abaddon threw a straight front kick that landed just above Vic's crotch, forcing him off balance. Abaddon rushed forward. He wrapped his arms around Vic's waist and lifted him off the ground, carrying him into the fence. Water droplets and rust bounced off the fence and into Vic's eyes and nose.

Abaddon tightened his hold. He pressed his head against Vic's stomach and used his entire body as leverage, attempting to squeeze the life out of him. It was hard to breathe.

He coughed and his mouth filled with blood. The familiar metallic taste coated his entire tongue. The world was fading. He only had a few seconds before he passed out. Vic gathered whatever strength he had left and brought his right elbow crashing down on top of Abaddon's head.

Abaddon let out a pained grunt and loosened his grip slightly. Vic rained down quick and violent blows, alternating strikes from his elbows. Abaddon's warm and sticky blood, orange in the amber light from the headlamps, exploded up from his scalp and covered Vic's arms.

After too many blows to count, Abaddon released his hold and staggered backward. Vic slid down the fence a bit and hesitated a few seconds, trying to catch his breath. Abaddon pawed at his face, trying to clear the blood away. After a few seconds Abaddon lowered his hands from his face and the two men locked eyes.

For the first time since the fight had started, Vic was aware of everything going on around him and felt a strange sort of clarity. Every sound and movement seemed magnified. He felt as if he could hear every word being shouted and see every raindrop falling from the sky.

Vic stared at Abaddon, covered in shadows and blood, and he knew this wouldn't end till one of them was dead. He reached into his back pocket and slid the fingers of his right hand into Teri's brass knuckles.

"Come on, Vic, let's finish it," Abaddon growled.

They tottered toward each other. Abaddon's eyes were glazed over, and he was unsteady. Vic threw two quick left jabs followed by a right cross that landed clean on Abaddon's jaw, just beneath his ear. The blow from Vic's brass knuckle covered fist sent Abaddon crashing backward to the ground, and there was a loud cracking sound when the back of his head bounced off the asphalt.

Vic rushed forward and mounted him. He balanced himself and started throwing punches at Abaddon's head and face. Fueled by images of Abaddon's merciless killing spree, Vic rained down blow after blow, pummeling him until his body was bloodied and lifeless.

The Williamsburg Bridge was a little over a mile long, so normally it would have taken Vic, Teri, Carolina, and Kai about thirty minutes to walk it. But with Vic battered and exhausted, it took sixty-five pain-filled minutes to make it across.

It was early Thursday morning when they stepped off the bridge in Manhattan. The sun had yet to rise, and the city was still blacked out, so the streets were dark and deserted.

"What will they do with him?" Carolina asked.

It was the first thing she'd said since the fight had ended. They'd walked in silence, everyone too exhausted to speak. Vic had figured Carolina had been processing everything that'd happened. He had his own processing to do so he hadn't minded the silence. He knew she meant what would Ray Ray and his gang do with Abaddon's body.

He'd found it odd that after he'd lifted himself off Abaddon, it'd been completely quiet. In the back of his mind, he'd expected the Savage Kings would go on the attack to avenge Abaddon's death. But as it turned out, self-preservation was a lot better motivator than revenge. Not wanting to be anywhere near a dead body when the sun came up, the once loud and boisterous Savage Kings had fled the area as quickly as they had invaded. None of them had made a move to check on their fallen leader.

Teri and Carolina had made their way over to Vic, and he leaned on the two ladies as the three walked back toward the Williamsburg Bridge's pedestrian entrance. Vic locked eyes with Ray Ray and nodded, but the two old friends didn't speak. Nothing needed to be said.

It wasn't like the movies where they'd all make a big deal about ensuring Abaddon's body had disappeared. There wouldn't be a trip to the East River or a tub full of acid. Ray Ray would lead his Ruthless Ones back home to Bushwick laughing and joking about what they'd seen, leaving Abaddon right where he lay.

Someone would find him whenever the lights came back on, and the cops would pretend to investigate. But, like every other John Doe murder that happened in The Fear, it'd go unsolved, and Abaddon's body would remain unclaimed.

"Nothing," Vic said.

Kai said his goodbyes at Norfolk Street, holding onto Teri's hand a few seconds past friendly. He headed south on Norfolk while the others continued west on Delancey Street. They walked another block before Carolina was able to flag down a cab.

The inside of the cab was more than warm and smelled like cigarette smoke.

"Where to?" the cabbie said tiredly.

No one answered for a few seconds. Vic wasn't sure what the next move was, and it seemed the ladies weren't either.

"Sixty-Third and Fifth," Carolina said. She glanced at Vic and Teri. "I hope you two don't mind. I'd rather not be alone."

"No, that's fine," Teri said.

They were turning onto Fourteenth Street and, with no buildings or bridges in the foreground, Vic had a clear view of the sun rising over the East River. The sun was just peeking out from the horizon, filing the sky in a rose and gold hue. He couldn't remember the last time he'd watched the gorgeous and serene spectacle.

"It's beautiful, isn't it?" Carolina asked.

"Yeah, it is," Vic said, keeping his eyes on the view.

"What's your last name, Vic?"

He was somewhat surprised by the seeming randomness of the question. But considering what they'd been through together, her wanting to know his last name wasn't all that strange.

"Espada."

"Espada. That's pretty. What does it mean?"

"Sword."

thirty-one
Saturday, July 16

JOSIAH USED a hotel towel to wipe the fogged mirror clean. He stared at his blurry reflection and silently lamented that the hot showers he'd loved so much in his youth just didn't feel the same. When he was younger, he'd turn the heat up so high his skin would be lobster red by the time he stepped out of the shower. But age had done to his skin what it had to his bones and hair—made it thin and fragile.

He supposed it was the same for every man living in the twilight. Too many moments spent staring at a stranger, analyzing his life's successes and failures. Good thing for him he'd had a lot more successes than failures. And while Josiah's most recent endeavor hadn't gone exactly as planned, it hadn't been a complete failure either.

Yes, Carolina had managed to escape, ruining his planned media firestorm. But the miscreants, as predictable and stupid as ever, had spent twenty-five hours killing each other and destroying the little they did have. Josiah had made sure to point his newspapers in the right direction before he'd boarded his plane. By the time he'd landed in Miami, damage estimates in the hundreds of millions and quotes of outrage from influential liberals had been plastered on the front pages of every major paper across the country.

His mayoral candidate Renfrow was all but guaranteed to win the election in November. That certainty, along with the manufactured maelstrom, would be enough to get Josiah everything he wanted. Now, all he needed to figure out was what to do with Carolina.

Josiah had left New York soon after he'd received word from The Council of her escape early Thursday morning. Despite his best efforts, he had not spoken with her. She hadn't answered any of his telephone calls, and his security team still hadn't located her anywhere.

Josiah didn't really care about her well-being, and he wasn't concerned about the optics of not speaking with her. However, he had no idea what she knew or what she'd seen, and that was a problem. He needed to find her and have some questions answered: Like how'd she escaped and what had happened to Oran? Was he still alive? If so, why hadn't he reported in? And then he needed to eliminate her. The Carolina situation had become too complicated, and he didn't like complications.

He was getting ready to brush his teeth when there was a soft knock at the front door. He was expecting room service delivery of his breakfast, so Josiah took his time. He was halfway to the door when there was a second, more forceful knock. He was annoyed at the gall of a server knocking more than once.

"I hope you enjoyed that second knock, my friend." Josiah pulled the door open forcefully. "It just cost you a tip—"

"Considering wages these days, not tipping seems like an overreaction."

"Gabriel?"

"Good morning, Josiah."

"What are you doing here?"

"We need to talk. Can we come in?"

Josiah noticed the tall, powerfully built man standing behind Gabriel. The man glared at Josiah intimidatingly.

"Yes, of course." Josiah stepped aside, allowing Gabriel and his companion to enter the room. "Can I get you anything? I have some coffee on its way up."

"No thank you, this won't take long."

"Okay." Josiah's eyes went back and forth nervously between Gabriel and the man with the hard stare.

Gabriel let out a small laugh. "Oh, forgive me. This is Kai. He does some work for me from time to time."

"Hello, Kai." He nodded coldly but didn't respond, keeping his eyes fixed on Josiah. Gabriel's sudden appearance had already made Josiah nervous, but Kai's menacing glare filled him with dread. "How did you know where to find me?"

"Knowing things is what I do, Josiah. You know that as well as anyone." Gabriel smiled. "Besides, where else would someone of your status stay while they're in Miami but The Fontainebleau?"

"Am I that predictable?"

"When it comes to their comfort, most wealthy people are predictable."

"Fair enough. Why are you here? I thought we were scheduled to meet next week in my New York office."

"We were. But this couldn't wait," Gabriel said.

"What couldn't wait?" Josiah heard the click of the hammer being pulled back before he saw the gun. Kai held the silver, cartoonishly big revolver down by his side, close to his thigh. "What are you doing?"

"Tying up loose ends," Gabriel said.

"Is that what I am? A loose end?"

"For The Council? Yes, you are."

"What are you talking about, Gabriel? It worked. Everything's in motion now."

"That's where you're wrong, Josiah. Everything didn't work. In fact, you just added a problem. And if I know that problem at all, he's going to come looking for you. We can't risk what you might say when he finds you."

"Who are you talking about?" Kai pointed the gun at him, and Josiah stumbled backward, bringing his hands up defensively as if he could block the bullets. "Wait. Why kill me? I have money, resources. I'm an asset. Keep it simple. Kill this other person."

Gabriel's lips curled into a wide grin. "Josiah, my friend, The Council has plenty of assets."

Before Josiah could react, Kai had a hold of his robe and was forcing him to his knees. Josiah closed his eyes on the way down, and when he opened them, he found himself looking up at Gabriel.

"Gabriel, please. We go back a long way. What are you doing?"

"Keeping it simple."

Josiah heard a loud bang, and the world went dark.

"How can you drink that in this heat?" Kai asked.

Gabriel held the *cortadito* close to his lips, blowing on it softly to cool its temperature. "Easily. It's delicious." He took a sip of the Cuban coffee.

After their visit with Josiah, Gabriel and Kai had stopped at Eden, a stylish Cuban restaurant two blocks from The Fontainebleau. They were seated at the restaurant's poolside bar, overlooking the beach.

"What is it anyway?" Kai asked.

"It's Cuban-style espresso with steamed milk. This is pretty much all I drink whenever I'm in Miami."

"There're a few Cuban spots back home. You can't get that there?"

"They don't taste nearly as good."

"Here you go, sir." The bartender placed a telephone on the bar top in front of Gabriel.

He lifted the receiver and dialed a number.

"Yeah," a male voice answered.

"It's done," Gabriel said.

"Good. And what about Espada?"

"I think we should hold off on that for a while. I believe he may be of some use to us down the road."

"Are you sure? He's been a pretty big pain in the ass so far."

Gabriel hesitated. "Yes, I'm sure. If he proves to be too much of a headache, I'll take care of him myself."

"All right."

The phone line disconnected, and Gabriel hung up.

He arched his eyebrows and sighed. "Looks like I bought Vicente some time."

Kai nodded. "What do you want to do now?"

"What else?" Gabriel finished the rest of his espresso in one gulp. "Go to the beach."

about the author

J.J. Hernandez was born in Brooklyn, New York and raised in Brooklyn and Miami, Florida. He is the author of the critically acclaimed novel *The Broken*. He is a graduate of Sam Houston State University and has been a law enforcement officer in Central Texas for over twenty years. He lives in Austin, Texas with his wife and two daughters. Visit him online at www.jjhernandezauthor.com.

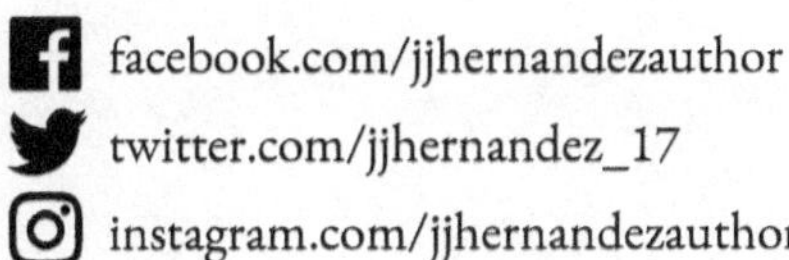

9 781737 101345